THE TRISIX COLONY

Wade Rivers

ISBN:0615728669
ISBN-13:978-0615728667

DEDICATION

This book is dedicated to my beautiful children and their generation, to their future, if they have one; and that with God's help, they may gain back what my generation has stolen from them.

Trisix Colony is also dedicated to AA, and with tremendous gratitude. Without AA, I would not be here, and you would not be reading my words right now. My only mark in life would be a short inscription on a tombstone in a decrepit graveyard where drunks go to feed their souls on moonlit nights...alone.

Thank you.

CONTENTS

Acknowledgments   i

The Trisix Colony   1

The Afterword   249

Revelations on a Stranger Passing Truth   259

Victims of the Night   261

MAXWELL   263

WILL YOU WALK THE STREETS   264

ALONE

Polar   265

WHO, WHO ARE YOU   277

Your mother and I   278

THE SWITCH ON THE WALL   280

THE FACTORY   281

An Afterthought to the Factory   292

SILENCE HAD BEEN LONG   294

AND STILL

About the Author   296

ACKNOWLEDGMENTS

This book could not have been written
without the help and assistance of my
loving wife Denise.
I spent many long hours researching and writing.
She spent many more hours editing and encouraging.
Though my name is on the cover it is absolutely a
joint project. A third partner in the project should
not be omitted either though He seldom takes credit
for anything. I can assure you this, without the vision
God gave us none of this would have been possible.
It is His vision that we had to share with you.

Wade Rivers

waderivers.com

CHAPTER ONE

He repelled down the building like a spider quietly lowering itself from its web. Over his shoulder, he looked at the city. It stood dark, alone, alienated. Empty. The once bright lights from the bridge, reflected meekly off the East River. He could hear a barge in the distance bellowing a fog horn as he touched down in the alley.

Quickly, he secured his gear; the ropes, pulleys and carabineers neatly under his trench coat. He took several deep breaths and stepped to the street. He listened for the Cage. The coast was clear.

In fear of detection, Travis walked briskly from Turtle Bay down Third Street keeping his distance from where tanks and armored personnel continually patrolled. He looked down the long corridor of streets at the tall building casting a menacing shadow. Travis dared not stop though he wanted to look; he wanted to observe what was going on, but he knew to keep moving. A moped whined up the nearly deserted boulevard as two riders whisked by him with toboggans flying in the chilly night.

He stopped. They passed. He re-lit a cigarette pulled from a crumpled pack as a camera lens zoomed in from the building across the way. He mumbled several expletives to himself pulling his hat a little lower over his eyes and quickened his pace across the street. Another block down, an old city bus crawled across the intersection like a mechanical caterpillar. He could hear the passengers, a crew of late night workers and drunks. He momentarily stopped listening for other vehicles then pulled up the collar on his trench coat and hurried on.

All was dark, except for an occasional street light on the corner; per order of the government; to conserve and save. A light rain had fallen earlier in the evening adding a chill to the night. Travis remembered his grandfather once had a shop there, not far from the old Empire State building before it was closed. Now they were just dark relics of a time that had passed. He crossed the avenue past a row of abandoned cars with a trail of smoke following him in the night like a long gray cape floating in the air. The pub was only another block or so away, and Marla would be waiting. He was anxious to see her; it had been six or seven years, maybe five…maybe nine. He couldn't remember. He had lost count; times had changed. Everything in the country had changed.

Travis walked along looking back occasionally over his shoulder; he reminded himself to be careful. He thought he could trust her, but he didn't know for sure. These were not times for love, only survival, and if one was lucky enough…escape. The "Big Bitch" was in total control. She, the government, ran everything. Travis walked down the street with the tingling sensation he was being followed. He stopped and turned around. At first, he thought it was a Big Dog lurking in the shadows, but he did not hear its distinctive mechanical hum. He looked again; it was indeed a dog, large and no doubt hungry. Travis waved his hand and stomped his foot. It took off. He heard it howl as it joined its pack down the street.

No sooner than he turned around, he heard the unmistakable sound of a Raven approaching from the next block and ducked into a dark enclave with a broad tattered awning extending to the curb. He listened to the dreadful sound of the mechanical drone humming up the street. It was moving much slower than most. He was amazed it was able to fly; it was going so mysteriously slow. Travis figured it was sending a live feed to a nearby remote location, probably to a cage waiting to arrest more people. He pulled out a small aerosol can from his belt and sprayed a shield around him and squatted low and turned his face to the corner. He moved not a muscle; he didn't even breathe. Travis knew he was out of view of the surveillance lens, but its heat sensor could still detect he was there. He waited motionless, listening as the Raven flew down the street.

Zzzzzrrrooommmm.

Its mechanical hum trailed like an angry bee down the deserted streets, and finally faded away. Again, he avoided detection and stepped back out to the street thankful he had escaped another close call.

Travis looked at his watch; he was late. He approached the corner cautiously and listened for oncoming cars. There were none as far as he could see; the coast was clear. Only the cameras positioned at the intersections could see him, but he was no more than a shadowy figure crossing a deserted street.

He passed by a number of marred buildings still baring the riddled evidence of resistance embedded by a fusillade of bullets across their fronts. It was like that in several of the older sections of the city. Up ahead, he could see the entrance to the Pale Horse Tavern, a scantly lit establishment still in business with descending steps to the basement of an abandoned furniture store. A crowd of a dozen or so people gathered outside. He hesitated and slowed his pace. It was not his first choice where they should meet; he had told her that in his note. He wanted to meet her by a park, but her message said that was not safe.

The faces in the crowd turned in his direction as he approached. They stopped talking. He was nervous, not knowing what to expect. He could hear the people inside the tavern; there was the unmistakable sound of a blues sax downstairs. Then, she called his name.

"Travis." Marla walked away from the crowd and ran up to him. She hugged him immediately. He could feel her plump breast against his chest. "Just act normal," she whispered into his ear. "I thought you were gone."

His voice, deep and raspy poured into her ear like a drink into a long tall glass, "I am."

She pushed herself back from him with her hands on his shoulders, and exercised her Midwestern volubility loud enough for everyone to hear, "Oh, my God! Look at you! Where have you been?" She acted surprised to see him. "What brings you to town? Business?"

Marla took him by the elbow and turned him away from the crowd and began walking him away from the tavern. She animated her words with the precision of an actress until they were far enough away that people couldn't hear.

Travis was amazed; she was still beautiful. Time had defined the features of her face with more grace. Her lips curled up on the edges in a friendly smile. They were expressive and teasing. They made his mouth literally water. Her voice was soft and fuller; it had always been sexy. It is what made her so seductive. Like an undertow, it wrapped around him and pulled him in. He was somewhat powerless when he listened to her. He stared at her and even in the marginally lit street her hair shimmered. It was a mixture of flaxen and caramel; transparent like a jar of honey when held up to light.

They stopped and looked at one another and both stood still. There was a momentary awkward pause. It had indeed been a long time, and she was glad he was there. "What happened to you? I have heard just bits and pieces?"

Travis was reluctant to tell her much, and though he believed he could trust her, no one was above suspicion. There had been too many disappointments.

She could tell he was nervous standing there on the street. The police could arrive any moment and check ID's. She felt his body, stiff and tense and could see the uneasiness in his shifting eyes. She noticed that his hair had turned from brown to shale since she last saw him six years ago. His eyes had almost a grayish tint. His hair was longer, and he had a beard. He looked good but had aged some; the times had been hard.

Travis took her chin in his hand and lifted her face up to the light inspecting her. She knew what he was checking for. He didn't say anything, nor did she. They could hear the crowd down the street at the pub. His arm slipped into her coat and curled around her back. He squeezed her closely to him and put his mouth over her ear, "I always told you I'd be back one day. Didn't I?" The deep sound of his voice resonated in her ear. His every word had texture, feeling, and the deepness of his voice immobilized her. The sound of his words moved slowly through her body and up her veins like heroin squeezed slowly from a syringe.

He held her tightly, and his arms felt warm on the chilly night. She felt his body relax. She could see a faint trace of a smile ratchet up his face; she kissed him. It was impulse, a reflex action, something she had not planned but could not stop herself from doing. Travis pulled her tighter; his hand curled in her hair, and then, in the distance, they heard a car coming around the corner from the next block. She felt his body begin to tighten like a fisted knot, and he pushed away. He listened. He knew by the sound, it wasn't a delivery truck, few as there were; it had to be the police. All private automobiles were forbidden after curfew.

Marla took him by the hand. "Let's go." She continued walking away from the tavern toward the end of the street, towards the sound of the car.

He pulled away, "What are you doing!" He jerked away, "That's the Force."

"Trust me." She smiled. She pulled off his hat and ran up ahead of him. He saw the police car cruise into the deserted intersection and could hear the dispatcher on the radio. It stopped. Its spot light roamed up and down the buildings, and then it scanned over to them. Very slowly, it began to turn in their direction. He screwed up; he couldn't run; it was too late. He knew they had seen him. Marla tossed the hat in the air and laughed out loud as the black and green patrol cruiser came down the block. Its light now blinded his face. He turned away trying to regain his vision, and his hand slipped down to his belt. Travis knew they would stop and check ID's. He was going to have to take them.

"Catch it!" She tossed his hat back at him over his head and laughed and then ran back up to him just as the Force was nearly parallel to them. Travis glanced over at the large letters emblazed on the side of the car, METRO FORCE. The words paralyzed people in fear. He picked up his hat and unfastened a strap on the back of his belt. She jumped into his arms and spun him around so that his back was to the street. The Metro Force slowed to a stop. The two officers watched. The glow of the computer screen mounted on the dashboard illuminated their faces. One puffed slowly on an e-smoke. They were looking at Marla, studying her body; men always did. The police always loved to check the ID's of beautiful women. The two cops looked at each other and grinned. One reached for the door handle and was about to get out when down the block the crowd was beginning to break up. Some patrons went downstairs, and others began walking very quickly away from the pub. The driver pointed to his spot light on the crowd as a group of four walked briskly away. "Come on." They drove down to where the crowd was dispersing and stopped again.

Travis exhaled a long breath. His heart raced.

She felt the palms of his hands; they were sweaty; she felt them twitch. Marla looked into his face and saw the stains of fear, "Oh my dear, what did they do to you?" He didn't say anything, but she could feel his heart beating. She never knew for sure what he had gone through. She only knew he had been on the run for a long time. He totally disappeared, no phone calls, nothing. Now he was here.

"Travis, why did you come back?"

He didn't say anything. His eyes looked over her shoulder down the street to the Force. She brushed back his hair. It hung down over his eyes obscuring his face. "Did you come back just to see me?"

He still said nothing. He stayed focused on the cops down the street.

"Look at me, Travis." He glanced at her for a split second and then flashed away. She shook him, "Look at me." They stood face to face; his warm breath poured across her mouth. She kissed him gently on the lips. "You are here on some kind of mission, aren't you? You're with the resistance."

He uttered not a word, but she knew it was true. The world had done exactly what he always said it would. It became the nightmare he had warned her about.

She thought for a moment he wasn't going to go with her. Marla grabbed his hand and pulled him, "Come on, let's get you off the street and some place where we can talk...follow me."

Up the block, two people were handcuffed and shoved in the back of the squad car. Travis stopped and watched. There were no sirens, no lights. There was no disturbance. Without a sound, the Force had apprehended two more. Without a peep, they turned the corner and disappeared.

CHAPTER TWO

For a split second, a twinge of Deja vu
bristled across his skin. The whole scene, the setting, was like
reliving a dream. It was like stepping back into an experience
he was all too familiar with. The crowd of people dispersing
on a dark and desolate street; cops shinning spot lights in
people's faces; citizens taken away in the middle of the night
never to be heard of again. Travis looked around. He had
been there previously at some time. He knew it. He had
crossed that street before holding her hand where she led him
into an alley.

Marla looked at him curiously distinctively arching her
brow, "What is it?" His eyes scanned the buildings
reconnoitering their shape and structure. His vision was often
myopic, what appeared before or in the future was often in
reality an experience from his past. He had been there he was
certain of that, but it must have been long ago when she
chauffeured him around town. "Have I been here before?"

She shook her head, "Yeaaah, you were always too drunk
to remember. Come on."

"Where are we going?"

"Why did you say you wanted to see me if you don't trust
me? Do you think I would turn you in?

He didn't answer.

"Come on. Follow me."

He hesitantly followed her up the block towards the Pale
Horse Tavern and then suddenly turned into a dark alley. They
passed by several dumpsters cautiously, and Travis looked

intensely for anything that might move. They came up to a back door with a metal awning peeling with paint that overhung a set of stairs lit by a single incandescent light bulb. There was noise inside. They were at the back of the pub.

"Wait here, I'll be back."

Travis was suspicious; he had to be. Against his better reasoning, he feared she had led him into a dead end alley with no escape. Against his better instincts, he had walked into a trap. Travis had been set up before, and some of them had been people he devoutly trusted. Nevertheless, no one had he ever trusted, like Marla. She had never let him down. Apprehensively, he watched her walk up to the street and turned the corner. He had been warned not to contact her, not to come back, and not see her. Marla walked back out to the street to the front of the tavern and made her way down the steps past a crowd to the entrance. The bouncer inside the front door knew her. "Hello, Marla, where you been?" It was noisy; they had to yell to hear.

"Hey Mac," she squinted her eyes in the light, "Long time, huh." She stuck her palm down under the scanner. A blue light flashed, and the machine dinged. Marla looked about the bar; it was packed. There were maybe thirty tables, some small, some large and at least a hundred people inside the dimly lit establishment. The crowd was into an old Jeff Beck tune that riveted through the building. Marla listened, amazed how authentic his cooing guitar sounded, like he might have been jamming in the corner of the smoke filled room. She recognized the tune from long ago, *"Cause We Ended as Lovers"*. She could almost feel his fingers dancing up and down the ebony frets, like they were sliding across her body. She hadn't heard the song in years. So many great songs had been banned, i.e. "restricted."

"Ummm, nice music, Mac."

He pulled back his ponytail and gave her a warm muscular smile, "Enjoy while it lasts, we may be shut down."

"Why?"

He yelled above the crowd, "We're out of compliance…again. Come back tomorrow night, two drinks for one. Live music too!" Marla always liked Mac, he was big and protective. He had walked her home on a couple of occasions and she told him good night at her door. There was one time she thought about asking him in but never did. Sometimes it is better to have a friend, especially one as big and intimidating as Mac.

He looked at her over the heads of another couple. "I might see you tomorrow then?"

Marla only smiled. The crowd was pushing her into the bar. She held up her hand above the patrons and waved good-bye. Mac waved back to her as she disappeared into the dark pub and checked some other people as they came through the door. "Two hundred."

"Two hundred!" A small guy with a skinny skank looking girlfriend quibbled about the price and then reluctantly stuck his hand under the scanner. It dinged four hundred.

"Four hundred!" He protested, "You said two hundred, man."

Mac pulled back his sleeves. He was powerfully built with massive forearms that rippled up and down as he spoke. "Aren't you paying for the chic, too?"

"No way, I'm not paying two hundred a piece. Not for her."

Mac laughed, most the women in the pub were hot but underneath piles of makeup he could see sores. She looked bad. He held the scanner over the man's hand and deducted the charge and then motioned with his head, "Beat it". They pushed their way back through the crowd grumbling. To Mac, punks that bickered about the cover charge would also stiff the waitresses on tips, and so he just as soon they not be there to waste perfectly good tables. Same with the SCABS, they were all bums, low life.

Marla elbowed her way through the crowd adjusting her eyes to the light, or lack of it. It was one of the last places that didn't have cameras and people felt comfortable smoking without the eye watching. There were plenty of signs around saying that it was a "*Smoke Prohibited Establishment*", but it was never enforced. Nothing was; it was a rogue venue where the anti-establishment went. Everything was like things use to be, if you didn't like it… leave. The Pale Horse was one of the last places that she felt secure. It was why she wanted to go there. The crowd wasn't accepting to the Force or the SCAB's. Marla walked through the crowd past the bar looking for a table. All the men took notice. Marla smiled at Henry the bartender and said hello. He was shaking drinks and talking with a joint moving about his lip with the precision of a conductor's baton.

"Well, if it ain't New York's finest", he grinned and poured an Armageddon, his special concoction of seven sprits. Henry lifted his lighter, and lit it. "Allah," it burst into flames. As smoothly as a sidewinder releasing a pitch, he slid the flaming drink down the bar to another patron waiting to get smashed.

"Hey Henry, long time no see."

"Shame on you doll, the drinks on me." He set two pitchers under tap and pulled the handle back. Henry took a hit and laid his joint in the tray. "Got a date or are you coming to spend time with me?"

"With a friend."

He shook his head in exaggerated disappointment, "That's the wrooong answer. Be careful, there are some SCAB's here." Henry pointed with his eyes to a group of guys at a table in the back of the room. "If they give you trouble let me know. I'll uh...me, and Mac will take care of them."

Marla appreciated him. Women were often harassed by the SCAB's and the Force. The Pale Horse was usually a safe haven though it wasn't exactly the cleanest place in town. The room was dark, but the bar was brightly lit and customers' faces glowed in the spectrum of neon lights. For some reason it always reminded her of a booth at a carnival. Maybe it was the peanuts on the floor, or the atmosphere of a fair, or even the people and the rank smell of the beer, but she thought it was Henry. He was quiet the entertainer. The bar was his stage. He was a very intelligent guy, a great conversationalist and sharper wit than most comedians. He had been a banker before the crash; Mac, his partner, had been a builder. They were against *everything* that had to do with the government. Henry in particular detested the SCAB's with a passion, referring to them as 'monkey cops' with IQs bordering primates. And the SCABs girlfriends, he didn't give them breaks either, referring to them appropriately as "sores". He had a never ending repertoire of jokes about them; 'How did the SCAB break a leg raking leaves?' Answer: 'He fell out of a tree'. 'What did the skunk say to the SCAB at the zoo?' 'Why do SCAB's lick themselves like dogs?'

With Henry it was never ending, he expressed his disdain in the only forum he had left, and he was one of the few still brave enough to do so. He was opposed to government control. And so was most everyone else there. The Metro Force were always coming in and checking ID's. And, if it wasn't the Force it was the Health Department; if it wasn't the Health Department it was Homeland Security or ICE or OSHA or the Alcohol Beverage Control Agency. Then it was the city inspectors and after the city it was the county and after the county it was the state. It was constant total harassment, regulations and fines. They all wanted handouts, special favors, drinks and food. They were *all* pigs, they were all corrupt. He had to serve them because *they were the government*, but Henry let them know in his own way they were unwanted. They got lousy service and bad drinks, real bad. Obviously none of them could smell that well. No ordinary person would want to drink the beers they were served.

Henry often opined how the agencies were like ticks and he was their dog they were sucking dry. He spoke frequently about it with the regulars. All the other places in town that compiled were by comparison inhuman sterile environments. Cameras were mounted everywhere, all the conversations were under surveillance, people couldn't smoke; the food was tasteless but met all the USDA approved standards. The music sucked. The other bars were void of character, consumption was monitored. It is where the "politically correct" went to be seen. Only an imbecile could have fun there.

Marla preferred the bodegas and felt violated when the government SCAB's came *there* to get drunk. She saw them in the middle of the room and immediately felt accosted by their eyes. Indeed they made everyone feel uncomfortable. She ignored their banter and grabbed a table just as a couple was leaving, then she pulled off her jacket and tossed it over the back of a chair. She heard a few comments as she adjusted her sweater which she ignored. Then she walked down the dark hall past the restrooms and acted like she was waiting her turn to go in. When no one was there she opened the back door.

"Travis."

He was gone.   She didn't see anyone in the shadows. She called again. He had split. There was no one in the alley. She knew she had messed up, she had taken too long. He was not the type to wait around for long for anything. "Travis!"

"Babe."

She looked down the alley but it was totally dark. "Where are you?"

"Up here."

He jumped down from a ledge and landed beside her.

She rolled her eyes, "You know *normal* people don't do that?"

"If I was normal you wouldn't be here."

"You're right."   She grabbed his arm, "Come on, we've got a table."

He could see the place was an old brown stone, and not that well ventilated. Smoke hovered above the sea of tables like a fog, a gray drape that swirled anytime someone moved. Their table was in the back, and one of the closest to the back door which suited Travis fine. He pulled his chair back and sat down with his shoulders against the wall so he could watch the crowd. He had had always been strange that way, he never sat where someone could come up behind him.   Marla waved across the room and the waitress soon arrived.

She raised her fingers, "Two beers."

Travis shook his head, "No beer, just water for me." The waitress made a note on her iPad and walked off. Marla took off his hat and laid it on the table, "Get comfortable, you look like you just walked off the set of an old spy movie." She paused, "So you don't drink anymore?"

She didn't know if he would say anything about it. She figured he didn't want to talk. He leaned over the table and lowered his voice to a crawl, "Prison had one benefit, sobriety."

She put her hand down on his leg under the table and patted him. She was curious and she knew it was painful. "So how long?"

"Sober, humm, about five years, almost six. The toughest part was not thinking about you."

She ignored his flattery, "No, I mean how long were you in…prison?"

"Forty-two months". Travis talked without looking at her. He studied the crowd. "Didn't you know?" He was almost hiding his whole face with his hands; they covered his mouth and chin. His elbows rested on the table. His eyes constantly shifted around the room. It annoyed her as if he was avoiding eye contact, but she understood the reason for his paranoia.

"Do you want to talk about it?" she offered.

"No."

Confused, "Then why did you come here?"

"This is the last chance I will have to see you." He spoke through his hand cupped into a fist over his mouth. Travis was a man who never had to say that much but he meant every word he said. She didn't know the circumstances of him being there, but she knew he took a great risk to do it. Marla scooted her chair closer to him.

"But why? I didn't think you cared."

"I always cared. You wouldn't listen, remember?" He grabbed her chair by the leg and pulled it up even closer to him. His head leaned over to hers so that he was speaking into her ear. "I know you wouldn't ever understand back then." He looked around the room as if to make a point, "But I am sure you do now."

She nodded coyly and slid a cigarette out, "I might have gone along if you would have explained what was happening." She nudged him with her elbow, "And been *patient* with me."

He responded in a voice that was quiet and sullen, "You were in denial."

She lit her cigarette and shoved the lighter over to him, "I don't think that is it. I don't think you trusted me." She squeezed his leg hard with a pinch as to emphasis her point.

Travis inspected her face in the flickering table light. She had the most perfect complexion. Her eyes were magnetic, drawing him closer. He looked away and pulled out a smoke from his pack. It was a burnt butt and twisted at that. He straightened out the crumpled end and lit it; it looked like he was toking a reefer the way the smoke curled around his fingers. "You weren't ready." He tilted his head down and looked at the small anemic light on the table as if he was looking at a crystal ball. It flickered across his face turning it a pale orange. She watched the white of his eyes hidden in the shadows. Travis took a deep breath and then turned his face toward her. He took a puff and leaned back. "Considering what has happened, it is a good thing you didn't go."

She knew he was right. She hadn't believed anything he told her. He had said all these things would happen but she never believed it would all take place so quickly. She thought a lot of it was just drunken talk, but if anyone would have known it would be him. He knew a lot about what the government was doing. More than most. The waitress came back to the table with the beer and water. "You want anything else? Chips? Sandwiches?" She put the coasters down and slid the drinks on top. As she was talking, the SCAB's were two tables over saying annoying things to the waitress, and it was obvious she was trying to ignore them.

Marla observed Travis, staring at them, which was not good. It was never good when somebody got under his skin. He looked hungry. She was going to ask if he wanted anything but then stopped. He would be too proud to tell her. Marla nudged him trying to divert his attention from the group at the other table. "I'm starved", she wasn't. "How about two burgers?" She didn't give Travis a chance to decline. "Both with tomatoes."

"No tomatoes, quarantine is still on."

"Hey, what time you get off?" The SCAB's laughed, "We want something to take home, a sandwich with you in the middle." They howled at the remark slapping each other on the back and sloshing beers down their faces.

Marla wondered how the waitress took the abuse, "How about lettuce, got lettuce?"

The waitress shook her head no, as if why even bother to ask.

"Pickle, onion?"

"We've got some cheese and mayo." She said with a twist of irritation and noted something on her pad. Then she clicked a scanner, "Now did you want soy or GM beef?"

"What's the difference?"

She showed Marla the price. "We'll take soy."

The waitress punched in the order on her scanner and then she showed her the total. Marla accepted. She held out her hand and the waitress scanned it. The scanner light blinked and "dinged." "It will be about fifteen minutes."

Marla nodded and looked away. She acted coy. She knew Travis was anti-chip; he became resolutely opposed to it. He hated it. There was an awkward pause between them. Neither said anything, they both sipped their drinks and looked around the room at the other people. Finally she asked him, "Why don't you just say it?"

He took a drink and acted like he didn't know what she was referring to, "Say what?"

She stretched out her hand across the table as if it were evidence. "Do you hate me because I did?"

"No, I hate them. I hate me. They forced you." He reached across the table and took her other hand. He held it up inspecting the diamond ring. "I thought you'd have thrown it away. You surprised me, or did you dig it out of your jewelry box just for ole time's sake?"

"You thought wrong about a lot of things."

"I don't blame you?" Travis pulled her hair back and spoke into her ear, "Babe, *you* weren't the problem. I know it was me."

She didn't expect him to say that; she thought he was going to chastise her because he had been so vigilant in his beliefs. It was then she realized Travis seemed different. She couldn't quite figure out what it was about him. His eyes were alert, and his hands gentle. She wondered if it was because he wasn't drinking. When he got drunk, he was a hard man to deal with.

They both looked around the room, especially Travis, making sure no one could hear them. It wasn't the best place to be talking about such matters. The annoying jerks at the other table were now looking her way. She squeezed his hand and then stopped; she felt breaks in the two smaller fingers of his right hand. She could see it in the light. The joints were grossly enlarged and out of place, they looked like knots. He didn't say anything. She looked into his eyes, and he rolled his wrists over. Marla was stunned; she pulled the cuffs of his sleeve back, "Oh my God." She felt down his arm and looking at his scars crisscrossing his wrist.

She could barely hear him; the noise in the pub was so loud. "So much for the constitution, huh?"

"They did this to you?"

"The results of Rule 922. Small cost when we gave up our rights."

"My God. When? Where?"

Travis took a sip and spoke under his breath, "Let's talk about it later."

Marla felt sick. She had heard rumors but she passed it off as mere exaggerations. The media only reported that resisters, "terrorists", were interrogated, detained. Travis was a citizen. He was a genetic engineer and computer programmer. He wasn't a threat.

"Why, Travis? What did you do?"

He didn't answer. He looked anxious to get out of there. The groups of belligerent SCAB's at the other table weren't helping matters. They weren't in their usual drab brown uniforms. They were off duty but that made them no less irritating. They were sadistic bastards that had a reputation for tasering anybody. Most were marginally intelligent; they had low paying meaningless jobs in the pre-chip world, if they worked at all, but that changed with the chip. The government hired them by the thousands to scan citizens. They detained anyone who did not register and used their authority with impunity.

All four of them were looking over Marla with belligerent drunken smiles. That was not unusual; Marla always attracted attention. She was the best looking woman in the room no matter where she was, and she had that body that instantly drew men's eye. Travis put his hand up to the side of her face and slid his fingers through her hair and tugged her gently to him. "They're watching."

She whispered back, "But they are watching *me*, not you…relax."

He listened to their raucous laughter and smiled. It was not the smile she liked to see; it was tense and uneasy, and a prelude to an agitator hitting the floor. Marla tried to amuse him, "Don't worry about them Travis. They are going to go home drunk to their dingy little apartments and amuse themselves, but you've got me." She shook his arm as if to get his attention. "Did you hear me?"

He didn't say anything. The waitress finally brought the burgers and she could tell he was hungry. He ate without saying a word, and it was obvious he was famished. Marla purposely only nibbled so that Travis could have hers too. She leaned over and whispered, "So you want to tell me about the Freemen?"

"Not now." He chomped on his burger with his eyes on the next table.

She was sure he had become a member. Marla had heard from an old friend that he had joined or was enlisted. The government blamed them for everything. The Freemen were labeled as a hate group along with some ten thousand other organizations. They were Christians in origin, but there were Jews too, and even others. The Freemen were viewed by the government as a threat. They were singled out as obstructionist, and it was the government's aim to destroy them.

She was curious and asked him again cautiously risking his ire, "Are you part of the Freemen?"

He nodded. "We're free, just Free. Get it?"

Her heart sank. She looked at the scars on his wrists and felt again the broken bones in his hand. She had heard they had released some after they recanted their beliefs, "Did they let you go or…"

He shook his head and took another bite.

"Then you escaped?"

He nodded and looked away. Marla knew that being in his company put her at risk. The penalties for her would be as great as the punishment for him. There was a zero tolerance policy; there was for almost everything. He had taken a tremendous risk seeing her. Now, she was taking an equally great a risk being with him. There was something about Travis that was hard to resist. He was not ordinary, or normal, or typical. He had always been different.

The place was getting too loud to hear without practically yelling. Both their chairs were next to each other against the back of the wall, an old Allman Brothers tune was playing, *"Whipping Post"*. Travis pulled out another crumpled cigarette and started to light it. She took it out of his hand and gave him one of hers. He struck a match under the table and lit both of them. They glanced around the room. Then, he turned toward her and put his elbow up on the table again so that his hand somewhat shielded his face. She understood why he was so secretive. He blew the smoke in the air and put his arm around her. "What do you want to know?"

"Everything."

"I thought you told me once you didn't want to hear about it, remember?"

"Now I know the facts, so what happened?"

Travis leaned his head to hers and began whispering. He told her that he became 'tuned in' when he realized what their research was actually designed to accomplish. All the systems were compromised and became corrupt. It was all about total control. He began studying everything, even the banking system. She remembered he talked about that a long time ago.

He discovered that billions were being stolen with the click of a mouse. All the systems were integrated; all technologies phased into one. The chip. There was an avalanche of abuse and corruption which led him to oppose everything Big Brother was doing. It is why the people in power imposed micro chipping. Referring to the government, he said, "It was like watching pirates taking control of the ship."

She listened utterly amazed. Travis worked on secret projects for the government; projects that he could never talk to her about; projects he was forbidden to, but if anyone would know, it would have been him. He said that hackers began feeding him information they retrieved once they broke through the security walls. It was all devious. She listened to his every word. He spoke about the privacy invasions, how every purchase at first was being recorded through RFID tags, and then, of course, the chip. The data were sorted through by bureaucracies. They were determining consumer behavior habits and developing and identifying citizens and contraband lists. People were being classified into 'modules of resistance'. This information was being shared with the military, police agencies and even foreign governments. He saw what it was becoming so he got out.

Marla listened and thought back reflectively and wondered how she could have missed it. Travis had warned her. She thought he was insane. She remembered his mad ramblings about the chip and everything it was going to do, which she passed off as drunken tirades. But, he wasn't the only one; she had other friends that were fearful. It had happened so subtlety. It wasn't in the headline news; or those micro thirty second blurbs once an hour on the radio stuck between the litanies of plastic rock songs. Still, the evidence was there. And then one day she came home, and he was gone.

Travis went out west to Colorado. He tried to get her to come, but she wouldn't leave New York. It was strange. He called and emailed, and then one day, he just disappeared. Vanished. He tried to leave the country, but they weren't letting anyone out by then. He wrongly figured they'd leave him alone because he quit his work and was no longer involved in the project, and then one day, out of the blue, he was pulled over. He was first questioned, then, detained. He was interrogated by various government agencies like some kind of criminal and then moved from a jail to a prison. Travis told her he wasn't allowed a single phone call; the Homeland Security Act prevented that. Still, it wasn't until he was transported to prison that he himself realized the magnitude of what was happening. Thousands, like him, were loaded on trains like cattle, shipped to prisons that had been built all across the country.

"But you escaped?"

"Yeah, over a year ago. But I was there for forty-two months."

She was shocked, "Forty-two months? So, you've been on the run ever since then?"

He shook his head, "Yes, and I've been in training". He snuffed out his cigarette, and she could tell he wasn't going to tell her anymore.

It was so strange; Travis had been gone for years, no communication, not a word. Several agencies came and questioned her, but she hadn't known anything about where he was or what he was doing. She knew nothing of the escape, and then suddenly he reappears. She looked about the room at all the people; there was noise, music and laughter. It was like people were in one world, and they were in another, separated from the crowd in their own little capsule, a sphere to themselves.

For Marla, it seemed oddly reminiscent of an experience she had as a child. Her favorite ride was the tilt-a-world. She would spin round and round with her sister; sometimes she would spin all alone. She remembered the feeling of the fair at night, the noise, the lights of amusements as she spun round and round unable to escape. Now, she felt the world was spinning uncontrollably around her, but it was her and Travis, and she was being pulled to him. There had always been this vector force she was powerless to resist. The rest of the world was becoming a blur the faster she spun. His world became the thing she held on to. It made her uneasy because she had been sucked in before until all that existed was the two of them spinning in their world, and then one day he vanished. Marla sat next to him; their eyes focused on each other. She knew if she was going to get out, she had to leave then. She had to get up from the table and walk away.

Marla tried to regain her thoughts. She struggled to remember what they were talking about stumbling for words, "Training? What kind of training?"

He didn't bat an eyelash. He looked straight at her with the most petrified expression, his gray eyes penetrating; "The end."

There was a long chilling silence between them.

She took a gulp of beer as if digesting the context of his words. Her mouth suddenly went dry. Travis never took his eyes off her. His voice was calm and steady, tranquil as any voice she ever heard. "You know what I mean don't you?"

She didn't. "I think so."

"This is all coming to an end". His eyes locked onto hers, "You may want to get out."

Her heart quivered. A lump grew in her throat. She

finished the rest of her beer hoping it might revive the dryness in her mouth, but it didn't. She knew one thing about Travis, he meant every word. He dealt only in absolutes. The end meant the end. She felt her legs begin to shake, and a cold paleness flushed down her face. She needed to think about what she was doing, where this was going. She got up, "I need to go to the ladies room."

She left somewhat off balance and walked down the hall. Travis wondered if she would come back. He wished he could have been more subtle, but there was no subtle way to say it. It was like telling someone they had cancer; you just have to get out there. He looked about the room at all the faces, people laughing and getting drunk. Their days were numbered. He knew time was about out. They didn't. Civilization was hurtling into a cataclysmic wall. There would be no survival.

Travis smiled at the insidious creeps, the four goons at the next table. The big one with the cheesy pointed goatee gave Travis a retarded look, crossed his eyes and started laughing. Not a smart thing to do to a guy like Travis. They were all laughing.

A few minutes later Marla came back and the SCAB's whistled and made grunting noises like a pen full of pigs. Travis ignored them. He put his arm around her, "You can leave. I won't hold it against you."

She shook her head, "What are we going to do?" The color had returned to her cheeks. She had put some blush on, but he could still see the evidence where she had been crying. He knew she was scared. He took her hand then picked her purse and set it in her lap. Travis eyes watched the big ogre get up from the table and stumble back towards the bathroom. He told her to go to the entrance, and he would be right back.

Travis followed the SCAB down the hall, and Marla made

her way through the crowded bar, "Goodnight, Henry. I might see you tomorrow."

He smiled and shrugged and mixed another Armageddon. "If we are here."

She stood by the door at the entrance and waited. The music was a thousand decibels too loud, and she could hardly hear anything standing where she was by the speaker. She watched the hallway across the smoke-filled room where the restrooms were down a dim hallway at the back of the building. A few minutes later Travis came out. He made his way through the concourse of tables and chairs, and she could see he was holding his hand.

"Let's go."

They made their way through the crowd at the door where Mac was. Marla stopped, "Mac, this is...Thomas. A friend from long ago."

The big guy brushed back his hair and smiled, "Good to meet you man." He stuck out his hand when he saw Travis's right hand bleeding between the knuckles. He looked at Marla puzzled. She put her arm around him and smiled, "Night Mac, take care."

Travis looked at Mac and nodded, "Good to meet you man. And by the way, your toilet is stopped up. Somebody may want to take a look at it."

"In the men's room?"

"Yeah. Something is stuck. He was too big to flush."

They ran out the door and up the stairs back out onto the streets. They walked briskly away for a block, and then they stopped. She pulled his hand out of his coat pocket inspecting it under a street light. "What am I going to do with you?" There were several gashes on his knuckles, and his ring finger was swollen. She sighed, "You never were very sociable."

Travis lifted her face up to him. He pulled out a cigarette from her coat and placed it in her lips. He lit it and without saying a word they turned away from the Tavern and began walking down the street. It wasn't till they walked several blocks that she noticed that he didn't have any bags, no suitcase, nothing. "You travel pretty light, don't you pard?"

"Have to."

Teasing him she asked, "So ah, Lone Ranger where you planning on spending the night?"

"With you."

Marla walked with him with her hand in his. All she planned on was seeing him, perhaps get a bite, and fill in the details of their missing years. It took less than an hour, and they were right back to where they were six years before. "This is scary Travis, so freaking scary."

"You mean about us, or about the world?"

"Both."

Travis looked over his shoulder back down the block, "You're right. I agree."

Two streets down, driving slowly in the shadows of the buildings without their lights on, was a dark car without inscription, following.

CHAPTER THREE

In all the years she had ever known him; it was the only time she could remember that she woke up before he did. She sat there that morning staring out her small living room window toward Central Park with her coffee in hand wondering if this was real. The old oil furnace was usually too hot or too cold, it hissed and rattled but that morning it was quiet, seeming just right, taking the chill out of the morning air. She hung her feet over the armrest of the divan and warmed them by the furnace, snuggled in her favorite tarry cloth white robe.

It was eight o'clock, a Saturday, and she was thankful that she didn't have to trudge off to work. All her feelings about Travis were back again. Like tulip bulbs that had been dormant for years, stored away in a dry safe place, until planted. That morning they were already blooming. It happened just that fast. Six years and three and a half months had passed since they were last together, but she didn't want to think about that. Not that morning.

Marla lit some incense. She loved the smell of fragrance and aroma of coffee in the morning whenever she had the chance. She never smoked until evening, a habit she had long had since she couldn't smoke at work anyway. The faint trail of incense crossed the room, and thoughts ran through her mind like water pouring down through a sluice separating the good from the bad, the past from the present.

Her body still tingled, thinking about last night. He was the slowest man she had ever known to make love. Most rushed through it skipping the more delicate aspects of it, and

29

on occasion he did too; but last night, time seemed suspended. It was like experiencing a ritual. She felt like she had been worshipped. It was a feeling she had forgotten; it had been so long since she felt so satisfied.

She smiled as her mind rolled about in carnal thoughts and then laid back and set her laptop across her legs. Instantly she felt its warm drive pulsating in her lap. Marla quietly hummed a rather octave less nonsensical tune and scrolled through the news with a mischievous grin transversed on her face. There were only a few sites that were authorized by the authorities, and it had become somewhat of a joke to everyone. News was never new; it was painfully repetitive. Everyone was numb to it; it was the same old standard government line. Everything was fine, yeah, yeah, yeah, of course it was; the economy was about to turn around; another stimulus was going to kick in. Have hope. It was all about the government. They were going to solve everything. She yawned and checked her text messages on her phone, returned a few, the rest she deleted.

Marla had very few women friends. It had always been mainly guys, though most eventually became jealous or possessive. Travis for some reason never was. He was strange that way, and she liked it. He was real, but when he hurt he told her. She always felt though that he was like from another planet, but she was too. Like somehow they both had been placed there, they were misfits, and on the surface mismatched. Yet, there was a connection that was hard to explain. She knew one thing, he always cared. He cared for her like no man ever had. He had told her once that she was his oasis. The world was a desert. His life before her was barren as was the life after. She related. He said they were time travelers, and this was their stop together. No one ever thought like Travis, except maybe her.

She sipped on her coffee and scrolled through her texts. Mac had texted her to see if she was fine. She wanted to text him back and say, "Better than ever"; instead she said that she was "k". She knew he had a thing for her and didn't want to hurt his feelings. Mac was always the guy she considered a possible. He was good looking and nice. He was a gentleman too; and perhaps too much. Other women went gaga over him, but for some reason he was always just a friend.

She scrolled down through the news bar on her laptop and thought about everything Travis had told her the night before. Somehow she knew that everything he said was true. In fact, it was Henry who had told her that the Freemen were the government's scapegoat for everything that had gone wrong. It didn't matter what it was: a train derailment, a toll bridge collapse, the plight of corn, the constant malfunction of traffic lights. The Freemen were the convenient blame for everything from satellites crashing to the squirrel flu, the pandemic that never happened. Nevertheless, the mandatory government vaccine cost 122,000 otherwise healthy citizens their lives.

It was all the fault of the Freemen. The government, the "Big Bitch", was responsible for nothing. Each event necessitated even more laws. There was a call for stricter security, more surveillance, more police, bigger agencies, more prisons. More, more, more, and every conceivable problem in infrastructure was caused by saboteurs. The people were reminded over and over again that they were at war with "terrorists that threaten American's freedom". Even the demise of the dollar had been blamed on the Frees for had it not been for the expensive war to eradicate the "evil in our midst," America would have remained strong financially.

Yeah, yeah, sure.

It all made sense now; Marla knew it.   She scrolled through the glib headlines.   Entire events were reduced down to a few sentences that undoubtedly had been authorized by some government agency.   The internet was swept clean of all subversive sites, and there was no news that could be ascertained on any event that was more than the most trivial sound bite.   All news had to be authorized to prevent 'misinformation and hate speech'.   There was no forum for WikiLeaks.   Information had to be disinfected through the purgatory process known as 'filtering.'   Only the government was allowed to 'filter' because only it was capable of determining what was disingenuous and divisive.   As a result almost no one watched the news media.   It was so sterile as to make one vomit, virtually useless mundane disinformation. Marla had lost interest like most other people and her world became infinitely smaller to the point that the only things that interested her was her tiny apartment and her monthly allotment of rations.   She hadn't really realized it till Travis came back, but she was living comfortably numb.   It was a term she heard that a sociologist used to described her generation.   It might have been attributed to the Pink Floyd song by that name.   Life consisted of not much more than breathing and eating.   Life was a process of function rather than purpose.   The Stanford sociologist, who was forced into exile, said that it happened day by day; it was by design.   He theorized that the masses could be tranquilized into complete obedience if all competing, or challenging maxims were removed.   A government could thence subdue a nation or people with minimum resistance.   By minimum, he meant one or two percent of the population.   The key essential elements to accomplish this feat were of course education and media.

Once they were firmly under the government's influence, if the proper steps were taken, it was just a matter of time.

Marla didn't want it to be so. She realized now she had grown comfortably numb. She thought she was numb; but in reality it was a nightmare, a nightmare that wasn't going to go away. She turned off her computer and looked in on Travis lying on his stomach with the sheets across his legs and his arms flung to the side. He was spread out with his arms to the side like he was lying face down on a cross. He only slept like that when he was very, very tired. She tiptoed over to him and was about to slip under the sheets to arouse him when she noticed several round reddish marks on his back. They looked like burns. There were dozens of them starting at his shoulders and going down his spine. She reached over to touch them and then stopped. He looked so tired; she decided to leave and let him sleep.

Marla shut the door and went into her kitchen. It was a quick reality check. Travis had paid for his freedom with a price, as did many others. This was not a theory, or article or course in college. The rumors, as awful as they were, must have been true. It was almost too much for her to comprehend. She seemed unable to grasp the total significance of it all. Her mind wanted to escape, to pretend it wasn't true. She looked out her window to the city; it was such a perfect morning. The sun was out; people were already going to the park. She felt torn, ripped right down the middle, as if her soul was being shredded into two halves. One involved Travis, the other a sublime indifference. She was prone to view things in an almost rhapsody fantasia without adherence to reality.

She couldn't cope with the thought anymore. She didn't want to think of the Freemen, or the world, or the government. She just wanted to enjoy the morning. It was a perfect morning to cook a breakfast, but disappointment quickly greeted her when she opened her fridge, a small mundane box about half the size of a filing cabinet with a freezer inside smaller than a shoe box. She had just one egg and a little bit of cheese, imitation at that. Marla went back to her lap top and checked her rations, and what luck. She had four more eggs that were allotted to her that month that she hadn't received, and eight ounces of cheese. She had bagels already in the fridge and jelly. If there was any fruit available at the market, they could have a grand breakfast just like old times. She scribbled down a note and left it on the counter that she would be right back; she had gone to the store. She put on lipstick and kissed the note, threw on her coat and was out the door. It was four flights of stairs to the street, and she just hoped Tannenbaum's would have what she needed. She didn't want to have to track four eggs all over town.

Marla knew the owner of course, and on occasion, he held something back for her. And perhaps, he did for some of the other women as well, but that didn't bother her; he was a nice Jewish man with a thick Yiddish accent. He liked Marla because she was so Midwestern, so All-American. If it had not been for the tiny inch long scar on the bottom of her chin Marla would have been destined for a modeling career, that and the ten extra pounds, which never did seem to bother the men.

"Morning, Mr. Tannenbaum."

"Vhy good morning, Marla. You look radiant. Good night sleep?"

"A good night, that's for sure". She smiled, "Have you got eggs and cheese?"

"Just in, and a surprise vor you", he lowered his voice. His eyes shifted around the store, "We've got bacon, can you believe it? Shhhh. It's been awhile, and since it's not kosher I thought…"

"How much?"

He wagged his finger at her and lowered his voice even more bending over the counter, "Tsk, tsk, tsk. You should know better by now." He pulled a pound of bacon out of the freezer and brought her a dozen eggs.

She looked around at the other patrons. They didn't get the special treatment that she received, and she was careful not to reveal anything. The government was very strict about rations and appropriations. "I only have rations for four eggs". He scanned her hand and looked at her monthly allotment on the screen behind the counter. He opened the carton and winked, "I see only four. Anything else?"

"Cheese?"

Mr. Tannenbaum opened up the freezer behind him and pulled out a pound of cheese, "Eight ounces coming up." He scanned her hand.

"Oh Mr. Tannenbaum, you don't know how much this means to me."

He grinned and put her things in her bag, "I think I do. I remember when I was young." She smiled and hurried out the store. It was only a block and a half away from her apartment, but she was worried that Travis might have awakened, panicked and left. She watched all the faces along the way making sure he hadn't bolted and lost himself in the crowd. When she got to her apartment building, she went to the elevator. It only came on every fifteen minutes per order of the Energy Commission. Like everything else, electricity was conserved. That's when the older people used it. Younger people were encouraged to use the stairs, and indeed, it did save a lot of energy. Marla didn't really mind; it kept her legs in shape. She walked by the folks in the lobby waiting for the elevator to start. According to the clock on the wall, they had seven more minutes to wait before the doors would open. She gave them all the customary greetings. They all liked seeing her; she was vivacious and friendly to them all and often helped them with their trash or their groceries and did odd chores, favors for them. In many ways she was like a surrogate daughter to them.

"Marla."

"Marla."

"Marla Jean."

"Good morning. Good morning. Good morning." She whisked by them and darted for the stairs, "I would talk, but I am expecting a phone call. Talk to you later. Bye."

"Marla."

"Mar...." She ran up the steps blowing the hair out of her eyes and was winded by the time she got to the fourth floor with a renewed aspiration to quit smoking again. She didn't feel totally relieved until she put her key in the door, and the dead bolt was still locked. He hadn't gone anywhere. She checked on him in the bedroom first thing. Travis hadn't moved, not one inch. In fact, he was snoring and talking in his sleep, murmuring things she didn't understand. She shut the door quietly and wondered if she should start breakfast then or wait until he awoke. She decided to wait and toasted a bagel to tie her over. It was nine thirty and the most beautiful day that she could remember in a long time. She sat on her couch and watched the people milling in the street. A beautiful spring day, chilly but sunny. It reminded her of how it once was. When they first met, Travis worked at St. John's University. He was older, and she liked that. He fascinated her from the beginning. His apartment was down by Battery Park, and she loved to go there. They spent all their time down there, picnics, bike riding, taking the ferry to the Statue of Liberty and Staten Island.

Marla nibbled on her bagel and watched the people going to the park. It was odd, very odd. It was like nothing changed, but she knew that wasn't right. Everything changed. On the surface things appeared as they always had, but there were signs that couldn't be ignored. Many of the buildings were boarded up, but that also happened in the first great depression. There were cameras everywhere that was obvious. She wanted to pretend that everything was normal, before the rations and all the controls. She tried to imagine that morning as it used to be; and as thoughts were materializing in her mind, she spotted a Raven hovering in the air over a group walking along the storefronts down on the street. It was taking their pictures. It flew about thirty feet above them; and when they crossed the intersection, it followed.

Reality set in. The world was not the same. It was haunting.

She couldn't remember when she first saw the Ravens, but she knew they hadn't always been there. They didn't spy on people when she was young. They weren't even around when she was with Travis. But one day they appeared, and not long after came the Wasps and Flys, and the Big Dog, and all the other government drones. One day she looked around, and they were everywhere, following and watching…. and chasing. The drones took over. Just like with the surveillance cameras, she couldn't remember when she first saw one; but one day she looked around, and they were on every building, every room, spying. Marla wondered how it happened. There was no more privacy; it became an obscure thought you couldn't even comprehend. She was thirty-three years old, and she knew it used to be different. People used to kiss and hold hands and without being monitored, observed; but it was so subtle the way it all happened.

She had been numb to it without ever realizing she was numb, which is probably the best definition of numbness, you don't feel it. You don't know it is happening. She sipped her coffee and leaned against the ledge of her window; and though it wasn't usually her habit, she lit a cigarette and cranked the window open. She hadn't reflected much on life in recent years; it seemed to have been getting away from her, dissolving like a sandcastle in waves, slipping away into an ocean of indifference.

Marla observed the people that morning from a fresh vantage point. The park was filling up with people toting umbrellas, and yet there wasn't a hint of rain. Street vendors sold them by the thousands, and now she figured out why. She couldn't believe she had been that naïve. The only way to have privacy was to shield one's face, and so thousands went to the park with umbrellas, or sunbrellas as they were popularly called, to shield one's face. Others wore floppy hats to protect what little identity they had left. People were taking measures to avoid iris scanners and remote cameras. What a shame, she thought, that people adapt to their conditioned environment.

Reality scared her. She nervously tapped her cigarette ash out the window.

Marla realized that morning that she had been pathetically naive. She never indulged in political discussion, finding it boring and irritating. Consequently, she never paid attention when the government took measures to tighten security; she never considered this would be the consequence. She was gullible and believed that such measures protected her freedoms, never suspecting they were actually doing the opposite; they were taking them away. Marla for the first time realized how easily she had been duped. She looked down at the crowd and wondered how many were just like her. How many were oblivious to the true motives. She took another drag and snubbed her cigarette out and then fanned her hand in the direction of the window. Normally she wouldn't take chances violating the code, but she needed a smoke that morning to calm her nerves thinking about the predicament she was in.

Her emotions had gotten the best of her and maybe something else. She was taking an awful chance having Travis there; and yet, she so badly wanted to be with him. It seemed so natural; it always had. It was like there just wasn't any use fighting it. She never was able to put her finger on it. She knew other guys more handsome, Mac was. But Travis was so fearless, fearless and determined. She had never met a man so sure of himself. Often, he didn't say a lot, but he meant what he said and because of that, when he did say something or expressed himself, it meant more than all the words of other men put together. Two large marble Angelfish swam circles in front of the glass trying to get her attention. It amused her; they were so graceful and gentle and yet so utterly dependent upon her. She looked at the permit on her tank. It was about to expire, and penalties and fines were quite severe. She didn't want to think about it. Marla sprinkled the fish flakes on the surface and watched their small mouths breech the surface. She could relate to them; her space was not that much larger than theirs. In fact, her space was quiet smaller when measured in proportion. Their window was much larger than hers from which they could view the world. A thought suddenly rushed up her arm tickling her skin. What if Travis could stay with her? He didn't have to leave; they could be like her two Angelfish. They seemed happy; they were fed. There was a possibility, she could work and come home; they would eat and enjoy each other's company. They could be together, and no one had to know it. What happened in the world didn't have to affect them any more than the fish in the tank. It was feasible; after all it happened to the fish.

Marla considered the possibility and it would work except that Travis would never adjust. He would be like a tiger in a cage, pacing constantly looking for escape. Other men would gladly wait for her all day but not Travis. The thought, the whole idea quickly vanished.

Suddenly she felt his presence in the room. She turned around. He was standing there with the bed sheet wrapped around him like a toga. "Hey, handsome."

He rubbed his eyes, "Watcha' doing?"

"Oh, nothing", she smiled.

Travis sat on the couch next to her and gave her a kiss. He looked at his watch and let out a long exhausting yawn and scratched his head. She stretched out her legs across his thighs and he pulled back her robe exposing her leg and kissed her the top of her knees. He didn't look at her but stared out the window in a post slumber gaze.

"I can't believe I'm with you."

"I'm the one that's shocked."

"I use to be pretty hard to get along with wasn't I?"
"You could be quite an ass." She smiled and patted his leg, "You pretty much cornered the whole market on buttholes."

Travis grinned; he couldn't help but chuckle. He brushed the hair out of his face. His gray eyes were strangely soft, "I am surprised *you* never left me."

"Oh, I tried," she sighed, "but I couldn't." Marla wanted to change subjects, "So, you want to go to the park today?

Look at how beautiful it is."

"Ummm. Let me think about it. This is what I never get to do". He kissed her.

"Sleep in?"

"Sleep in a bed. Relax. I am always on the move."

"Why don't I get you breakfast?" She got up and handed him her laptop, "Want to look up anything?"

He leaned back on the couch, "I will later. I just want to look at you."

She kept glancing back at him intermittently playing tag with her eyes that morning as she cooked breakfast. It was peculiar, like she was watching a movie reel from six years before. He sat back on the couch just like he always had with the same manners, his hair was longer. His build was almost the same, if anything he was leaner than before. It was odd, though, like somewhere there were years of missing movie reels on the floor. They talked the rest of that morning about the good old times, both carefully avoiding the more difficult subjects. He did not talk at all about their breakup, and he never asked her about her boyfriends though he knew there were many. He did mention 'Collier' a few times, a guy she worked with that never quite materialized into a steady after Travis left. She corrected him with a bit of irritation in her words, "His name was Collins," but then she quickly dropped the subject after that. He did too.

She noticed that when Travis got up he never stood directly in front of the window only to the side. He let down the blinds and adjusted the slats up as to prevent anyone looking up from the street. He mentioned to her how well he liked her apartment. He said he liked the view even more than the place they use to have down by Battery Park, and complimented her on how she had it decorated. There were lots of books and of course the fish tank that hummed quietly in the corner. He looked through her collection of albums. He pulled out an old Lennon album and put it on her ancient Phillips turntable. The music started to play. They both hummed and sang along, with her in the kitchen. She cooked; he walked around the room admiring her collection of art. He studied with intense curiosity several Eisher lithographs on the wall and admired the collection of Salvador Dali's prints.

It was a wonderful relaxing morning for both of them as they laughed and enjoyed her breakfast. They looked at each other with the same amazement. After they ate and washed dishes together, Travis picked up a deck of cards and did some tricks for her, same tricks he had always known. In the old days he would do them in bars for entertainment and get free drinks for the two of them wherever they went. Then…she remembered his favorite trick, the one no one else could do.

"Can you still read minds? You remember that thing with the telephone book?"

"I have forgotten. It has been too long."

She could tell he was reluctant. "Let's see." She reached under the counter and pulled out her old New York phone book and tossed it to him. "Remember these?" He flipped through the pages for no more than thirty seconds.

"Okay, but I am probably rusty". He handed it back to her and asked her to give him three numbers between 1 and 9.

"Nine, three, eight."

Travis reversed the numbers and then subtracted eight, three, nine from nine, three, eight. "Turn to page 99." She did. She stood far off from him with her back to the wall and he told her to view the whole page. She looked down page 99 grinning.

"I'm going to freak if you can still do this."

"Marla Jean, you have to concentrate or it won't work. Clear your mind and look at the whole page." He waited. "Now look at me."

Travis looked into her eyes for about twenty seconds starring in perfect unblinking stillness. "Go to the third column and look at the nineteenth name from the top. Are you looking at it?"

"Yes."

"Is it Bell, Art 212-267-5645?"

"NOOOOO Way!"

Travis started laughing. Marla was jumping up and down in hysterics repeating, "I can't believe this. I just can't believe this! That is freakin' impossible."

A broad smile ratcheted up the side of his face, "Thought I lost the touch didn't you?"

"Do it again."

He shook his head, "You know how this drains me."

She did a kiss with puckered lips, "Please."

"Alright, give me three more numbers."

"Four, one, seven." She was careful not to pick any of the same numbers.

He reversed them and subtracted the small one from the big one, "Ah, okay, turn to page 297." She did and scanned down the page. Travis was a good fifteen feet away from her stretched out on the couch. He held his fingers to his temple and squinted his eyes. "Go to the second column, fifth name down. Look at it. Is the name, Martin, Alfred 212-788-9600?"

Marla's jaw dropped open. "Oh my freakin'—amazin'!" She shimmied her neck and shoulders. "How do you do that?"

Travis rubbed his temple, "Practice."

"Don't give me that 'The brain is trainable crap'. You can't train the mind to do that."

Travis smiled, "Only about a third of your brain is consciously aware..."

"Yeah, yeah", she mocked. "Do it *one* more time. One more, I am begging you. I haven't seen you do this in years. I've told lots of people about this trick, I just want to see it again."

"Babe, it drains me. You don't have any idea how this wastes me. No."

She weaved back and forth in her bath robe, "You know how this turns me on."

He shook his head no. Marla jiggled her breast beneath her robe and smiled. "Please...I'll be good."

Travis caved in and laughed. "Last time. Give me three numbers."

"Seven, three (she paused thinking) and five."

Travis reversed the numbers and subtracted. "I may not be able to get this one because I am losing energy." He sighed, "Go to page 198."

She flipped through the pages and came to page 198. She looked up and down each column, and waited. He rubbed his head and moaned. "I am having a hard time focusing. Look again at the names." Marla looked down at all the names on the page.

"I'm looking."

"On the first column is there something like ferment?"

"No." She had seen him miss it before. "Wro'ong", she said in a snippety ding dong tone.

He held up his hand, "Wait. Go back. In the middle of the column. It is coming in. I see something...lemme look. It's coming in." He paused squinting his eyes, "Is there a Ferman, Erin Rae?"

She dropped the book on the kitchen floor and put her

hands over her mouth. She couldn't believe it. Three times in a row.

"Fooled you. Don't ever underestimate me."

"You are freakin' awesome, Travis." Marla came around the counter and laid a big kiss on him. She rubbed her hips against him. "You have no idea what that does to me."

He smiled. "I have a clue." His hand rolled across her butt, "But was I seeing what you are seeing? Or did you see what I was seeing?"

She looked confused. "You are seeing what I am looking at, right?"

"That's merely entertainment honey. It is just numerical gymnastics. But when I can *make* you see what my vision is, it is something else."

"What?"

"Power."

"I guess they didn't *fry* all your brains did they?"

There was a momentary awkward pause. She felt his hand lose its grip. She couldn't believe she said something like that. She didn't mean to; it just slipped out. She put her hand gently on his chest and untied the loop in her bath robe. "And guess what the prize is for you?"

"Later."

Apologetically, "Travis I didn't mean that. I don't know why I said it."

"It's okay, really. I'm going to take a shower."

He slammed the door, and she heard the water running for about thirty seconds. He always took the world's quickest showers. A minute or so later he walked out drying his hair. She looked at him and shook her head and then went into the bedroom. She came out and tossed him a shirt, a red and brown plaid shirt. "Try this on, it's clean." Travis looked at the back of it; it was a size 46, he wore a 42, or use to. He had dropped about fifteen pounds from what he had been. He slipped it on.

Marla then held up his belt with various gadgets holstered to it and a sly smirk crisscrossed her face, "What are you? Like Commando Dan?" The leather belt was more like a four inch wide strap with a dozen or so attachments. "Humm, let's see…audio jammer, video detector, ice spray, wire cutters, looks like an all in one ratchet and screwdriver set, night goggles…"

He grabbed the belt out of her hand, and she held up two leg shin straps, "Don't forget these, Mr. Gizmo."

Travis look annoyed, "I've got to charge some of these." He laid the belt by the wall and plugged several devices into the socket.

"What, no guns or knives?"

"My coat."

"Oh yes, the average fifty pound overcoat that is so popular these days." She pointed to the couch, "Okay now, tell me about it. I want to know everything. I want to know about your wrist and the scars on your back. We are not doing anything else till you tell me."

He hesitated. She buttoned the front of his shirt and pulled his face down to hers, "I want to know, and I'll never say anything inconsiderate like that again."

Travis shrugged; he didn't seem to be smarting over her comments. Travis was one not to ever let little things get under his skin. He had faults, but that was never one; he was the most resilient that way. He looked at his watch, and it wasn't like he had anywhere he had to go. He knew he had to explain some things so he zipped up his pants and sat down on the couch. Marla took his head into her lap and he laid there relaxed looking up at the ceiling. She ran her fingers through his damp hair playing. "Tell me about Rule 922."

"You want to know *now*?"

"Yes, and forgive me for that dumb thing I said."

"Forget it." He sipped on some water and slowly began to recant the events prior to his arrest. He talked about the time after he left and moved to Colorado. He bought a small ranch and for a while kept trying to get her to move out there. She remembered the time well; she thought he had become a survivalist nut and had even quit reading his letters because she didn't want to hear about it anymore. Then Rule 922, the Citizens Registration Act, became law. Travis told her that the people that refused the V-chip lost citizenship rights. That much she knew. He continued, "People were treated like illegal aliens. Didn't matter if they had served their country, paid their taxes; did all the things good citizens do. They were stripped of their rights." Without citizenship rights, properties were confiscated, businesses closed, bank accounts and assets seized. Many stayed under the radar for a long time, but eventually all were reported and detained. Rule 922 made non-compliance a seditious act, a federal offense.

"So you weren't trying to overthrow the government or anything?
That's what the papers made y'all out to be."

"We wanted what all the generations before us wanted. Freedom. That was taken away. The people that passed the law were the ones guilty of sedition, not us." He said people were first sent to detention centers just like they would if they had entered the country illegally. All she knew was that Travis was detained; there was an occasional censored letter with half his words blocked out, but nothing more. It was strange, and she couldn't get any information. She was told by authorities that he had become a terrorist. Travis told her she was fed disinformation. The truth was that mock trials were held; but there was one lawyer assigned to every five hundred cases, and the appeals process was a joke. But the government was able to maintain to the press that no one's constitutional rights were violated. According to them, every person had 'representation'.

Travis took a deep breath and reached for a smoke. "But that was just the beginning. There was no physical torture in the detention centers, the torture didn't begin till we went to prison". He anticipated that about eighty percent of the people in the detention centers eventually cut deals, some with the promise they might get their homes back, others caved in just to be back with their families. He held no grudge against those that gave in. "I only hold a grudge against those that gave false witness."

"Is that what happened to you?"

She could see him clinching his fist. The thought upset him. "Yes. The Nazi's did the same trick. They coerced people to tell lies." He was denied the chance to address his accusers in court. Travis said there were even written statements by people he never even knew saying that he was planning the violent overthrow of the government.

Still skeptical, "But you weren't?"

"Oh sure, I had a 22 rifle and some shells. I was planning on mounting a ridge and picking off the tanks. Had a bucket full of potatoes too when I ran out of bullets. Figured I could knock their freakin' heads off. They said I was trying to secure a 30/30 rifle, and I was. It's a hunting rifle for Christ's sake; it ain't like I could take down a cruise missile."

She offered an apology, "I didn't know." She felt stupid for asking and realized she had also hit a nerve. That was understandable considering what he had been through. Hesitantly she asked, "So what happened in prison?" Then added, "But you don't have to talk about it if you don't want."

Travis told her somewhat vaguely that he was found guilty of sedition, planning subversive terroristic activity, though they never said specifically for what. It was a life sentence, which to her seemed shocking *if* he had done nothing. She didn't interrupt him, though, and let him talk. Travis said the authorities knew he hadn't done anything; they knew that none of them had. Though she was a bit suspicious of his story, she had never known him to tell her anything but the truth. Travis said his torturers, interrogators is what they were called, were sadist. They enjoyed it. Part of the torture was putting them in cells with real criminals and not just criminals but the insane psychotic disturbed criminals. He described being put in a cell with a serial killer. The man had been given three life sentences, "I won't bother going into the details for what. He was the most grotesque individual I have ever known in my life, and every night I went to sleep with him in the same room."

"I can't even imagine."

He lit another cigarette and flicked the ashes in the tray. "He eventually got shived by another inmate in the mess line. Everyone hated him; I mean there is a reason we should have a death penalty."

"Was it planned?"

Travis then changed the subject. He said his new cell mate saved his life; he was a member of the Frees. He had been in prison for seventeen months before they met. After that everything changed. He discovered what his purpose was. Everything in life up till then had been a total selfish waste.

She took his hands and looked at the scars that wrapped

49

around his wrists. Her fingers gently moved across the surface. "Can you tell me about this? And your back." She didn't want to push him, but she wanted to know because she wanted to understand, why? How? She felt such abandonment, she needed to know why?

Travis eyes examined her. He was looking up at her from her lap. She looked rather peculiar with her face upside down. He hesitated. He was thinking. He spoke very slowly in a deep quiet voice reflecting back on the means of torture. He then discussed how they continually asked him to provide information. He said he had none. He felt like they had other motives. He was never part of any organized effort. They accused him of feeding information on the projects he worked on to the 'saboteurs'. He knew nothing about anything they accused him of. The more they asked, the greater he resisted. He would not give them the satisfaction of breaking him.

He said all the prisoners were tortured but none of the criminals. They used many types of torture like water boarding, sleep deprivation, and electro shock administered to various parts of the body, the feet, the back, the head, and the genitals. During all the tortures, they were stripped down. They took place in a cold room with tile floors and a drain to wash away blood and feces. Sometimes there would be three or four interrogators; sometimes there would be a crowd. They would often laugh especially when the prisoners screamed.

"Did you scream?"

"Are you kidding? We all screamed. We are human. The body can't take what they administered, nor can the mind." He said when they tortured the prisoners late at night; he could hear them scream all the way from the basement. It was maddening having to listen. "It was harder for me to hear another man, a friend, than to suffer myself."

"And what happened to your wrist?"

Travis got up and went to the window, glancing through the blinds. She could tell he was hesitant to say anything. He stood there quiet for a long time. Very slowly he began sipping water and taking long slow breaths. He explained that they had a torture called the "pole". It was a rod that attached from wall to wall which was adjusted to fit men's various heights. They tied piano wire around a wrist and then around the other with about a foot and half of space between the two hands. They slipped the bar in between and raised it to a point mounted on the wall. If a man stood on the tips of his toes, the wire wouldn't cut through his skin to the bone. He hung naked like meat hanging from a hook for hours. He stayed suspended from the pole until his ankles and toes could take it no more. After a long time, sometimes five, sometimes eight hours cramping would begin. It felt like his feet were breaking, crushed from his own weight. When he could take it no more and he could not hold up his own weight, the wire began slicing through his wrist like razor blades. The pain was beyond excruciating. Blood at first started dripping slowly down his arms, in steady drips; then, as the cuts deepened it poured. Blood splat across the top of his head, drip, drip, drip. It drove many men insane, and some died hanging from the pole. But he lived.

Marla couldn't see his face. He turned away looking down to the street. She wanted to touch him, hold him; but he stood there at a distance. "How did you survive?"

"The worst that could happen to me was to die. Pain is hard to deal with, but I've been through pain. Once I accepted that, then there is nothing else to fear."

"So you overcame the fear of death?"

"There is something worse than death and destruction. It is something we should all fear. It is being consumed. Little by little, day by day. It happened to me, it has happened to you. It has happened to our country. The greatest indignity is to give up and not fight back. I hung naked and bleeding in a cold room. Depraved men mocked my pain. Little did they know, I had been through hell before, worse in many ways. Drinking consumed me, it nearly destroyed me. It mocked me without mercy, but I did not give up. All they did was inspire me to fight back and I figured out how I could. It is why I'm here."

She pictured him in the room. It was beyond horrible what he described. Tears began to well in her eyes. Her lip quivered. Marla chewed nervously on her lip.

Travis let out a long exhale and rubbed his brow. She could tell it was difficult for him to talk about. "It took a lot for me to realize something; I was stripped to nothing. Understand? I faced evil. I have felt its breath upon my face. It was then I vowed to fight it. We all make a choice at some time. To be destroyed by it or to resist it. I made a choice. They wouldn't break me. There is God and godlessness, and nothing in the middle. I had to choose a God who knew about suffering like me. I can't relate to anything else. My God was abused like me. Does that make sense?"

"I think? So you converted?"

"Yeah. I will do everything I can to fight evil. I became a believer, if that is what you want to call it. As much as I could. I still have many flaws, some anger issues, temper."

"And patience."

"Yes, and I've been a...".

"Jerk."

"Thank you for reminding me. But I no longer drink,

okay. I am more cautious about my language. More considerate. There have been small strides of progress."

"I've seen. So you don't blame God for being there?"

"Of course not."

Travis sat back down and picked up another smoke. Marla lit it for him. She rubbed her finger across his wrist and then kissed them.

"I have a question, are you a Christian then?"

For Marla it was hard to believe she was even asking him the question. This was not a conversation that she normally would have with Travis. He was a scientist. He only thought pragmatically. He told her in essence that everything else was phony. "I'm not the traditional Christian, babe. We're in a war, have been for a long time. It's a war that must be fought. We pay with our lives. I've given what's left of my life to the cause, which is Him. He has my total allegiance, but he also gets all my faults. That's the great thing about my God; he doesn't turn anyone away, no matter what they've done. He accepts me just as I am. Doesn't freakin' matter to Him". He shrugged his shoulders, "Where else was a guy like me gonna fit. Marla, you don't fit either. You just don't know it yet."

"What do you mean? Like we are time travelers and this is our stop together. I believe that." She brushed the hair out of his eyes and kissed him.

"No babe, you were never meant for this world. You are too beautiful. You are to me; you are to God."

She smirked, "Oh Travis, you are putting it on thick. You don't have to say that just to get some." She giggled.

He shook his head. He was serious. "No, I mean it. It is why I've come back. I've come back to get you. To save you, if not for myself, for God. You are very precious to Him. There is no way I could forgive myself if I didn't."

She was stunned. No one had ever talked to her like that. Not even Travis. He was always deep, but never that deep, and for him to talk like that just took her breath away. Marla exhaled a long breath, "Do you mean this? Is this really why you came back?"

He nodded and looked at her with the most forlorn look. "There is a lot more that you're not telling me isn't there. Is it going to get bad? Get worse?"

He bit on his lip which he sometimes did when he got nervous. He turned away and scratched his beard, another sign he wanted to change subjects. Then he rubbed her legs, "The sun is out. Let's go enjoy it."

She hesitated as if drawing the thought up from a well. "You escaped. How did you get out? Was it just you?"

He didn't want to tell her the details. He refined his answer to a simple, "Eight tried, three made it."

"So what will happen to you if they catch you? Will you go back?"

He scoffed, "There is no going back. There is only termination."

"You mean it is life or death?"

"Marla, there are lots of things far worse than death. Death is favorable to what they've got planned."

"And what is that?"

"It's the Colony, the end of human existence, as we know it."

She felt like air evaporated from her lungs. "The Colony?" Her nails dug into his arm. Marla's countenance changed into a whiter shade of pale. Her heart rushed to her throat. She felt like she was going to choke. "You're scaring me, Travis."

"I shouldn't have said anything." He patted her on the leg, "I don't want to think about it now. Not today. Come on.

Let's go to the park."

Marla's enthusiasm vanished. She leaned her head against him. Her voice was barely audible; it was meek as a child. "Hold me."

Travis took her into his arms and gave her a reassuring hug. "No Travis. I mean hold me like you *can't let go of me.*"

Her smooth sultry leg rubbed against him, and her eyes roamed across his face. Marla's eyebrow rose mischievously. She unbuttoned his shirt. "Make love to me, like..." She kissed him down his neck, "there won't be tomorrow."

CHAPTER FOUR

Too few are the truly blessed days of
our lives. If we are lucky enough, we all have some days
that are magical. For most of us, they are very infrequent.
They are never often enough or long enough; but if they were,
they wouldn't be magic.

When Marla woke the next morning, Travis was in the
other room. The early morning dawn shadows of the cities tall
buildings leaned down across the nearly deserted streets.
Travis sat quietly in the chair finishing a drawing of her that he
did while she slept. He didn't say a word as she came in the
room, only smiled. She put her arm around his neck and
watched his pencil round out her shoulders and he then took
his thumb and smudged the lines together. He worked the
contours of her body until the shadows where perfected and
soft. He handed it to her.

It was beautiful. "When did you learn to do that?"

"I did hundreds. This is the only one I've done that
wasn't from memory."

She couldn't believe it was so good, "Oh my gosh, Travis,
it is wonderful. Aren't you going to sign it?"

He thought about it, contemplating. "And what shall I
write?" He took the drawing from her and signed it in Italian,
'Amante'.

Marla was stunned. No one had ever done a portrait of
her before; many, however, wanted to take pictures. Nothing
had ever thrilled her as much and especially considering it
came from Travis, a creation with his own hand. He was

indeed an oxymoron, an enigma.   Like his drawing of her, there were no distinct lines, smudges, variances of shades that together made a single portrait of a person. She was amazed. This wasn't the same Travis she had known before, not by a long shot. He was much different, more passionate. Marla looked at the portrait and at him. She couldn't believe he was so good.

"This means more to me than if you had given me a Rembrandt." She started to look around the room wondering where she could put it once she had it matted. Travis got up and went to the window and adjusted the blinds.

"Hey, Marla Jean, another day. Still want to go to the park?"

A sly grin curled in her lips. "You look a little whipped." Marla smirked, "Sure you have the energy?"

He quipped, "I don't think I have the energy to stay *inside* with you all day. I'd like to get some sun and maybe see Times Square and Grand Central Station tonight."

"You sure? We can just stay in; it's fine with me"

"Let's do the park."

"Think it's safe?"

"No, it's not safe, but no place is safe for me. And I've got things to see."

"You sure. I think we are better off staying here". She chuckled and patted her butt, "I need the exercise."

Travis was still peeping through the blinds, "Geez, hon, gotta give me time to reload."

She laughed and walked over to him bowlegged with her hands on her hips. She mimicked a country accent, "Well, you reload your pistol Sheriff; I'll go fetch me a saddle."

Travis grabbed her real quick by the arm and pulled her tight, "I've got plans for you little fella."

"Oh yeah?"

He slapped her on the butt, "Fetch me breakfast and I'll…"

She spun out of his arms, "Save it for later. Just make sure those bullets of yours have bang."

She went to the bedroom and a few minutes later she came out wearing a gray John Lennon shirt. It was a portrait of Lennon in the park. "Remember this?"

He was shocked, "You still have that? Is that the one I gave you?"

"Oh yeah, I only wear it on special occasions…and today's a special day." She fixed a quick breakfast; and within an hour they were leaving, but not together. He left a few minutes before she did, slipping down the stairs at the end of her hall and leaving out the backdoor of her building into the alley. Travis wore the clothes she had given him the day before along with a baseball hat. He waited for her across the street from the Dakota, milling around through the crowd that had gathered that morning at Strawberry Fields. There was the usual assortment of vendors selling T-Shirts and hats, sunbrellas and souvenirs. Travis saw her coming across the street and watched her for a while to make sure that she wasn't followed.

She saw him in the crowd with his baseball hat and then followed him as he walked away. He walked down a pathway through an esplanade with trees hanging over the pathway, and then he stopped at a bench. She walked by him and acted like he was a total stranger. He let her pass without saying anything. She walked further, and he waited to see if she was followed. She wasn't.

He came up behind her and handed her a glove. "Let's go. Put it on."

"What's this?"

He put it on her hand, and they walked through a series of winding paths before they came to a great field and eventually walked around a lake to a spacious lawn. It was their favorite spot to go years before. Travis stretched out on the grass and she laid her head down on his stomach as they watched sailboats skim across the water.

"Isn't it beautiful?"

"Hard to believe. Almost looks normal."

"So what's with the glove? Feels like it is lined in lead."

"It is."

She had heard about them. GPS signals could not transmit through the lead. People wanting to avoid detection used them, mainly the elite. They looked like ordinary black patent leather gloves and in the winter didn't seem out of place; but, of course, in the summer, they would raise suspicion.

"Can't I take them off?" She wanted to run her hands through the grass.

"No." Travis pulled a dandelion twig from the grass and stuck it in her mouth. "Not unless you want them to know where you are."

"You think I am being followed."

"You've been watched. I know that."

She sat up. "Who is watching me?"

Travis didn't say anything. He turned his head to the side as if listening. "Hear that?"

She listened. She didn't hear anything; and then, off in the distance, she saw it coming in their direction hovering over the lake. Travis pulled his hat lower. "Look down."

It was a Raven crossing the lake humming straight for them. People everywhere turned and pointed. Its hum grew louder and louder, sounding somewhat like an electric weed eater whirling in the sky. Then, the drone turned and crossed back over the field in the direction of some people playing ball. They listened to its sound fading away. She let out a long sigh. "I hate those things!"

He didn't say a word. He just looked around which really annoyed her. He pulled stems from the ground and chewed. "You didn't tell me who is watching."

"If I told you, you probably couldn't sleep."

She was frustrated, "Okay, then can you tell me about the Colony?"

He hesitated, "I don't think you are ready. I don't want to talk about it today."

"Try me."

Travis was hesitant, procrastinating about the subject. She could tell he didn't want to discuss it. He paused looking around him as if looking for men in suits or the MF. There were none. Nothing stood out. He pulled up his pant leg and looked at a device he had strapped to his shin.

"What's that?" she inquired.

"Video detector." He pulled his pant leg back down. They weren't being watched.

He observed the people milling around; teams played ball, and families flew kites. It was warm, and the sun was radiant. He unbuttoned the top few buttons of his shirt and picked up a spring daisy and twirled it in his hand. It reminded him of a song with a simple melody and of a movie he saw as a kid when a computer was programmed to sing the song like a man.

Travis stalled but Marla wasn't budging. She insisted on knowing. "Are you going to tell me or not?"

"I guess you need to know." He slowly began telling her in minute details and with the authenticity of a professor.

Travis explained that the chip, like the one she had, the V-chip, was just the beginning of the government's plan. "The V-chip was implemented to control the masses. It involved all the governments, world governments and big business."

"I think I figured that out by now", she said somewhat sarcastically.

"The first chip didn't go far enough; their intention was always more control. It had met resistance and some demonstrations, but they were always put down."

Despite the propaganda to the contrary she knew that, she knew that major cities became urban battle grounds, Dallas and Memphis, even Boise became nightmares, virtual lockdowns, for months nothing in and nothing out. She had watched it all on T.V. Tanks surrounded the pockets of resistance across the nation. When the resistance broke down, hundreds of thousands, perhaps millions were rounded up. She had watched reports on the news, but what was reported was not the way Travis told it. The media said that resisters were terrorist cells trying to bring down the government. Travis said that it was the other way around; it was the government that had turned against the people. Food supplies were interrupted, roads were closed, and utilities were shut off, the government blacked out the internet. He shook his head, "We wouldn't do that to ourselves. Do you honestly believe we would stop our own supplies, come on?"

She sighed realizing her naivety, "So what I was seeing on the news…"

"Was a lie. All propaganda. We weren't the ones closing the roads, shutting down utilities. We weren't the terrorists; they were."

The government he said used a time tested module. People first say nothing because a position becomes unpopular. Then, they say nothing because they fear retaliation, losing a job. Then, they remain silent for fear of going to prison and finally "they are mute for fear of death."

"Weren't you there in Denver when it happened?"

Travis rolled over and looked around at the people strolling in the park. "No, I lived in the country, peacefully, till they came after me."

"Then you weren't there when those cities burned?"

He denied it. Travis said he was already in detention when the chaos started. He was taken in the first wave of the crackdown. He heard from those coming in what was happening in the streets. The atrocities grew worse; and as it did, the media grew more fearful of covering the truth. It only took a few months and the "Days of turbulence" was over. The door had slammed shut on liberty.

Marla took a deep breath. Much of what he said she knew was true. She knew of people who weren't radicals that resisted. Some were detained, questioned. Most eventually complied, and some went back to their jobs. She didn't understand then what all the fuss was about. She believed the chip was about tightening security, protecting the borders, and it would put an end to identity thief. That all sounded good and logical to her, so she never understood the rebellion. But obviously Travis knew about things she didn't. She wanted to know the whole truth though. She asked, "What about the Colony? What is it?"

He wanted to avoid the subject, but knew he couldn't. One thing about Marla, she was persistent. Travis took a good long breath; he knew it would take a while to explain. He said the Colony, that's what it became known as, was always their main objective. The government knew from the beginning the V-chip, the one she had in her, was flawed. They knew that when it was designed, but they had to have it first to get control. Everyone who had the chip was very familiar with its problems. It never performed all the functions the government promised it would. It didn't stop identity thief, far from it. It escalated theft, made it easier. It was a piece of crap. People's entire bank accounts were wiped out due to the chip. Rations were stolen on a frequent basis by petty thieves. Citizenships were deleted either by accident or on purpose, and of course, medical records often just disappeared. The worse thing about the V-chip was the constant outages. Marla was very familiar with those. It was a nightmare. Every storm that roared through the east seemed to knock transmissions out. People couldn't buy anything, couldn't get gas or food until the system was operational which sometimes took days or weeks. It was an awful mess. Authorities promised it would get better, but after the people took the chip what choice did they have? It was too late to go back to the old system, because the other system was destroyed. "Rule 922 in effect marched society across a financial bridge, and they burnt the bridge behind them. Gone forever was the cash society."

She was confused, "But Travis, why would they want to give us a flawed system?"

"To prepare you for the new system. It is about supreme control. It involves a series of steps, corners, and turns. There is the ultimate plan they've had all along. Their strategy is to create problems so you are forced to take their remedies. Create a problem, provide a solution. Create a problem, provide a solution. It is a calculated plan, though repetitive. The 'solutions' always gave them more control. It is all by design. Once it is in place, the human race is finished as we know it."

"You can stop it now. I've heard enough."

"You sure. Okay, I'll stop."

"No, kiss me." He did.

"Do you want me still to stop?"

"No, tell me more. Just hold my hand when you do it. You are talking about the new chip, right?"

"Yes."

She had heard about it, the "advanced chip", but she hadn't paid that much attention. She hadn't ever heard the name, or what it was called. "Is that the one they put in the forehead?"

"Yes. It contains all the information of the V-chip, but it will do a heck of a lot more. It will completely enslave you."

It felt like the oxygen was sucked right out of her lungs. She struggled to get the words out, "What do you mean by enslave?"

Travis pulled up his pant leg and rechecked his monitor. "Marla, the new chip is the epitome of slavery, but it is a very advanced form of slavery. Slavery of the mind. You see, the body will do what the mind tells it, and that's been the problem with slavery all along. This new chip is every despots dream. The problem with all previous feudal societies is that they could only enslave the body but not the mind. Revolution was always inevitable. People will eventually find the courage to fight. But if the mind is enslaved, revolt is eliminated because it is an unthinkable option. The new chip will control not just your finances and identity, but your thoughts."

She was trying to understand, "It will tell me what to think?"

"Not exactly. It will tell you what *not* to think. Every resistance impulse you have, the chip picks up and evaluates. It monitors sudden conditions and changes in your body. The thought of resistance is similar to what happens when you lie;

in fact, the lie detector was the precursor to this technology. When a person is given an order or command, if there is a thought of resistance the chip sends a signal to the auriculotemporal nerve. It releases impulse shocks via a tiny neurotransmitter. It is called a stinger. They are short but incredibly painful."

"A stinger?"

"That is just a nickname. It is a microchip, very, very small. It is administered through a syringe." He pointed to her temple, above her ear, right at the hairline. "The main chip is only about four inches away at the top of the scalp. It sends a signal to the stinger when resistant factors are detected like lying or disobedience."

"And this works?"

"The auriculotemporal nerve is hypersensitive. It is a weak point in the composition of the human anatomy. Martial arts experts are trained to strike there. It immobilizes people instantly. It is also where migraines originate from."

She pulled her hair back and raised her eyebrow somewhat skeptical. She might not have believed anyone else, but she knew that Travis was a scientist. He was smart, very, very smart; and he thought differently. If anyone would have been knowledgeable about the field, it would have been him. But she had her doubts and when she did, she always scrunched her lower lip and the scar on her chin curled into a question mark. She was skeptical, "They have this? This is what the new chip does?"

"Yes, believe me Marla; it was researched for years. It is already being administered, but the government is not making the same mistake they made with the V-chip. They are not going to risk another insurrection. They aren't stupid; they know how unhappy everyone is already with the V-chip so it is being administered selectively. Carriers are being picked. Most are in government so there can be no dissension in rank. Key press members and business leaders have quietly been taking it, and most not by choice. Nevertheless, when the chip is in they have full compliance. Many agreed to take it under the pretense that it is temporary, just part of a test. They were fooled. Once it is in, it is too late."

"Oh my God.

"Do you know where it was first tested?"

She guessed, "In school?"

"Some place where they didn't have to worry about volunteers. In the prisons. *We* were the perfect subjects. I saw some of the most defiant prisoners become no more than mindless robots. After just a few days, they lived just to obey the commands. I saw it happen with my own eyes. I saw them order around men in the yard like they were dogs. I mean literally like dogs. They would be ordered to sit, roll over, and beg. The guards laughed, and the men did it. No one has the power to resist this chip."

"It makes us inhuman."

"That is the purpose."

They laid there together in the sun in a patch of daisies. Travis was tempted when looking at her breasts to pull up her shirt and moisten his mouth. She looked at him slyly and grinned knowing what he was thinking. They watched a bee land on the spring blossom. Travis observed it, "See that bee? Look at it."

Marla watched the little honey bee landing on the petals, flying diligently from flower to flower collecting nectar. "It goes about the day systematically doing what it is programmed to do by nature. It doesn't really know anything about pleasure and enjoyment like we do. These things never enter its mind.

The bee doesn't question its job or position, or state of happiness. It has no thoughts about tomorrow or even today. It is void of all ambition or desire. It never considers escaping or flying off someplace. It knows nothing of independence. Emotions never register in its brain though it does have one. Watch it."

Marla lay in the warm grass staring at it as it moved from petal to petal. The skyline of the city was like a mural all around her.   She watched it going from flower to flower collecting pollen. "You see," Travis continued, "the bee is different from every other creation. It is the most perfect example of what they want the human race to become."

"Example of what?"

"Of a colony. The new chip is designed to make us as obedient as bees. That is the grand design. Concepts, such as democracy, freedom, choice, individuality are all obsolete. Religion forever crushed. The Constitution, a relic of a time that past."

Marla jolted as if she were shocked. Her eyes were wide open; her face became a frame of fear. She pushed away, "No way. Tell me it is not true."

"Haven't you wondered where all this technology was going? We've been pushing to fulfill every tyrant's dream. Can you imagine if Stalin or Hitler, Mao or Hussein would have gotten their hands on this technology, but it wasn't there? This is every tyrant's dream, to rule completely obedient masses. The world would function so perfectly if we would comply and obey. Now they have it, the Colony is here."

"Tell me, you are just screwing with me". She grabbed his shirt, "Tell me, Travis."

He didn't say anything. He pulled the bill of his cap lower and looked down at the grass. She knew he was telling her the truth. She had heard rumors about things which she had ignored. But, he had never once told her a lie, and she knew he wasn't now. After a few minutes of silence, she finally asked, "What do they call it? Does the Colony have a name?"

"It is the name of a man and a number."

"A man and a number?"

"The system is called the Trisix Colony."

"Trisix?"

"Yes, like the number. Six, six, six. It is a number and a man's name."

Her mouth dropped open as if gasping for air, "Travis!"

"Shhhhh". He rolled on top of her and pressed his lips to hers. "Listen to me." She was shaking, trembling. He knew she was about to cry. "Listen Jean, this is why I am here. Listen to me carefully."

"I don't want to hear anymore. Stop."

"Listen to me. You have to know. You need to know why I have come back." He held her down literally until she stopped shaking. Tears began to form in the corners of her eye and leaked out; they rolled one by one down her face. Travis wiped them off with his finger.

Marla laid there quietly for a long time looking at the sky, not moving as if the information paralyzed her, finally she asked, "Who is Trisix?"

"It is the code name for the man who created it. I can tell you this; Trisix didn't have to invent the technology. All that needed to be done was to assimilate existing technologies that were already there and put it all together."

"If you are lying, tell me now; please tell me this isn't so. For God's sake, tell me this is not real."

"Have you not wondered where we were headed? Have you not wondered about the consequences? Just follow the dots, and you'll see."

Her expression was flat, "Can anything stop it?"

"Only one thing, but it will require extreme measures." Travis reached his hand down to his boot checking something and looked around over his shoulder. "The major corporations of the world are in on this; all the governments have been waiting for this to develop. Trisix doesn't have to know what a person is thinking to have mind control. The person's own thoughts are what control them."

"How? I want to know exactly how it works."

"It is not complicated really. Genius always makes the complicated simple, functional." Travis gave her an easy illustration. "If you were to light up a smoke here in a restricted park, the part of your brain that knows you are breaking the law will generate negative or what they call resistant impulses. These are fear factors; and they vary from person to person, but generally are associated with slightly elevated blood pressure, increased heart rate, rapid condensation of moisture on the skin, and other various factors that can be monitored and detected. The polygraph moves a needle; the Trisix chip emits an impulse shock. So, if you had the Trisix chip, after you lit the cigarette you would be shocked by a neuroactivator that is attached to the temporal nerve. You will continue to get shocks until you put it out. It monitors virtually every reaction in your body; it's perfect. The chip has the same effect as shock collars on dogs. After several shocks, people won't even think about crossing the line. It eliminates disobedience."

She rolled over on her back and groaned. "Get me out of here!"

"I didn't want to tell you, but you asked. This is the New World Order; it is perfect order, see? Imagine employees at work stations like yours. The boss is gone for the day; no one will know the difference. The employees start to leave early or to goof off, but they can't. The moment they register the thought, they are shocked. You see, this is what I mean by complete obedience. No one can resist it."

"Then we will be like those bees. Work, work, work, right?"

"Exactly, the world will have the most perfect work force. Corporations love it, and they will have the perfect consumer. The governments will get what they want, a completely compliant populace with absolutely no descent. There will be no debate, no resistance, no free thought. Just complete compliance. Think about it Marla, if you were a world leader and the country which you ruled could control subjects under your complete authority with no possibility of insurrection, would you do it?"

"Of course not. I love freedom."

"I wouldn't either, but the mad men of the world would. And who has run this world if not mad men? This is the ultimate power; it is what they crave. This is what Babylon aspired to be. A godless world is a world where man makes himself god."

It was obvious by her expression she was still battling with denial, "They couldn't be that callous."

"Oh really, know your history. Stalin killed twenty million of his own people to gain complete control. Did you know that? So much for liberation, huh? Mao is said to have done even more. Look how many leaders in years past would have instituted it immediately, Saddam Hussein, Gaddafi. Greed is incurable."

The scar on her chin hooked back into a question mark, "But surely no leader could want this. They would be slaves like everyone else."

"You're right...*if they* took the chip. Marla, there will always be masters. The masters aren't taking it. They aren't stupid! They will say they are, but we know their plan. They will take a placebo chip. It will appear to function as a Trisix chip; it will have GPS and all the other technologies, but the impulse transmitter will not be activated. These people have every detail planned out. This has been in the works for years, and it gets even sicker. There are elites in this world; I won't tell you who they are, but you know some of their names. They have cloned themselves."

She shook her head in disbelief, "They outlawed human cloning, Travis."

A snide expression arched up his face. He scoffed, "Laws? Do you think *these* people obey laws? Are you serious? They call it a "DNA reincarnation", sounds better than cloning, doesn't it? Of course, there were thirty years of failed experiments, but every experiment has flaws, right? Just throw the mutants in the trash because they weren't entirely human, yet. The botched clones that didn't turn out perfect with all the desired qualities were destroyed, but you know, what the heck...keep going. All science is progress, or is it?"

"So you think this is going on?"

Travis looked at her perturbed, "Geez honey, you didn't hatch from an ostrich egg. Surely you've been watching what has been going on."

She felt offended by his tone, "No, I haven't."

"Then you believed everything you've been told?"

"I didn't think about it, Travis. What do you want me to say?" Marla resented his condescending attitude. "It didn't involve *me*, alright."

"If it involves our world Marla, it involves you. You can't

spend your life living in a cocoon."

She folded her arms in protest and turned away, "Look Travis, I didn't know it was going on. It's not my job to look out for these things, okay?"

"Well, it has been going on. Embryonic stem cell research wasn't about cures; that was a guise, it was about clones. They called it SCNT, Somatic Cell Nuclear Transfer". His voice was still noticeably sarcastic, "But what are a few failed experiments, right? I mean who can argue with their ultimate objective, the creation of a man- made eternity where *they* will be able to reproduce themselves and live forever, and rule."

A headache suddenly came on her. She didn't know if it was the sun or the pollen, or whether it was what he was saying, but Marla pressed her fingers to her temple hoping to alleviate some of the pain. She squinted her eyes in the light and massaged her head.

Travis looked concern, "Are you alright?"

The throbbing began to subside. She sat up and looked around. Marla took a couple of deep breathes and nodded, "It's better. Tell me more, I need to know."

"Are you sure? Maybe I shouldn't say anything else."

She nodded, "Go on."

Travis continued on but softened his tone. He explained the details of Trisix and its capabilities. There was a connection between it and cloning. He said that for over a hundred years, but especially since the mid 1950's, elements of society have plotted and planned a more perfect world. It was a world in which not only they would be in control, but they needn't ever worry about insurrections. The technology finally arrived, and it took massive coercion and corruption to bring it about. "While they are reincarnating, cloning themselves, just like a queen bee remakes a clone of herself, Trisix subdues the masses."

She looked around the park at the buildings surrounding the enclave, the green space relegated to use of subjects. She could see clearly what he was saying. The truth was beginning to sink in...slowly. "And us?"

"And you, well, because you have the desired qualities that men crave, the beautiful women will probably become their personal slaves. That or you'll function in your mundane job until you grow older and are no longer useful. Then, you'll be terminated. You'll become a bee either to work in an office or..." Travis turned away as if he was listening for something.

"Or what?"

He looked back across the lawn studying the people. He observed his surroundings and spoke almost as if he was ignoring her, "A mate, a human for pleasure, you'll reside on something similar to a sex farm. All human life will be a matter of function, not of purpose."

She wasn't sure she heard him right, and wiggled her finger in her ear, "A what?"

"A sex farm. There are slaves already in this world now. Aren't you aware of that?" Travis looked a bit annoyed; irritated he had to explain something he figured she already knew. "There are nations and palaces where women are virtually slaves, have been. A woman like you, they would probably clone, make a dozen of you. When they wear out one Marla", he shrugged, "they'll have another. They may actually want one of you when you are thirty five, another at twenty five, another, who knows, maybe at fifteen."

Travis paused. She buried her face in her hands. He picked up a flower, and she lay there silently. It was obvious she didn't know what was happening. All he could see was the top of her hair. Her golden honey hair draped like silk across her shoulders.

She felt sick. He could hear her sniffling. It was so ironic; it was such a beautiful day, and yet never in her life had it seemed so dark. It was so gorgeous and yet so awful, all at the same time. Travis lay on his back looking up at the clouds passing over. He looked at all the buildings with their windows. They almost look like hives, tall glass hives. Before long, people would go in and out, to and fro without thinking of anything but work. Their world would consist of agri-bees, industrial bees, and services bees. Population will be controlled, as would all resources, food, and habitat. Functionally, the world would be perfect. There would not even be crime. Masters will control it all. The entire planet will consist of a hundred hives, maybe a thousand. There would be no wars, or so they thought. The obvious flaw, evil men are incapable of creating a utopia. The problem is they always thought they could.

Marla wiped tears from her face and turned away. "It can't be as bad as you say."

He didn't want to tell her. It was worse. Travis then rolled back over and looked across the way when he saw something coming. "Oh no!" He grabbed her arm, "Let's go."

It was a Big Dog.

Marla sat up and turned around; she saw it marching across the field. She could hear its menacing machinery marching across the lawn. Marla pulled him on top of her, "Be still, stupid."

She kissed him watching it out of the corner of her eye as it crossed the field coming in their direction. Its head, a black squared titanium skull with a lower jaw, turned robotically toward the people it passed along the way. Its sensors, red lights located in its eyes, scanned their codes into its system. It could stun violators immediately into submission with its tasers. She watched as a crowd at the baseball bleachers stood petrified, then suddenly out of the bleachers jumped a man. He fell to the ground and took off running. The Big Dog turned and gave chase. The man was sixty yards away, but it was pointless. The Big Dog gained ground quickly. A hush went through the crowd as it chased the man down, and then stunned him with tasers. He rolled into a ball screaming as the beast stood over him. It was pathetic and senseless pleading with a machine. Someone else yelled from the stands, and the Big Dog turned after the man was immobilized and walked in the direction of the stands. The man lay on the ground unable to move but still screaming. She knew it was their chance.

Marla stood up, "Let's get out of here."

Travis looked back over his shoulder. He could see a cage speeding across the field to pick up the man on the ground. Then, there was another, and then another. People were running from the bleachers. And across the field way over by the pond, he saw another Big Dog charging toward the stands. He had to resist the urge to turn and help. There was nothing he could do. They zigzagged through the path of pedestrians getting away. He felt just a brief modest twinge of conciliation, in a matter of days, if the mission was successful, they would be able to escape.

There was one place left in the world he knew they would be free.

CHAPTER FIVE

The shock of what they witnessed lingered for a while, deadening their sprits like anesthesia. After they were back, neither said much, the day seemed ruin by the event at the park. Marla was upset, very upset, and preoccupied herself with an assortment of tidy chores. Something she always did when nervous.

Travis got on the computer. He plugged a device into a port that allowed him to "piggyback" an adjoining signal onto the net so that his transmissions could not be monitored. "What's that she asked?"

He glanced at her with her mop and broom, "I'm tapping in."

She knew that was another name for hacking, and she didn't ask anything more. For the next two hours, she went on about her chores going from the bedroom to the kitchen, kitchen to the bathroom, bathroom to the living room. Then, he heard the water running in the tub. Travis finally had had enough. He turned off the computer and walked in to where she was scrubbing on her hands and knees.

"Alright, what's going on?"

She was sobbing, "I can't handle this." Her words started breaking up in heaping sobs, "You know, everything was fine … until … until … you…told me…a…about…."

He knew what she was experiencing, truth shock. It is what people experience when they discover the truth. A common reaction when someone discovers infidelities. It is a sickening reaction like when a priest, or someone they trusted, molested their child. They immediately feel dirty, angry, used.

It is a normal human response, like when people discover their local Congressmen is nothing more than a perverse narcissist who digitally exposes himself for some sort of self-love gratification. It is disgusting when you find out, but it is truth. Sometimes even truth makes one feel dirty. Travis took her by the hand and lifted her off the floor. She was trembling. She sobbed, and he held her. The brutal arrest they saw in the park brought her emotions to the surface. She was coping with the shock in the only way she knew how. It felt like a knife plunged against her heart, and the sharp edge of fear began to press through her ribs.

Travis had seen grown men, battle tested military types, break under the pressure of the enormity of truth. Under most normal situations, she was quite strong, but she was also sensitive as a flower. If she had not been that way, he never would have come back. She was the one person he had known that hadn't become hardened by the world. He saw her not in the light of naivety, but in beauty, innocent beauty. Because of that, she was the only woman he would risk his life for.

After a while, she seemed better. She regrouped. But, she wasn't talkative. Her demeanor was subdued and exhibited lethargic symptoms similar to the flu. She was very quiet. Neither wanted to talk about it any longer. The subject of Trisix wasn't discussed anymore. Finally, as it began to get dark and the sun set across the city, Travis said there were places he needed to check out in town, and he told her he could go alone or she could go with him. He figured she needed some time alone but to his surprise Marla didn't hesitate. She went to her bedroom and came back wearing a black silk V neck blouse and leather coat. She also had on boots, "I'm going with you."

"You sure?"

She smiled and pulled out her back lead gloves. "Let's do it."

He asked her again if she was sure, positive, and she said she was. It just took her awhile to digest everything. Marla was ready to move on. He went out the back, and she went out the front. They met at the Dakota and started walking down Central Park West. The street was bustling with people. At that time of the evening, it was like it used to be, cars were honking, traffic was congested, and they walked briskly through the crowd. She questioned him if he was aware of how long the walk would be to Grand Central, and then she realized walking was probably all he did. He looked at her after a couple of blocks and grinned. He could tell she wasn't use to his pace. They came to a street light; traffic had stopped. There was a delivery truck waiting for the light to turn green. There were no cars behind. It idled at the intersection. Travis motioned to it.

"Wanna cop a ride?"

She shook her head nervously, "Oh no. We can't do that."

Travis took her by the hand and crossed the avenue to the truck stopped at the light, and unhinged the back door. With a shove, he lifted it sliding it up the rolling rack to the ceiling. He looked over his shoulder. There were only a couple of people on the street watching what he was doing. The truck was empty; it had finished delivering bread for the day. Marla was about to run, but he grabbed her by the waist and then tossed her up to the bed of the truck. She was shocked, and he leaped up beside her, laughing.

Suddenly the truck lunged forward and began heading down Central Park West. Marla pulled back her hair smiling, "You're crazy. We are going to get caught."

Travis hung out the back of the truck with his face in the wind. He smiled. He looked at her with a devilish grin and grabbed the strap to the door and started pulling it down.

"What are you doing?"

"You know." He pulled the door down to nearly the bottom. The light vanished, only a spectrum came through just enough to see his feet.

"We can't. Not here Travis."

"Can't?" The truck jostled, and he pulled her to him; his arm tucked around her waist. Marla's heart was racing. The noise of traffic was all around. The hum of the city just right beyond the truck panels. The headlights of the cars in traffic cast shadows around her feet. She couldn't see his face, but she felt his lips slowly stroll down her neck. He pressed her against the wall of the truck forcefully. His hand went down between her thighs squeezing. A sensation began to rush through her.

"Stop."

He didn't. His hands gripped her even firmer. "Don't." He paid no attention. He could feel heat radiating up her belly over his hand. She tried to push away, and then she relaxed. Marla finally grabbed his hand and moved it to her belt. He unbuckled it, and his hand began to massage her. She couldn't believe what they were doing and where they were. "Oh my God, Travis. Travis!" He wasn't listening. Marla forgot about everything else in the world, it didn't exist. She felt his hand move across all the right spots. He had her literally in the palm of his hand. She started panting down his shirt. The more he rubbed, her legs began to quiver. She began huffing loudly in deep breathes across his neck. She bit down on his shoulder all the way through his coat. He thought she was drawing blood but still didn't stop. Then, her mouth covered his entire ear panting like a thoroughbred fresh from a morning run. "Don't let go. Don't let go!" He didn't. Then, she engulfed his lips sucking the breath from his lungs like he held the last bit of air in the universe. Her tongue swirled around his. Marla kept sucking and panting, she was hyperventilating. She grabbed his hand and pressed it against her harder and harder until finally she let out a long convulsing gasp. He felt her body tremble, shaking, convulsing, moaning. She shook for a long time until finally she stopped. All her weight collapsed against him. Her fingers… let go. She hung from his shoulders like an adult size rag doll. Her arms went limp. Marla slid down the wall of the truck to the floor. Neither said a word.

He let her lay there for a while and just listened to the traffic. They were at a stop, and then the truck's engine revved and it took off again. The driver obviously was unaware they were there. Travis grabbed the wall to steady himself. He felt her glove rub his leg, and he knelt beside her. He could barely see the outline of her face in the dark and brushed away the hair from her mouth. He could hear her sighing, long relaxing breathes. The truck jostled again in traffic. Both of them listened to the sounds of cars honking and the sound of taxis' dispatchers giving directions for another fare. Her hand squeezed his hand; she was coming out of her trance. "Jean, you alright?"

She kissed his hand, "Don't ever leave me, again. I don't care where we go as long as I'm with you."

"We'll see. I've missed you Marla."

She squeezed his leg, "Not like I've missed you."

He leaned down peering out the door and looked at the cars behind them. He wasn't for sure, but he thought they probably had made it down to the Port Authority or close to it.

He grabbed her hands and stood her up. The truck was still moving. "Let's wait till the next stop." Finally, it came to another intersection. He got down on the floor and looked out inspecting the traffic, to see if there was the Force. He didn't see any.

"Aren't you scared there may be cops?"

"Yeah, but aren't any."

"How do you know?"

"I have my ways," He looked at his watch, "Let's go."

Travis pulled the door up and they jumped out and darted through traffic. A few cars honked, and Travis waved. They both were trying to adjust their eyes to the sudden glare of lights. They disappeared into the crowd and were somewhere around 50th Street; they were heading for Times Square. As they walked along she tugged on his arm, "Promise me one thing, if you ever leave, make me a mold of your hand."

Travis laughed, "Oh, what love, I'm feeling the love."

It was like old times. They walked hand in hand down the street, passed all the familiar buildings. Few things had changed in that area, it had been one of the neighborhoods least hit by the Depression. The crowd on the main thoroughfares was nearly as congested as it used to be, but many of the side streets were dark and looked desolate. Several blocks down, there were lots of abandoned cars; many ratted out in make shift homes. All the vagrants had been moved out, but the city hadn't gotten around to disposing of all the vehicles yet.

They came to an intersection, and Travis stopped. His instincts told him to avoid Times Square. They went by Rockefeller Center and St. Patrick's Cathedral instead. Two mopeds turned the corner and whined up the block. It was surprisingly empty, not many cars were there; they were already thinning out. They walked along a row of buildings with glass fronts. She glanced at their reflection passing by and fantasized that nothing had changed. It was reminiscent of when she was still in college. Marla looked at their reflections in the windows as they passed; the lighting was flattering to them both. Travis looked like his usual self, tall, cool and handsome in his overcoat and hat. And she, she still looked like the college girl ten years before when she had fallen in love.

They walked briskly towards Grand Central and then turned in a different direction. "What are you doing?"

"Fight like a lion, run like a rabbit."

"What?"

"Never go anywhere in a straight line."

She wasn't sure what that meant, but she followed him anyway. They circled the block until Travis became satisfied they weren't being followed; then, they came up to Grand Central. She tugged on his arm, "You sure you want to go in? It's going to be crawling with MF; it's swarming. I don't think we need to go." He look dispassionately at the huge stone building that he had been in countless times before. He always avoided highly policed areas; but he had orders, and he needed Marla for a cover.

"Let's go, let's get some coffee."

The atrium of Grand Central was always one of his favorite places. They use to go together and sit for hours and just watch the crowds. There was something distinct about the building beyond its décor and architecture. Travis loved the sound. To him, it was not a building, but a piece of art alive with people inside. But now, it was different. Evidence of the Bitch was everywhere. On every wall were cameras. It was no longer a place to go and observe; it had the laboratory feeling where humans were dissected under a microscope. There were tiny robotic eavesdropping devices that pick up the most discrete conversation 200 feet away. Travis knew they were planted throughout the building. There wasn't the usual clamor that he remembered; Grand Central had lost its attraction. It just seemed hollow. There was no laughter. It was more like a museum, or library, a morgue. Faces all around looked glum, and there was good reason, SCABS stood at the turnstiles where people entered a Future Attribute Screening Technology module (FAST), to detect possible terrorist. Primarily, they just harassed innocent people boarding trains, and the Force patrolled the balcony with assault rifles dressed in their coal black uniforms.

Travis acted as coyly as he could, but he was nervous and for good reason. Most members of the Force didn't carry guns except for the snipers. They carried something just as lethal and more terrifying, "the glove." The glove had an electronic pad in the palm that could deliver a five million volt charge on voice command. It was attached to a battery pack on the inner forearms. The smallest of MF officers could take down the largest of men with a single command. It was designed supposedly for restraint, but nearly everyone had seen the MF hold a person down administering the torture with pleasure. It gave them power, and they abused it. He had witnessed citizens jerking and convulsing in pain on the streets that had been zapped by the glove, defecating on themselves in front of others. The public was in absolute fear of them. You were instantly at their mercy. It was terrifying.

Marla was very uncomfortable there, but you would never know it; she was under such circumstances a good actress. They walked by the MF, and she acted like she was on her cell phone. Travis could have been stark naked with a rose stem gripped in his teeth and the Force never would have given him a second notice. All the men's eyes were on her, especially those on the balcony. She could feel their eyes looking down at her breast as they walked through the atrium. She handed her phone to Travis, "They want to know why you didn't get the tickets?"

Travis took the phone aware they were being watched, "Hey, I am sorry man. They were out, what can I do? We'll go another time."

They carried on with their charade conversation when suddenly a man in a wheel chair collided with Travis.

"Hey man, why don't you watch what you're doing?" The guy looked angry and agitated. The collision knocked some books of his down to the floor. Travis knelt down apologetically and quickly picked them up.

"Sorry man, I didn't see you." It was obvious the guy ran into him. Travis picked up a book that had slid under a bench and put it on the stack.

The small man with a blanket around his knees shook his head and grabbed the books back out of Travis's hand, "Yeah, they all say that. Just watch it, why don't cha." The man wheeled across the foyer and left.

Marla shrugged her shoulders and looked around at the guards, "That was strange." They walked up to a deli bar and stood in line. She ordered two coffees and a sub. Travis handed her back the phone; and the lady behind the counter rang up the total. "Oh, let me get that." Marla slipped off her glove while still talking on the phone. The total dinged. "I promise we'll go next week alright. Okay, un huh, I'll get a baby sitter for the kids." She hung up the phone. They walked casually back up the steps and out the door pretending to be discussing the mock conversation while they passed the sub back and forth.

They casually walked back out onto the street and headed toward the New York Public Library. After about a block away, he stopped and wiped a bead of sweat from his forehead. His heart felt like it was skipping some beats. "My God, that place was thick."

"Told ya. The Port Authority, Times square, they are all crawling. You should know that". She handed him the sub, "Here, I got it for you. Why did you want to go?"

"I had to check it out; I've got business there this week."

"Business? Like what, some kind of fugitives' convention?" He could see the smirk on her face.

Travis didn't respond; he chased the sub with his coffee and tossed the cup away. The two of them walked past the steps of the Library; they didn't stop. There was a park up ahead where there used to be concerts and even outdoor movies. Travis pulled her closer. Both of them kept their eyes on the park. It was dark and nearly all the parks were overrun with packs, small bands of hoods that roamed at night looking for victims to terrorize. Packs had replaced the larger gangs. Ironically, the Force didn't do much to stop them. In a way the packs served a purpose, they kept people off the back streets at night, and that's what the MF wanted.

Marla had a girlfriend that was brutally raped by a pack that pulled her into a park in Midtown, and since then she had steered clear of the parks at night. "Let's hurry." She squeezed his arm and quickened her pace. "Let's get out of here."

They realized they were the only ones on the street. It was completely dark; all the lights in the park had been busted all the way down the block. As they past Bryant Park and were almost to Broadway, Travis heard some noise behind them. He glanced over his shoulder, there were six maybe seven.

They were just dark shadows that stepped from the trees into the street. Suddenly, they came out of the woods like wolves. He couldn't see their faces; they were too far behind them. They didn't say anything. Travis lengthened his stride. A car came down the street as they made it to the bright lights of Broadway. He looked back; they were gone. Times Square was only a block away. He wanted to avoid the Square before; but with the dangers posed on the back streets and Marla, it seemed better to go there. They crossed Broadway, and he wondered what would have happened if she had to walk down the street alone? He realized it had been terrifying for her to live in a city where she felt like prey.

They looked down the Square; it was only half lit, most the buildings were closed, some were boarded shut. It was not the same Times Square he remembered. The crowd was sparse and thin. A group of Jamaican musicians were playing reggae, and women dressed in bright kimonos danced on the sidewalk. A group of Chinese tourists were taking pictures. Travis couldn't help but notice the irony as a mammoth billboard flashed Xing Jeans with a cowboy and a horse. They stopped and listened to the drums rhythms pulsate. From a block away, they could see the coal black uniforms on patrol. They looked like ants looking for someone to sting.

"I don't want to go Travis; it is too risky."

They only had a couple of more blocks, and they would be at the Port Authority. He was kind of surprised she said that; normally she would have wanted to go and dance. Travis turned around, and there were two men about a half a block behind them. They were in dark suits. They were being followed. There were other people on the street, but Travis knew when it was a tail. They hurried along without trying to appear they were running.

"Remember the rabbit?"

She nodded. "I see them."

They turned south in the other direction away from the Port and ran across the street. Travis looked back over his shoulder. The two men in suits turned the corner behind them, about 200 feet to the rear. He looked at Marla. She looked at him.

"You ready?"

"Let's do it." They took off. They could hear the shoes give chase behind them. They made it to the corner and turned the block practically running over a group of people. Cars were double parked blocking the street, and Travis and Marla leaped across the hoods and landed in the road. Up ahead were buses at the Port. Traffic was stopped, congested with cars and taxis lined in front. They ran between two buses idling and disappeared into the mob of people coming out of the Port. Marla and Travis practically flew down the steps with their coats flying and then ran down through a long corridor where they took another turn down some more steps and turned the corner again. There were bathrooms. Travis started for the men's restroom, and she grabbed his hand, "No stupid. In here". She pushed him into the women's bathroom. The door flew open and two women were by the sink. "Shhh", she said gasping for breath, "My husband is out there. He's a cop. If he finds him with me, he'll kill him. He'll kill us both."

The women looked at each other obviously shocked. Marla pleaded, "If you see him, you won't say anything will you?"

They shook their heads. Marla opened the stall door. Travis sat on top of the commode and she sat on the toilet. A few minutes later a knock came on the door. A man came in.

Marla could see him through the crack in the door. He asked the two older women if they had seen a woman and a man. Her heart raced; it was grinding through her like a buzz saw.

"Man, what kind of man?"

"Medium height, about fortyish. He's wearing a dark overcoat."

"No, we haven't seen anybody like him. What about her?"

"Never mind. If you see them, report them to the Metro Force or Port Security. They are dangerous". The man left. She watched him outside as the door slowly closed.

Marla was shaking. "Thank you ladies", she whispered. She looked through the crack again. The women were gone; she didn't see them leave; it was like they vanished. She thought about what the man said, 'dangerous?' They were dangerous? What had they done? What crime did they commit? Eat a sandwich?'

They stayed there for the longest time. Women came in and out going to the bathroom and touching up their make-up. Travis was texting on his phone to someone and kept checking his watch, and then finally after about forty-five minutes he whispered, "Let's go."

The bathroom was empty. Marla came out of the stall first and went to the door. She opened it slowly peering out. She didn't see anyone in uniform or the men in suits. "It looks clear. Come on."

They quickly milled in the crowd. They hustled down a long flight of steps to the turnstiles at the bottom. Travis followed right behind her. She came up to the turnstiles and swiped her hand across the scanner screen; then, she grabbed hold of him tight, and they both spun through the turnstile together. "Come on. Hurry!"

They ran down the concourse to the subway platform and leaped on just as the doors were closing. They plopped down in the seat together, and she looked over her shoulder out the window to see if they were being chased. There were no men in suits huffing through the crowd with guns drawn and badges waving in the air. No shouts to *Freeze!* They managed to escape. In seconds, they were hurtling through the dark tunnel and rocking back and forth in their seats. "I want to know what is going on. Why are *you* so important to them?"

He didn't say anything. She nudged him and whispered out the side of her mouth. There was a young black man that got on when they did who sat across from them; he was texting. A man and woman were engaged in a conversation at the other end of the aisle toward the rear. She nudged him again. Marla put her hand over his ear, "Tell me. Are you a terrorist? What are you?"

Travis looked down at the floor. She looked at the scars on his hand and the bruises from the Tavern. He clinched his fist repeatedly like he was trying to get circulation back in his hand. He was totally ignoring her. Marla put her hand over his to quell his movement, "Travis I need to know."

He looked away. His voice was barely an audible whisper, "No."

"So what is this about?"

He pulled her close and put his lips to her ear. She could barely hear him; his voice was a raspy whisper, "We, are the Solution." His eyes glanced around studying the other faces on the train. "We are going to stop everything. The end is near."

CHAPTER SIX

The train jostled over the tracks into the next station. Marla sat like a woman in a coma. Her eyes were open. She was stunned.

She sat silently wondering if perhaps Travis was the one with a turgid mind, or was it them? Was it the system, the establishment, like he said? Was it him, or was it the Bitch?

The train came to a stop. The doors opened. Marla didn't say a word. She put her arm in his and leaned against him shoulder to shoulder. She didn't know what the solution meant, but if the "solution" would stop Trisix, she would do anything to help. She would help him fight. She would give him her life and her heart. There was nothing in the world more important. She had come to believe that the future of civilization depended on that, but still she was confused, and scared. They both sat there under the bright fluorescent overhead bulbs humming dully on the train. She clasped her hand in his.

The couple at the end of the car got off. Some college age kids jumped on. The train hissed and sat still in the station idling. The black guy sitting across from them was bobbing his head up and down listening to music and texting. He looked like a nice guy, nice face, about twenty, but it was hard to tell. Travis peered down at the two guys and a girl at the other end. One of the guys had a Columbia University sweatshirt on, the other St. Johns. He and the black guy looked at each other. Travis acknowledged him with a nod. Neither said anything, and then the trained hissed and took off again.

They rocketed through another tunnel; the lights flickered

on the old train. The seats rattled evidence of the depression and of broken promises to be repaired. After ten years of a dismal economy, the public knew there was no hope, but at least the trains were running. Travis was just glad they had escaped the men following them. He had had too many close calls. He leaned back and listened to the college kids talking, whispering about the "message". The noise from the tracks was too loud to pick up much of what they were saying.

The voice came over the speaker, "Next stop, Fourteenth Street". The students stood up in the aisle and held onto the straps over head as the train came into the station. Travis and Marla could smell something in their bag. It was the distinctive odor of paint. When the doors opened, they got off; and as they left the train, some rowdy looking thugs barged on. Marla stiffened. It was a pack; she could tell. There were five of them. The train sat in the station for a minute, and then the doors shut, and the train took off again. Just as it was leaving the station, Travis caught a flash of something written on the subway wall. The college kids were running away up the steps.

"Did you see that?"

"What?"

"The message on the wall. It is what they were writing. It said 'MENE, MENE, TEKEL, UPHARSIN.' It was in big bold letters."

She seemed unmoved, obviously unaware of what it meant. "It's everywhere". I've seen that on lots of buildings."

The black guy looked up from his phone, "Yeah man, where *you* been? We got it over in the Bronx, too. They painting all the stop signs, now they all say stop 'the Bitch'". Marla noticed that he had a silver crucifix around his neck. He saw her staring at it and smiled, "Where you headed?"

Travis shrugged, "Ah, Battery Park."

"This time at night?" He glanced down at the hoods, "You sure man?"

Marla's head leaned against Travis's chest; she looked tired. The black guy shook his head and looked over to the five that had just leaped on the train. They were starting in with their taunts. He could hear them talking. They all wore black leather, and their heads were tattooed. Of course, they wore the spiked wrist bands, and together their chains sounded like keys rattling. Their ages ranged from about eighteen to twenty-five. Marla looked away disgustingly; one of them had teeth that were completely rotten. He didn't have anything but a couple of sharp spiked edges in his mouth. He reminded Marla of a possum with beady red eyes and a pathetic, whiskered mustache. The slanderous abuse started flowing from their mouths. They were laughing, "Slut." "Tramp." "Hoe."

Marla squeezed Travis's hand tighter. They were walking their way, or her way, laughing and taunting. Travis could feel Marla trembling underneath her coat. She was right again; they shouldn't have come out at night. She pulled him closer to her and whispered, "Don't do anything. We'll get off and get a cab."

Travis sized them up. Obviously, they had no idea what he could do. Travis figured that the tall one, with his face hidden in the shadows of his hood, would be the first to go through the glass, followed by another. After two, he'd see what would happen to the rest. Travis visualized the big one hitting the track perhaps in the path of an oncoming train. He had a stun gun in his pocket, and he visualized ramming the gun into the side of another's face 'bolting' him till his eyes popped out. The others he figured would scatter quickly after that unless they were packing guns. Knives didn't bother him;

it was a gun he worried about.

All five walked down the aisle to where they were sitting. They were hanging onto the ceiling railing pushing each other around laughing. One of them kept staring at Marla, making gestures with his mouth; she wouldn't look at him. Travis sat still. He gave him a superficial grin. The punk smiled, "What are you looking at freak?"

Travis grinned even more. The guy was about six feet away standing with his buddies. Travis looked at his snotty nose ring pierced through his nostrils. "Come closer. I'll show you."

Marla pulled on his coat, "Travis NO."

He pulled his coat away and stood up. The train jostled and jolted. The breaks began to hiss as it came into another station. "Christopher Street. Houston Station next stop."

The door opened, everyone on the train turned around. The man was huge, dressed in a coal black uniform. It was a MF. The pack separated as he stepped on. Marla tugged on his arm, "We need to go." Travis sat back down.

The MF walked by the pack and went to the back of the car where he looked through the window into the next train. They all got quiet and sat down. He turned around and walked back. He was barrel chested, probably played football, would have had to been a lineman. His face was wide, and his hair cropped short. He stopped in front of the black guy who never looked up at him; he just kept texting. The cop smiled at Marla. She had learned when to give them a coquetting smile in return. He nodded silently without saying a word, hardly noticing Travis sitting next to her. He turned and gave an inspecting glance at the pack. The big

MF then raised his hand and tightened a strap on his glove.

Without saying a word, he walked to the back of the car and opened the door to the next car and left.

The black guy leaned over, "Did you see that guy?"

"Be hard to miss him."

"He's got the fang."

Travis said he didn't know what that was. Marla nudged him, "His glove." The pack was laughing. The little one with the nose ring puckered his lips at Marla mimicking a kiss.

The black dude looked back at the cop in the next car. They could see him through the Plexiglas door. "Yeah man, that ain't no ordinary glove. He got the fang. It shoots two spikes out, got a range of twenty feet and they slam so hard they can break your bones. If they hit your skull, man your dead." He shook his head, "That is one bad dude. He got one on each hand."

Marla looked over into the next compartment, "Oh, no!"

"What?"

"He's checking Id's. We have to get off." The MF was moving down a line of people with their arms stretched out. He was checking each one for the chip with a scanner. She knew that he'd be finished with them in a matter of moments. She whispered to Travis, "We have to get off at the next stop no matter what. He's coming back. I know it."

They just passed Canal Street, and the train was roaring. The MF appeared to be checking the last person in the compartment, a pretty mulatto girl with braided hair. She saw the MF smiling at her playfully; they could hear his boisterous laugher. She knew the routine. The MF got the information they wanted on the scan; and later, if the girl was single and lived alone, it wouldn't be long and the cop would be at their door. They would say they just stopped by to say, 'hi'. It was very intimidating and lots of women relented and just let them in. The MF turned and looked back through the window. He saw Marla observing him, and then he noticed her black leather gloves. She saw his eyebrow rise in curiosity, and then he looked at Travis.

Marla whispered out of the corner of her mouth to Travis, "We need to go". The big cop pulled his belt up higher over his stomach and started walking their way down the aisle. She whispered again, "Travis, let me handle this, please. If he..."

"Franklin Street. Next stop Chambers."

"We've got to go." Marla grabbed his hand and they stood at the door as the train sped into the station.

The black guy shook his head at Travis, "Don't go man. You are better off here." He motioned to the pack with his eyes. "Trust me."

Travis looked at the MF just as he was opening the door to their compartment. The pack was standing in the aisle pushing their way toward the door. Travis wasn't sure what to do; one choice was going to be as bad as the other. Finally, the train came to a stop, and the door opened. Marla grabbed him by the hand, and they hurried through the station. The pack got off too and followed right behind them. Immediately, the taunting started.

She kept pushing him along, "Keep going. Keep going. We'll get a cab."

The station was nearly empty. Their laughter echoed off the subway walls. "Hey Freak, gonna share that girlfriend?"

Marla kept pushing him toward the exit, and he realized that maybe they would have been better off to have stayed on the train, but it was too late. The train was gone. They walked briskly through the station with the pack right behind them. Travis said not a word. As they approached the stairs they heard more laughter, this time it was coming *down* the steps. Travis and Marla looked up to the street. It was another pack, four of them, all wearing black leather and trench coats. Their chains rattled underneath their long coats. He couldn't see their faces, just their silhouettes at the top of the stairs.

One of the punks yelled behind them, "Hey De'mon, watcha doing t'nite?"

"Trolling." The four of them stopped on the steps in front of Marla and Travis. "Well, well, what have we got here?"

Travis took Marla by the hand, "Don't let go of me." He stepped in front of her and bounded up the steps in his long strides right at the four punks coming down. The pack stopped at the handrail in the center of the steps blocking their path. Travis pulled Marla behind him and went straight for them, and then suddenly, right as he approached them, he managed to sidestepped them to the right; and with his arm, he literally lifted Marla off the ground and swung her up ahead of himself in a swift fluid motion. Instantly, the pack, (all of them), were now behind them, and they crested the top of the stairs to the street. It was empty, desolate, not a soul in sight. There were no stores open; no cabs in sight, and no buses running. He could see ten blocks in both directions; no one was there. The city looked completely abandoned.

Travis knew he had made a huge mistake. They couldn't run. If they did, they'd be exhausted by the time the packs caught up to them. He knew better than to waste his energy in flight. He quickly studied his surroundings. There weren't many lights around; most of the street lights had been busted out, and the buildings were sparsely lit. Across the street was a small park, completely enshrouded in darkness. He wondered if there were more packs in the park waiting. This was their hunting ground; Marla was their prey.

Travis walked down the center of the street and pulled something from his belt. She saw him slip it in his coat pocket. The pack came swarming out of the subway like rats, and then they ran down the street and up ahead of them. Travis stopped. She counted them; there were nine. The one they called De'mon had red and purple spiked hair and a spider web tattoo across one side of his face. His eyes looked like he was wearing mascara. There were dark shadows under his eyes, but she couldn't tell if it was tattoo or just the lighting. He walked steadily toward them as the others formed a circle that began to tighten. De'mon whisked back his coat like it was a cape. His boot tops came above his knees and was studded with silver down the side. He stomped the pavement and pointed to Marla, "Give us the slut."

Another one pulled out a pair of handcuffs and dangled them in the air, "Party time." The rest of them laughed.

They circled the couple like animals, like hyenas chattering and arguing between themselves over who was going to be first. Travis was walking backwards in the street with Marla at his side; then he stopped. He had backed up far enough. There was but one single bulb streetlight at the corner that gave him just enough light to be able to see them relatively well. They were all pacing in a circle except for De'mon; he stood still, and Travis figured he had to be at the top of the chain. He'd be first. He knew that they all probably had knives and most likely one or two had a gun. He knew that there wasn't any way out of this. Travis inspected them carefully. Normally, he would take down the big guy first, but the small one with the creepy nose ring kept getting closer. He stuck his tongue out twitting it between his charred teeth. Marla didn't say a word. Travis was stone silent.

The little one, the rat, stuck his face out toward Travis, "Hey Freak", he laughed, "gimme …"

He never finished his sentence. Like lightening, Travis snatched him by his coat and shoved a stun gun into his neck. His body exploded in riveting jerks the second the voltage hit. He screamed like a cat and then collapsed. Travis whirled him by his collar completely off the ground and spun him around and tossed him against the others. Another one charged Travis from behind. Marla screamed, and Travis ducked and spun around catching him under the chin with the gun. The charge sent him reeling backwards jerking and convulsing on his feet. Then, they all pulled their knives, first one and then the others. One of them, with long braided hair with aglets, charged Travis and then stopped just out of reach. He taunted Travis with the blade, rotating it in his hand. It was at least ten inches long and serrated along one edge. He lunged for Travis but missed. He lunged again, and Travis spun catching him perfectly with his heel to his head. His feet went into the air, and he dropped to the street. He was out cold completely. There were six to go, and Marla was still by his side.

"Give us the slut, man, and you can go."

They weren't laughing anymore. They were still circling. Then, the one with the hood, the tall one from the subway, stepped forward from the rest. He pulled a gun from his coat and pointed it straight for Travis's head, "Drop it!"

"Don't Travis." They were standing about six feet from him and Marla whispered, "Don't let go of your gun". Suddenly, Marla shoved her hand straight out, aiming something for the guy's face. They all looked. She had something in her hand. It was too small to be a gun.

"It's acid!"

"She's got acid!"

She held a small spray canister in the palm of her hand not much bigger than the size of a pepper shaker. Marla had it pointed directly at his face. They started backing away except for the one with the gun. Marla's voice trembled, "You Drop it...*punk*!" Her soft voice was suddenly filled with rage. "NOW!"

Travis could see it was an old 22 revolver. The sight was missing. It looked forty years old but still probably operable. He stood with his gun pointed at Travis; she stood with her spray pointed at his face.

The gang told him not to drop his gun. "Don't drop it, Scars."

"Waste him, man!"

Marla could see his face beneath the hood for the first time. It was grotesque. From his eye to his chin, the skin had been burned, melted, *'aced'*. He had been sprayed with acid before. His eyebrow was gone, and his eye peered out a hideous layer of skin that drooped down. Marla took a step forward, "I said give it up," she commanded.

Slowly, Scars laid his gun down on the ground; and just as Travis bent to pick it up, a shot was fired. Travis felt the bullet pass within inches of his face. He froze and looked around; it was De'mon. He stood about twenty feet away with his gun drawn. The smell of gun smoke was in the air. He looked at the gun on the pavement; it wasn't but three feet away. It might as well been a mile. Travis figured he could lunge and get it, but the odds, they weren't good. He didn't even know if the old gun would fire. Then, De'mon pointed his gun to Marla's head. He warned Travis, "She'll get it first?"

Travis knew it was useless. Her spray was only good at close range. He was too far away from the gun, and Marla would take a shot to the face if he tried. De'mon cocked the trigger back, "She'll be ugly, man. Real ugly. She'll look like Scars."

Travis was frozen in motion, half way to the gun, and half way backing up. He was about to back away from the gun when someone yelled. "FREEZE!"

They all turned around. Out of the shadows, behind them all, walking up with a gun was the black guy from the train. His pistol was pointed right to the back of De'mon's head. "You move man, and you gonna be missin' the back of your head."

De'mon kept his gun pointed at Marla. The black guy warned him again, "Drop the piece, or your dead."

De'mon still had his gun pointed at Marla. He didn't move. "You might miss her, but I ain't missin' your punk ass." He walked closer.

De'mon finally uncocked his trigger and put the gun down slowly on the pavement and began backing away. Travis quickly scooped up both the guns and gave one to Marla. Two guys still lay on the ground; the rest dropped their knives. Travis wasn't finished. He walked up to Scars and pulled his hood back. The sneer was gone from his grotesques face. Travis looked him in the eye. They stood there face to face. His voice crawled out of his throat like a chain dragging across gravel. Travis pointed to Marla who was standing behind him, "What do you think you were going to do to her?"

Scars didn't say anything. Travis raised his gun to his temple. "I asked you a question."

"Don't!" Marla screamed. She was clearly upset. "Let's just leave."

The black guy concurred, "Yeah man, we need to just get out of here."

Travis ignored him and grabbed Scars by his head. "Open

your mouth." Travis slapped him, and Scars opened his mouth. He then jammed the gun in, chipping a tooth and busting his lips. Blood poured out of the side of his mouth.

"Come on Travis, let's go!"

He ignored them and cocked the hammer back. "Say, bye bitch." Blood trickled down his chin. Travis tapped on the trigger with his finger. "Come on, say bye."

They could all see Scars shaking. Fear swept across his face, and his eyes closed, squinting, expecting the end. It became completely quiet, not a sound; then, they heard the dripping. Underneath his coat, a pool of urine spread out from his boots across the pavement. Travis stood back away from him, "You coward." He then turned around to De'mon.

Marla begged for Travis to leave. "Come on, Travis! Let's just go."

"Yeah man, this place might be swarming."

It was as if Travis didn't hear a word they said. He looked like a man possessed. He walked over to De'mon and flashed a smile. Travis turned his head sideways and chuckled holding the gun in his left hand. De'mon's face appeared almost camouflage in the web tattoo. He was hard to read, even his eyes. They were dark and utterly void of expression. He revealed no emotion. Travis knew he was a killer. He killed without blinking. They would have raped Marla without mercy in the park across the street, and then he would have slit her throat. Probably, would have gone for a beer afterwards. For De'mon, it would have been just another night on the town.

Travis grinned, "Your turn. Open up, let's see what you got."

De'mon didn't say a word. He didn't open his mouth either. De'mon had his hands in his coat pocket, and Travis pulled his arm out. He put the gun right under his chin and reached down in his pocket and pulled out a cell phone. Travis read the text.

"Calling some of your girls for help?" He dropped the phone on the pavement and smashed it with his boot. "When they get here, all they are going to find is your cold dead body on the ground."

He cocked the trigger back.

Marla screamed, "Travis, Stop! Please."

He looked away from De'mon and back at Marla as if coming out of a trance. Travis shook his head. He stepped back and then slammed his fist into Demon's gut dropping him to his knees. He put the gun to the back of his head. She was sure he was going to execute him right there on the street. Marla was in total shock. She couldn't leave, and she couldn't watch. Then, Travis smashed him on the back of the head with his fist, knocking him to the ground and into the pool of piss. De'mon didn't move.

The black guy looked around nervously, "You done man? Cause we better go. This place is gonna be swarming."

Marla pulled on his coat and pleaded, "Come on, Travis. You got your revenge."

"Follow me, man. I'll get you a ride." Travis put the gun in his coat and backed away. He wanted to kill every one of them. He wanted to waste all nine of them right there in the street, and would have except for Marla. He knew she would never be the same. He didn't want her to see it, so he backed away. Then, the three of them quickly left. They walked two blocks one way and a block another way zigzagging through a mostly deserted hood. There were abandoned cars everywhere and very few lights. There appeared to be a few occupants in all the buildings, but obviously, most the tenants had left.

Night time, everything was closed shut. As they walked along, Travis said almost nothing; he kept glancing over his shoulder as if expecting more trouble any moment. Marla though, as she always was, was more sociable and attempted to engage in some casual conversation. She asked the guy his name.

"Freddie."

"Thank you, Freddie."

"Thank me when we're safe."

They walked another four more blocks or so through a literal war zone and then came to a street where they heard some music and kept walking in the direction of the sound. There were a bunch of cars parked on the street, mostly cabs. Then out of the dark, a legless man on a board wheeled his way down the sidewalks toward them.

"Hey Freddie."

"Hey Wheels. How's it going tonight?"

"Kinda quiet. Ain't seen the Force at all. No busts."

A man across the street pushing a shopping cart yelled out, "Is that you, Freddie?"

Freddie waved to the man in ragged clothes and a long beard. It was obviously a hub of activity. Three more black guys were out front of a bar smoking when they walked up. It was like they didn't even see Freddie or even Travis for that matter. They heard blues playing inside, live music but nothing that Travis recognized. When they got there, Freddie didn't say anything to the men. It was like he ignored them and walked right past and led Travis and Marla down some dark steps to the entrance to the club where Marla stopped. "He can't go in."

"Why not?"

"He just can't."

Freddie looked at Travis and nodded, "I figured. Stay

right here, I'll get you a ride. Don't leave."

Freddie went down the steps into the club. They weren't real sure what to think. After a few minutes, he came back up and told them that a cab driver named T Dog would be coming out in a few minutes and he'd give them a lift.

Travis lit a cigarette and leaned against the brick. He offered one to Freddie. He declined, "Kill yourself, I like living."

Travis took a deep breath and then put his hand on his shoulder, "Say, I want to thank you for what you did back there."

He smiled and shook his head, "Lemme' guess, you was expecting a different color for a hero?"

"No...it's not that."

Freddie pulled a crucifix out from his shirt and kissed it, "It's alright man; I was expecting a different color too."

Marla looked curiously at Freddie. He had such a pleasant looking face, "Why did you follow us?"

"You two got trouble written all over you. Some say it is my job."

She thought that was an unusual statement, but Freddie was an unusual guy. Travis huffed down his smoke and they talked for a few minutes more killing some time and listening to the band. When the song was over, Freddie said he had to go somewhere and disappeared up the steps.

A minute later a black guy came out and started up the stairs. He looked up and saw Marla. His eyes widen. She asked, "Are you T Dog?"

"Sure am, honey. And who are you?"

"Marla. Freddie told us you could give us a ride."

"Freddie? You seen Freddie?"

"He just went in to get you."

T Dog just then looked at Travis standing there, "Is she with you?"

"Yep."

"Just my luck. Where you two want to go?"

"Central Park West."

He smiled, "You're a long ways from home pretty lady, but I'll get cha' there."

All the way back through midtown Marla kept talking about Freddie. She didn't say what had happened outside the station, and Travis said virtually nothing. T Dog listened as she rambled, and Travis sat quietly observing everything as they drove through town. T Dog finally looked at Travis in the backseat, "Is she always this crazy?"

"This is a good night. She is usually a lot worse."

Marla elbowed him, and then folded her arms. She looked tired. The streets were desolate all the way through SoHo and Greenwich Village. The only traffic that was out were the few remaining Taxi's on their last fares before curfew. They passed through intersections that had lights with no cars. Occasionally, a bus passed along its route, and he saw a few MF units along the way. Travis looked down at Marla; suddenly, she got quiet. She looked exhausted. It had been a long night, and she leaned her head over onto Travis's shoulder. T Dog kept making small talk. Travis saw a few stop signs that had been spray painted. Other than that, there wasn't much sign of resistance. It had been terminated.

T Dog and Travis talked for a while. Marla was nodding off but not completely asleep. T Dog talked about the police harassment. He complained about the Ravens flying everywhere taking pictures. The thing he hated though was the dogs, the Big Dogs. "Can't go anywhere without one of them looking at you. They scare the crap out me, man. Some of the new ones have got lasers, and the beam will blow a hole right through ya. Its laser can't go through glass or metal, but they sure burn a hole through your flesh."

"You've seen it happen?"

"Oh, yeah. A brother messed with one, and it blew right through his mouth a crater about the size of a quarter. He put up his hand to protect his face, and it blew two fingers off. Just like that."

Travis looked down at Marla. Her eyes were closed. "You saw it?"

"I was standing next to him. He won't hardly go outside no more."

Travis thought about the one in the park that subdued the man. Must have been the older model, or maybe it wasn't. Maybe he was screaming because he was hit with a Taser instead of a laser? Maybe that's why all the ones in the crowd started to run? Travis looked up, and they passed by another pack walking down the street. T Dog could tell he was nervous and pulled out a rather large hand gun and laid it on his dash, "Don't worry man," he looked back at Travis in the rear view mirror, "Cabbies are loaded. You're safe with me."

Travis looked out the window as they passed by several dark streets with punks drinking and smoking. One flipped the cab off, the others laughed. Travis looked around behind them, and he could see the Force driving through the intersection. "They don't do anything do they? They don't try to stop them?"

"That's why she is a Bitch man. A brother would help ya". He looked back at Travis, "Did you know it was gonna be this bad?"

"Worse than what I heard."

He put his gun back down on the seat next to him and

turned onto Tenth Avenue. "It has all changed man. She rules everything, and ain't nobody get a break."

He was right; everything had changed. It was not the same city, and it was not even close to the place it had been. The conditions had deteriorated worse than what was reported. Travis put his arm around Marla until they arrived back to her apartment. She had fallen asleep. Travis told him to stop about a block from her place and then woke her up. "I'm going to go in the back way. You go in the front."

Marla mumbled, "What?" She yawned and looked around, then, she kissed Travis, "Are we safe?"

"Almost." He told her they would watch and that he'd be there in a few minutes. She swiped her hand on the scanner and got out. Travis and T Dog watched her walk down the street to her building. "Um hum, that is one fine looking woman."

"Yes, she is." Travis looked to see if anybody was tailing her. There was no sign that anyone was following. He saw her make it to her front door. They talked for a while after she made it to her apartment, and then Travis told him, "Drop me off at the next street."

"You both some crazy people you know that." T Dog handed him his card. It said TOP DOG TAXI, BUSTIN MY TAIL FOR YOU. "Make sure she gets this," he winked.

Travis put his hand on his shoulder and squeezed firmly. He put the card in his inside pocket and got out. "When I call, you pick me up here on this corner. Is that cool?"

"Cool with me, boss man."

"Good. See ya, TD." Travis walked in the opposite direction of her building, circled the block and came back to her street. He, then, walked down past her building looking to see if there was anyone sitting in a car watching. He saw no one; the street was deserted. He continued past her building but on the opposite side of the street, then, he crossed the road and ducked into an alley that he followed to the back door. He tapped on it twice. She opened it.

They weren't in her apartment five minutes, and Travis looked in the bedroom. Marla lay on her bed past out, still fully clothed. He took her shoes off and shut the door. He went back to her computer. He had lots of work to do, and time was running out.

CHAPTER SEVEN

When Travis woke up that Monday morning, she had already gone to work. Breakfast was in the fridge, the coffee pot still on, and a half pack of smokes lay on the counter. He got on her computer again and did some research. Then, he cut his hair in her bathroom trimming it meticulously into a business man style. He shaved, and then he went to work.

It was not at all a customary day for her. Nothing appeared the same anymore, and she had the most unusual feeling inside. It was a peculiar type of craving. She took a walk at lunch and bought a couple of cards. She kept hoping that she would turn around, and he would be there, even if he was in disguise. She knew she couldn't call him, though she wanted badly to hear his voice. It was weird, really weird. She left that Friday from her office and returned Monday morning a completely different person. She no longer thought the same, or acted the same, or felt the same. She didn't know if it was her or the world that was different. Maybe both had simultaneously changed.

Marla looked at the people in the crowd, their faces. She viewed them now not in the same context. It was like *she* was from another planet now; her whole sphere of thought was different from theirs. They jabbered nonsensically about the about the most trivial mundane things: shows they watched, sports and celebrities, gossip, fashion. *What are they talking about?* She wondered. *Don't they know what is going on?*

They were all so oblivious. Lemmings, sheep. She sat on

a bench in a park and ate her measly lunch by herself. She looked at the cameras on all the buildings, everywhere, with their tiny robotic ears. Travis was right; it was all about control; the government didn't trust the people. The system didn't trust anybody. The evidence was compelling. It was undeniable. She watched the MF patrolling the street. A new cage unit circled the block and then stopped to talk to the MF on patrol. This cage unit was larger than the predecessors. The unit could hold up to ten prisoners in back. She hadn't seen the inside, but she was told it had hooks attached to the wall with cuffs. That made it easier to apprehend citizens, especially groups, so convenient for crowd control. The front of the unit looked like an armored car; indeed, it was armored with a new bullet proof exterior, although that was hardly needed since very few people had guns anymore except Cabbies and hoods.

Marla watched the MF talking to the guys in the unit. One guy had been watching her. She hoped he wouldn't come over and check her I.D.; that got so old. She didn't want to have to deal with another cop knocking on her door. The unit finally drove off, and she grudgingly went back to her office. No one followed. The remainder of the day, she sat at her desk waiting painfully for the clock to get to five, and then left. She had a lot to tell Travis about what happened, but when she arrived at home, he wasn't there. That didn't surprise her. There was a note on the counter. She looked at it. For a moment her breath was taken away. Her heart raced. He had promised he wouldn't leave her like that again. She had brought home some gyros; they were still warm in her hand. Something had told her he wouldn't be there when she came home. Marla put the sandwiches down on the counter and picked up the note. Her hands trembled. She opened it.

"I miss you."

He had written down instructions for what she was to do. She looked at the time and waited. At seven, she turned out the lights in her apartment. One minute later, she turned them back on. Thirty minutes later, she went down stairs to the back door. He was there. At first, she didn't recognize him; he was dressed in a business suit and had on glasses. She hugged him, and they kissed as soon as he walked through the door. "I missed you."

"I missed you, too. Come on, I think you're being watched."

They went up the stairs together; and as they were about at her door, an older lady came out of her room across the hall. It startled Marla. She was nervous. "Oh hi, Mrs. Goldstein."

"Why hello, Marla." She looked at Travis and smiled, "Who's this nice man."

She had a short little old lady perm and wore bright orange earrings and way too much lotion and powder, "I'm Joe, Joe Maddox. Marla and I use to work together."

"You worked with Marla at the agency?"

"No, I worked on another floor. That was a long time ago. I live in Baltimore now. I don't get back to the city much."

Marla looked like a teenager caught sneaking out her window. She was blushing all over and fumbling with her keys trying to get in her door quickly. Mrs. Goldstein walked over to her and patted her on the arm, "We all just love Marla. She is such a nice girl". She looked at Travis in the gray flannel suit. He looked like a lawyer or broker, "You staying in town long Mr. Maddox?"

"At least a couple of weeks," Travis whispered in her ear, "but please don't tell anyone."

She looked at Marla and then back at Travis, "You'll have to bring Mr. Maddox over for dinner some evening. I've got rations for a Cornish hen."

"Well, I, um, I…" She dropped her keys. Travis picked them up and opened the door. "I'd love to, maybe Saturday night?"

"We could sooner."

"Saturday would be fine. How about you, Marla?"

"Um, well, ah sure. We could do Saturday. I could bring a plate."

"Good." She stuck out her hand, "It is so nice to meet you Mr. Maddox."

"Joe."

"Call me Bernice."

She went down to the hall to the elevator. It was almost time for it to start up again. Monday nights were her bridge nights. They got together at Marlene Offerman's on the second floor. Marla shut the door and locked it. "Why did you tell her we'd be there Saturday night? You are going to be gone, right?"

He kissed her, "You think she is going to keep quiet?"

"Of course not."

"If anyone checks on you, I don't want them to have a clue you are going to be gone. I want them to think you are going to be around for a while. Do you see?"

"Not really." She took off his coat, "Sit down, and eat." She slid the gyro in front of him. "So tell me."

"You are being watched." Travis took a big bite of his sandwich and wiped his mouth, "I am pretty sure of it. I saw you today at lunch, saw you on the bench."

"You were there?"

"I was in the crowd. When you got up and left, two guys

came over a few minutes later and looked under the bench to see if you left something. I think I saw them one time before, but I didn't say anything. Tonight, when you turned off the light, I saw a guy get out of a car and start walking up to your building. When you turned the light back on, he stopped and went back to the car. There was another man in the car. A few minutes later, I walked right by them. They had a camera mounted on the dash."

Marla lit a candle and turned down the light, "So if they think you're here why don't they just come and get you?"

"*If* they do know I am here, which I am not sure they have figured that out yet, they are hoping I will lead them to my contacts. They think we have a headquarters here in the city, but we don't. That's what they are after; chances are they will probably just conduct surveillance for a while."

"What would they do with me, if they found you here?"

"You can probably figure that out. As bad as it was on me, it is always worse on women."

Marla pushed her plate away, "I don't care anymore, Travis. As far as I am concerned, after what I saw today, I don't have anything to live for anymore anyway."

"What happened?"

"I tested Charlotte, my boss. I am sure she has it. I didn't notice it before, but she has a little bump on her forehead right at the hair line. It is what she did that convinced me."

Travis took another bite, "Go on."

"There is a girl in our office that is getting married. So I went and bought her one of those cheesy beef cake cards during lunch. You know with the guy that is practically undressed, wearing nothing but a bow. Well, I showed it to Charlotte to have her sign it. We are not supposed to have any more birthday parties at work; it's a drag, but anyway I told her that we were going to have a guy come up and do a dance for her before she gets married. Travis, it was hideous. Her head jerked back when I showed her the card. Her left eye flittered. Her knees actually buckled for a second, and she grabbed the desk. She raised her hand in front of the card and looked away. She told me that there would be no birthday parties in her office, and told me to go."

"And…"

"I did. I have never seen her like that. For a second, I thought she was going to fall down. She has it, right?"

"Hard to tell. I don't know what her normal personality is like. When the guys took it in prison, the biggest toughest guys we had become like mealy worms. It was amazing; these guys talked revolution all the time, and in a few hours they obeyed every command they were given. They were unreachable from that point on. I tried to talk to them; they were gone. They weren't there anymore; it was like they were soulless beings. They never laughed again, didn't talk about their families, nothing. They lived to serve. It was all they did."

"They didn't tell you about it?"

"They never mentioned a word. They can't. When they are given Trisix, they are instructed not to tell anyone; and of course if they do, they are shocked. They may try it once or twice. After that, they aren't going to open their mouth. Just like a dog with the electronic collar. He gets bolted once or twice going to the fence; he's not going there anymore. So if they even think about a thought that will trigger the impulse, they won't think that same thought anymore."

Marla's shoulders slumped, "She has to have it. Travis, she seemed terrified when I mentioned the party. You should have seen the look in her eyes."

"Hummm. We have heard that they are developing a second version, one that doesn't have the strength of the original impulse chip. The first chip, the one that was used on the prisoners, is possibly too strong for someone like Charlotte. They don't want it to be obvious that people are being implanted with it; they want a much more subtle reaction. Much of this is still in the experimental stage; not that it is going to prohibit them from moving forward. They discovered that people have different thresholds for pain. They want it to be less obvious, to dispense pain but not obvert where it can be witnessed by others. But you know what really makes me sick?"

"What?"

"They are working on a chip just for children, but they are not there yet. They will be. They don't want to give the human race any time to develop a resistance."

Her mouth dropped wide open, "Are you serious? That would be so cruel."

"Beyond cruel. But you see there is a fundamental problem and that is they have discovered that electronic shocks to mammals in the development stage cause numerous problems. It has caused deformity both physical and, of course, mentally. Dogs are often retarded when they were exposed to shocking when they were young. They became basically untrainable because of the severity of the mental disorders."

"That's sickening. They would do this to humans, too? Children?"

Travis went to the window and peered out. He pulled back his sleeve looking at a meter on his arm, and undid his tie. "One of the problems that they didn't completely understand or anticipate was that the human brain goes through developmental stages. The brain of a two year old is not the same as the brain of a six year old. It changes again in adolescence before it matures into an adult. The reasoning, cognitive thinking doesn't begin to form until the early teen years. Too early an exposure destroys the ability to function at all. They won't be able to make the most basic decisions."

"Like, what do you mean?"

"Like if there is a fire in a trash can. They won't be able to decide to put it out with water or a shovel. You see, the rationale portion of the brain that makes those decisions will be damaged due to exposure to impulse shocks. This phenomenon would destroy the purpose of Trisix because they do want an obedient society, but they also want a functional society. You see?"

"So they can't administer Trisix until that portion of the brain develops naturally on its own, right?"

"Correct. So the dilemma for the government is at what age it can be administered because if they become adults and can think on their own, they will organize and destroy it."

"So they are in fear of the next generation."

"Absolutely. The young will not be fools, not like our generation."

"I hope not…" She clawed her lip with her teeth, "What I saw was too horrible to describe."

"Did it last long, the shock?"

"Just a second."

"That's all it takes. Believe me, babe; she will not even entertain the thought of breaking their rules. She will be a perfect worker. She will do everything on time. She will labor endlessly, and that's what they are looking for. It will make us all human bees instead of human beings."

Marla handed him the rest of her sandwich. She wasn't hungry.

She was confused, "So do you think they know you are here? You never told me exactly. What are you doing? You told me, y'all have a solution."

He didn't say anything. His eyes looked away from her.

She gulped and asked hesitantly, "So, are you a terrorist? Do you plan on destroying the government?"

"The terrorist is our government."

Her heart began to race. He could see the drink shake in her hand. "Are you here to attack it? Is that the solution?"

"Attack and defend are subjective. It depends upon one's perspective. If a person rushes to help a person being mugged, is he defending the victim or is he attacking the assailant?"

"He's defending, of course."

Travis lit a smoke, "There is your answer."

"But you are going to attack the government?"

"We are going to *free* the people." He could tell she was scared. It was too much for someone to comprehend so suddenly. He knew he couldn't tell her anything else; it would be dangerous for her if she knew. Travis told her not to think about it anymore; he would tell her later. He didn't want to talk about it. Then, he got up from the table and began washing the dishes. She helped him and neither discussed it the rest of the night.

When they were done putting things away and drying off the plates, she ran her fingers down the buttons of his shirt, "Okay, next question Mr. Joe Maddox. I am guessing that you didn't go shopping on Fifth Avenue today, so you can at least tell me where you got the suit".

"Like it?"

"You know I do."

He smiled, "I do most my shopping at the subway. In particular, in the restroom." Travis laid a gun on the counter.

"Travis, you…"

He put his finger on her lips, "Uh huh, it's Joe", he laughed, "Nice guy. I really wanted to leave him my clothes, but it is always best when I leave them naked. Gives me more time to get away."

Marla laughed, "You did what?"

"Robbed a guy. Took his clothes". He smiled, "You have to remember; hon, I can't buy anything. I have no other choice."

Surprised, "You took a man's clothes in a subway? You left him naked?"

"All the way." Travis shrugged, "Just a regular day at the office for me. Not for him, though."

She laughed, "I guess not, and then what did you do?"

"That, I can't tell you. I was busy, though, very busy."

Marla started undoing his belt, "Well, I must admit I like Joe Maddox. You know what it does to me when I see you in a suit." She pulled his belt through the loops and tossed it on the chair.

Travis looked at his watch like a businessman standing at the station, "You know it is only eight-thirty? A little early."

"You've had a hard day at the office, me too."

Travis felt exactly like she did. The world was ending, and all they had was each other. "Are you insane, Marla? Are we both insane?"

She blew out the candle and grabbed his hand. "Yes."

"Good. Because I wouldn't love you if you weren't crazy."

"Bring your water". She walked him to the bedroom. "You've got some business to take care of, Mr. Maddox."

CHAPTER EIGHT

Travis was gone when she woke up the next morning which didn't surprise her. Normality was on a sliding scale. She had come to expect the unexpected. He did leave a note, "I'll be late. Take an umbrella; it will rain." It did.

By noon, the bright early morning sunshine had vanished and given way to a dismal gray, raining, overcast afternoon. It was a sobering day for Marla. She looked out her window at downtown Manhattan; the people walking back and forth with umbrellas in the drizzle. Most were black umbrellas, but some had color. They looked like ladybugs and ants moving about back and forth. Some stood at the lights so still, waiting for the signal hand to turn green. It was all so orderly. She could see it so clearly now. The tall buildings throughout downtown looked like big honeycombs in glass jars, vertical in shape. They were just modern hives with workers going to and fro. It wouldn't be long, and it would all be perfected. City after city, country after country, the planet would be a colonized.

It was difficult for her to focus on her work that day. She didn't want to be there, but she couldn't leave. Before the chip, she could have said she was sick and gone home. But in the new system, it was all so strictly regimented. Now, there were procedures; her chip tracked her every move. If she left now, she had to go to the clinic that took hours; she'd be there all night. She knew she wouldn't be granted authorization for an absence. Others had tried to fool the health department and failed, and subsequently demoted. She didn't feel like working at all, but she did her best to get done what she could. It didn't help with the constant presence of her supervisor lurking about. She felt strangely claustrophobic, paranoid. Every time she looked up, it seemed like someone in the office was watching her. Were the cameras not sufficient enough?

She couldn't believe how they *all* so easily submitted, how the plan came about. Marla thought back; she remembered that first the government started chipping dogs and cats for identification purposes. They passed ordinances and restrictions with penalties imposed on those that didn't comply. She couldn't believe how easily society had been indoctrinated. Even she had been for the chip; it seemed reasonable at the time. Then, it was all the government workers turn; they were next. Everyone in her office took the V-chip. Comply or lose their job. The economy was bad, and so they all submitted just like that. Now she understood. It was just one of the steps in creating a totally submissive society; first dogs, then cats, then people. Marla wanted to just get out of the whole system. She wanted to break free from all the restraint. She had the urge to run downstairs to the middle of the street in all the traffic, in the rain with all the people looking and dance. She wanted to raise her hands to the sky and scream to them all, "I'm NOT LIKE YOU!"

The reality was she wasn't different though. She was a slave just like them. She looked at her right hand on the keyboard with the little bump underneath the skin. It was her chain. They could shut her down for anything at all, at any time. She would no longer be able to buy anything, even a ride on the subway. Her rations would be deleted. When checked, her identification would flash "WANTED. APPREHEND SUBJECT IMMEDIATELY". She was in the electronic cage; she had walked right into it, and she never once complained. She complied completely. She had thought like they all did; it would benefit their life, protect their security, and make everything more efficient.

Marla felt nauseous; her stomach felt queasy thinking about it. She looked at the data on her screen. She was behind on her quota of reports to complete. A little calculator on her monitor appeared periodically to remind her of the time and how many reports were left to finish for the day. It was always pressure, pressure, pressure; numbers, forms, data entries. Her head was pounding with each click of the digital clock. Her anxiety intensified, and the emails from her co-workers didn't help. They needed her reports. "Was there a problem?" Delete. "Was there a reason for the delay?" Delete.

Marla's mouse raced in her hand across the pad. She kept watching the digital clock, click, click, click. Send, send, send, until finally the monitor flashed across her screen, "DATA ENTRY COMPLETE".

It was 5:45, nearly all the staff had gone home. She was ill from the day; her stomach empty. All she had to eat all day were the USDA's approved salt less saltines. It was like eating chalk; they just made her sicker.

Charlotte came by her desk with an arm full of files, "Marla, was there something wrong today? You seemed to be getting behind?"

She brushed the hair out of her face, "I thought I was working fast enough. It seemed like I had an unusual amount of work to complete."

"You are a category eight; you should be able to handle it."

"I'll try better tomorrow."

Another worker came up to her desk, Al, a short balding man in his mid-fifties. He had probably been there longer than anybody else at the agency. He had thick glasses and notoriously bad breath. Women always stood back from him, but Al was usually good for a joke.

Marla grabbed her coat and umbrella, "Hey Al, how are you?"

"Good." He showed Charlotte something on his computer. "We are having more technical difficulties with the system again, but it is not a virus." He didn't even acknowledge Marla which was unusual for Al because she usually had to back away from him because he used every opportunity he could to pen her in her cubicle.

As Marla squeezed by them, she couldn't help but notice his scalp and the way it reflected in the light. She saw it! It was clear as could be. There was a bump on his forehead where his hair line used to be. His eyes looked different too, and there wasn't his customary smarmy smile.

"Is something wrong?" Charlotte asked.

"Oh no," she smiled, "Just tired, long day."

"Get some rest. Go to bed earlier and come in sooner if the work load is more than you can handle."

"I will try that Charlotte. Thank you."

Marla took the subway back to her apartment. It was still raining and dark by the time she got home. No Travis, no note. She hung her rain coat up as soon as she walked through the door and collapsed on the couch. She couldn't remember being so exhausted. Her eyes ached from staring at her monitor all day, and the bright light in the kitchen irritated them even more so she lit a few candles and placed one on the window sill so Travis would know she's home, that is, if he was watching.

She didn't know how he would contact her. He used a phone, but never to call her. She knew enough about him, though, to know he would figure out a way; he always did. Marla closed her eyes and laid her head back. She still had a headache from the day. She didn't realize she had even gone to sleep until she woke back up much later and looked at the clock; she was hungry. There wasn't much to eat, her refrigerator was practically bare. She fumbled around the shelf and found a container of seafood bisque, though it wasn't really seafood anymore; ocean fishing had been banned. It was a genetically modified substitute. Marla looked at the ingredients on the back of the plastic container; "Ferrous Sulfate, Thiamin Mononitrate, Riboflavin, Folic Acid, egg white, cornstarch, cooked mechanically artificial shrimp compound, Monosodium glutamate, autolyzed yeast extract, and maltodextrin".

Though she was hungry, she poured the less than appetizing compound down the drain. 'Hum', she thought, *so this is an authorized recommended meal by the Nutrition Council.*

"Yum."

She sat down at her kitchen counter and nibbled on a dozen stale saltless saltines. She looked out over the city at the rain still falling and ate quietly under the glow of the candle. She was beginning to get worried now about Travis.

It was at that moment, that for the first time, she actually understood it all completely. She envied him. There were millions of people in the city; they were all prisoners of the chip, but Travis was free. Even though he was on the run, looking over his shoulder, he possessed something she didn't. Marla got up and went to the window and lit a cigarette looking down on the traffic below. She listened to the busses and cars stopped at the light. In another hour, it would be curfew and hardly anybody would be out. The street would be nearly quiet. Everyone was rushing home like bees returning to their hives, but not Travis. Wherever he was, he was free. They hadn't put the electronic chain around his neck. That first night she saw him at the Tavern, she thought he was the one that needed empathy. Now, she thought different. They needed empathy. They were trapped, and he was free.

Marla flipped through some CD's. Jewel, Kings of Leon, B.B. King. She put on an Adele and unbuttoned her blouse and stood at the window in the dark. She opened it slightly and listened to the music, and the cool air felt good blowing in across her breast. She wanted her freedom back. She wanted life like what it had been. She wanted to eat real food, and if she wanted to eat junk, she didn't want some agency to tell her she couldn't. She wanted it to be *her* choice. She wanted to be able to walk the streets again, without worry of rape or murder. She wanted to drive a car anytime without curfews. She craved liberty. She didn't want to be watched all the time by those insidious cameras and Ravens flying down the street. Marla wanted to be a human and not a freakin' bee.

She realized that all she had left in the world was her apartment. It was no more really than just a little cage. She felt like a bird put up for the night; there weren't bars around her cage, but there might as well been. She looked around her tiny apartment, and the pain of reality hit her. She had worked nearly ten years at her job, and this is all she had, a little cage. At that very moment, she would have rather been anywhere, a farm, the woods, on a hill, even riding in a boxcar on a train looking out across the desert on a moonlit night. Marla wanted her freedom back. She didn't know why she so easily gave it away. She finished one cigarette and then lit another hoping to see Travis coming down the street. She saw nothing but parked cars and the rain falling across the city. She was tired and all the things going through her mind wore her down. She started visualizing Travis, where he might be. She couldn't believe how much she missed him. Marla looked at the clock and fretted where he could be? Did they catch him? Did the Force chase him down some street? Did they shock him with the glove? Was he jerking on the ground in front of a group of spectators? Did they haul him away chained like an animal? Was he somewhere being shocked senseless, beaten, interrogated?

She listened to Adele sing a sad song about love and realized it had been missing from her life all these years. Only the time she spent with Travis did she ever feel alive. All the rest of the time, it was like somehow she was numb. Things happened, events occurred, but it was like living in a white box. She felt oddly like one of her dolls when she was a kid. They had a playhouse with furniture and other dolls. They mimicked pretend conversations but nothing about anything that was real. That's what her life was like without Travis. It was a playhouse world where nothing mattered. It was senseless.

She was thirty-three, and her life was pointless.

Marla snuffed out the cigarette and went to her room and collapsed on her bed putting the pillows over her head. She tried to think of something else, anything. Then, she heard the front door open. She rose from her bed frightened, her heart pounding. Someone was in her living room. It was dark, and then it moved into her kitchen. The refrigerator door opened.

"Travis?"

"Shhh...keep the light off."

"What are you doing? You're driving me crazy; you know that. How did you get in?"

He walked in to her bedroom and sat beside her on the bed. She could barely see his face in the lights from the street shining through. She felt his coat; it was wet, and she took it off and tossed it on the floor.

"How did you get in? Where have you been?"

"It's a simple lock." He sipped on a bottle of water. His voice was low and soft. "You are being followed. I can't stay." He told her that he watched her from the roof of another building down the block. The same car that was parked on the street the day before was still there, just moved to another spot. After she went into her building, another car drove up next to the first one, and they talked for a while. Then, the second car drove off. "I have to go babe, but I need to get on your computer first."

"Stay with me or take me with you. Don't leave me alone."

Travis stroked her face with his thumb and sipped on the water, "Be patient. You need to go to sleep. Maybe tomorrow."

"Maybe? You are only going to be here for a few more days, and you tell me maybe. How can you do that?"

"It is too risky. They are on to you."

"Well, let's go someplace, get a room. We can lose them, don't you think?"

"If they know you are trying to lose them, they'll just shut you down. The system will turn you off. Trust me, I know."

She grabbed hold of his arm and pulled him to her. He knew she was trying to get him to make love to her. He put his arm around her waist, "You know I want to, but I can't babe. Don't you understand?"

"I'm scared. They are in my office; they are watching me. It's awful. Isn't there something we can do? I...I...I don't want to be without you."

"Lemme think." Travis leaned across her knees and looked out her window. Her fingers stroked the back of his head with one hand and his leg with the other. He knew she was being monitored; they could swarm her building at any moment or it still may be days. Finally, he turned around and knelt down on his knees beside her on the bed. "This is what I want you to do. Invite somebody over tomorrow, that guy Mac. Have him over early, fix him supper and make sure you are both seen in the window. It would be great if you met him downstairs. At 8:00 turn off the light, go out the back and meet me at the corner".

"What about Mac?"

"How good a friend is he?"

"He'll do anything I ask."

"Tell him the truth; you need him as a decoy."

"Travis, I don't like this. Why don't I just meet you someplace?"

"They'll be everywhere you go. That phone of yours is traceable; you know that, right? You leave it here tomorrow night and take the glove." He handed her another phone. "Use this."

"And who did it belong to?"

"Somebody that won't miss it, for a while. Do you think you can remember a quick code?"

"Code?"

Travis showed her a system, elementary, but it worked. If she got a text that said "Red", it meant go. "Green" meant abort. "Yellow", wait. It would be followed by one word. The word was the key for deciphering the code. Vowels were represented by symbols: * for a, % for e, ! for i, @ for o and ^ for u. Ten of the most used letters in the alphabet were replaced by numbers, 1 for b, 2 for c, 3 for d, 4 for g, 5 for h, 6 for l, 7 for m, 8 for r, 9 for s, 0 for t. The rest of the letters were the same. "Meet at nine would be 7%%0*0n!n%". He wrote it down and gave it to her. "Use it a few times, and you'll get used to it. If you get a message over thirty-six characters, it is a fake. It is a trap. Don't respond. Do you understand?"

She nodded, "And, how do I text you?"

"You don't. I am watching you, and I am watching them. I've got a whole lot to do, and I'm running out of time."

Her head sunk down exuberated. She wanted to convince him to stay, but knew it was no use. He handed her a pill and told her to take it. "You need a good night's sleep", then he set her alarm.

"When will you tell me what is going on?"

"We are down to just a few days left. Go to sleep. I'll see you tomorrow." Travis kissed her on the cheek and she laid back. He looked out the window from the shadows of her curtain. She was sleepy and didn't even hear him leave. The next thing she knew it was morning; her phone rang. It woke her up. She scrambled around the sheets looking for it, the message said, "RED !l@v%y@^."

She looked at the phone and pulled out her code. It took her awhile, but she got it. She smiled, "I love you, too."

It was all she needed to hear.

CHAPTER NINE

Marla did arrive early Wednesday morning. There was something peculiarly strange about the people on the subway downtown. It was unusually quiet, and when they got off at the station, it was uncustomary orderly. She walked three blocks to her office, and because it was early, there was very little traffic. At the first intersection she came to, the pedestrian light was red so she waited with the others, but there were no cars. There were ten to twelve people waiting for the signal to change, only Marla and another guy crossed. As she went down the street to her office, she looked back over her shoulder, and they were still just standing there. There weren't any cars. Other people came up and crossed but not the ones that were already there. She was almost all the way down the block before they moved, and they probably would have stayed there all day if the light didn't turn green.

She went straight to her desk and started on her work immediately before everyone else arrived. One of her problems is that she was friendly; men especially liked to come by and chat, but the women did too. Popularity has its draw backs. She postponed the talks that morning till break because she couldn't afford to get behind. She called Mac at mid-morning and invited him over for dinner though she didn't tell him anything of course about what was going on. She felt shame for using him like that. She knew he would be disappointed, but he had always been a friend. If anybody would understand, it would Mac, or at least she hoped.

Marla was able to concentrate on her work much better than the day before, and though she wanted to text Travis, she knew that if she started doing that she wouldn't be able to think about work. She actually felt better than she had in a long time, and though it was silly, she kept thinking about his text that morning. She couldn't remember if he ever told her that he loved her before, and though he said it in a text, a coded text for that matter, it lifted her spirits throughout the day. She actually finished her reports about an hour early; and she wanted badly to leave, but she couldn't. She sat at her cubicle relieved to be done and thought about what he had told her. He said there was much more going on. Trisix was much more than just a super chip; there were plans. How could that be possible she wondered? Marla peeked over her cubicle wall at Charlotte in her office. She looked like a bad caricature of a wax figure staring motionless at her monitor. Her eyes fixated on the data flashing across her screen.

Marla sat down and clicked on to the net. She put her earphones on and clicked to the news that she hadn't seen in a long time. She hadn't missed much; it was all the same. It was the same for as far back as she could remember, government, government, government, a touchy human interest story before the break. It was the same format it had been for years. Nothing changed. After the commercials, the talking heads came back on and cut to the "big story of the day". Standing on the capitol steps were all the props, microphones and podium, the cast of dark suits, white shirts, blue ties and manicured haircuts. In the background, were lifted wrinkled faces splashed with make-up and an assembly of photo ops smiles. More lies; more bills; more legislation that were going to save us again.

According to the report, months of negotiation and debate were complete; another bi-partisan law passed and waited the President's signature. Hooray! Marla looked at their faces and then peeked over at Charlotte. She looked back at the screen again and back at Charlotte. They looked the same.

She leaned back in her chair and clicked to another channel. It was the same story. She clicked to another station, again the same story. It was all the same. Even the faces of the reporters were the same or at least the words they mouthed were nearly identical. When the story ended a commercial came on and she clicked back through the stations again; commercial, commercial, commercial. Same products, same commercial, same everything.

Individuality was deceased. It had died without a funeral, and though the sun shined outside her window, it was a dreadful dreary day. She looked at the tall glass hives, helicopters flying to and fro landing on the helipads on top of the roofs. Bees. Just like bees. All they needed was a supreme ruler, a queen, a king, and then everything would be complete.

Marla grabbed her coat, and at 5:00, she was in the elevator going down. It was busy with traffic, typical rush hour. She went by Tannenbaum's to get some items for a meal and was disappointed. There still wasn't enough to make a good salad. They had lettuce and onion but no tomatoes or carrots, no celery either.

"Anyone special?" Mr. Tannenbaum smiled, "Got some macaroni salad. Just made it; it's fresh."

Marla looked around at the deli; it was not what she was hoping. "What would I serve with it?"

"Corn beef and peas. I got some fresh French bread just an hour ago. I can cut it extra thick. Use garlic and lemon. Cook it about thirty minutes. Trust me."

He smiled over the counter. The bell rang at the front door. A nice dressed man in a suit came in. He stood by the counter, "Hello."

"Hello." She paid and then left. "I'll let you know if Mac likes it."

Marla hurriedly along to her building and stopped in the foyer, looking back. She saw the man in the suit leave Tannebaum's. He was on the phone, but he had nothing in his hand. That didn't necessarily mean anything, maybe he didn't see what he wanted, and maybe he only bought cigarettes or some gum. He looked back up the street toward her apartment but then turned the other way. She knew she had not seen him before in the neighborhood; he had the kind of face that women just don't forget. He also didn't seem like the type that would be with the secret police. It was hard to pinpoint, but there was something about his manner; he appeared cordial and relaxed. He was by all means a very sexy man.

Marla raced up the stairs to her floor and began cooking. At seven, Mac buzzed her downstairs. Normally, she would have just let him in, but she went down to greet him. He brought a bottle of wine. They were able to catch the elevator and take it to her floor, and as luck would have it, Mrs. Goldstein was coming out her door at just the same time.

She looked surprised, "Why hello, Marla", she looked at Mac with his long dark hair pulled back in a ponytail. She glanced down at the bottle in his hand, "Friend? Is he here in town for business *too?*"

"Bernice, this is Mac."

She stiffened her lip and stuck out her hand, "Well, you have a nice evening, sir."

"Well, I hope to," he smiled.

Mrs. Goldstein gave Marla a look of noticeable displeasure and coughed, "You look tired, hon. Maybe you should rest more. Night."

Marla ducked into her apartment before any other nosey bodies came out. She double bolted it "Geez that was not good."

Mac popped the wine, "What was that all about?"

"Sit down, Mac. I will tell you. You know that guy that I was with last week at the club?"

He poured her a glass, "Thomas, right?"

"Yes," she set the plates on the table with the napkins, "He's in trouble, and I must help him."

Mac took off his coat, "Uh, huh, go on".

"He's why I called you."

Mac poured another glass and took a sip. "I'm not following here; you lost me."

She stood by her window and looked out, "I'm being watched. They are looking for him."

"I knew you were being followed. The other night when you left, a guy left a few minutes after you. I heard him on the phone mentioning your name."

"They are all over. Will you help me, Mac? Please don't be mad."

He wasn't happy, "I wish you would have told me."

"I couldn't, not till you got here. They are even listening on my phone".

"Crap," he slugged the drink down his throat and poured him another glass, and sighed, "Well, I thought this was too good to be true."

"I'm sorry. Won't you help?"

"I'm here," he sighed, "What do you want me to do?"

"We have dinner. I turn out the light and leave. You stay here till I get back."

"That's it?"

"Oh, and if somebody comes to the door," she grinned,

"answer it naked."

"Like we are um…"

"Lovers."

"Where are you going to be, lover?"

She told him the truth; she didn't know. They ate, and Mac had a couple of more glasses of wine. When they finished, Marla took him by the hand, and they stood in front of the window. "Let's give'em, a show. Kiss me, Mac, and pretend I told you something that really turned you on." His big arms wrapped around her, and his hand grabbed her butt and pulled her tight. His chest was huge and muscular. She could feel him up against her. She reached over behind him and closed the curtain. She blew the hair out of her face blushing; she was flustered, "Mac, you're supposed to be acting." She was taking short little breathes. Marla lit a candle and turned out the light. "I'll be right back." She went into the bedroom and turned on the light and shut the door. She closed the drapes and changed into some jeans and grabbed a bomber jacket off the rack and turned the light back off.

"If I'm not here in two hours, go ahead and leave."

Mac sat on the couch with his shoes off, and legs stretched out, "Someday, you'll explain what this is all about, right?"

"Someday."

"You have my number. Call me if you need me…for anything, Marla."

"I can't. I have to leave my phone here. Bye."

Marla crept down the hall, but instead of going down the stairs, she went up the stairs to the roof. She crossed her roof to the next, and then the next, until she was four buildings down; then, she slipped down the stairs to the street. She could see the same black sedan that Travis had pointed out but couldn't tell if anybody was in it. She pulled a baseball cap down over her face and ducked around the corner. About a block away, Travis was waiting. She recognized the cab.

"How are you, T Dog?" Marla jumped in and kissed Travis.

"TD. Friends just call me TD."

"So, where are we going?"

TD rolled his eyes, "Ask the mystery man; I ain't got a clue."

"Take us to Wall Street. I'll tell you where to stop."

"Wall Street, what's at Wall Street?"

He looked at the window as they were pulling away, "A robbery."

"Robbery? I ain't going to no robbery man. Count me out."

"We're the ones that got robbed. By our own freakin' government."

Marla raised her eyebrow and leaned against the door. She studied him. "Travis, you didn't tell me about this."

"There is a lot you don't know."

She shook her head. "You just don't *ever* stop; do you? There never is such a thing as a normal date with you." She blew the hair out of her face and turned away from him and stared out the window. He knew she was fuming. He looked at his watch and checked the time. Travis smiled. He knew not to talk to her for five minutes. That's how long it usually took to get over it

CHAPTER TEN

It looked like they had driven into Ghostville. It was so desolated where the cab pulled over to the curb, but it was perfect. They were just a couple of blocks from Wall Street. Travis told him to stay there, to wait for him, but TD said that was a bad idea. It was going to look suspicious for a cab to be sitting there without fare. He was right, and so TD returned to the club where they met before. He'd wait for Travis to call, and it would give him time to down a couple of beers.

Travis and Marla walked along the street; a noisy cage patrolled the next block. They could hear commotion, some kind of celebration, coming from the district but neither knew what to expect. The closer they got they could tell people were partying. Travis stopped by a trash can and rummaged through it till he pulled out a bottle wrapped in a paper bag; he sprinkled some bourbon on his clothes and wiped some on his face. "Come on, let's see". They rounded the corner to Wall Street. In front of the New York Stock Exchange were a line of limo's and on the steps of the Exchange were guards decked in camouflage uniforms and blue helmets. Marla wanted to leave immediately; she knew better, but Travis had hold of her by the arm. He stumbled a few times, and she grabbed him before he fell.

"Travis, let's get out of here."

He looked passionately in her eyes and took a deep breath, "Baby, we need to see this". He grabbed her by the arm of her leather bomber and pulled her along until she no longer resisted. They walked toward Nassau Street past the old Federal Building with the statue of George Washington. He couldn't believe what he was witnessing, neither could she. There were flags on all the limos; all of different countries and the one that caught their attention first was a red flag with a familiar hammer and sickle. Another limo had a green flag with a crescent moon and leaves forming a globe. Expensive luxurious black sedans were on the street as well adorning UN plates and the all too familiar UN flag on the front. Travis leaned against her as they walked down the street past a big black limo. A large man in a black overcoat got out. He had a beard that was well trimmed and a dark sable hat. They could tell by his accent he was Russian. They were on one side of the block; he was on the other. He was smoking a cigar, and he walked boisterously down the street with two other men, one in a gray suit and the other in a dark brown suit. They were laughing. One man was Middle Eastern; the other might have been Slavic; it was hard to tell, but his voice had that distinctive eastern European accent, and his skin was pale with pock marks left by acne.

The big Russian had his eye on Marla. Travis didn't know what he was saying, but the Russian walked pasted a few limos and patted each on the hood. They could see inside them, and the occupants were mainly older seditious looking men with young provocatively dressed women. There was lots of laughter, drunken laughter. The Russian motioned to a couple of the UN guards standing by, and he nodded across the street to Marla.

Travis and Marla acted like they didn't see him, but of course, they did. She murmured to Travis under her lip, "Travis, I told you that we should have left."

Travis foot slipped off the curb and he staggered back up trying to straighten himself. Two UN guards came over with Uzi's strapped to their shoulders. He held up the bottle.

"Greetings!"

"I'm sorry. He's my fiancé; he's drunk." She smiled brilliantly and tossed her hair over the collar of her jacket. She teased the guard bashfully with her playful lips. "Don't worry we're going."

The darker guard that looked Arabian with coal black hair and white teeth inspected Marla. He checked her out approvingly with his eyes, "This is a restricted area. Do you need a ride? We can give you a ride." He pointed with the barrel of his gun to the limo.

She acted embarrassed. "Not tonight, I've got to get him home. He lost his job today."

The guard looked at Travis as he disgustingly wiped his mouth mimicking a drooling drunk. He turned the bottle up and grinned. The guard rolled his eyes and handed her a card, "In case you change your mind." It read Finance Minister Bank of Moscow. The Russian waved his hand from across the street and smiled.

Travis growled, "Lemme see that card. Lemme take a look."

She put it in her inside pocket and winked, "Maybe tomorrow." Then, she whispered as Travis's head drooped from her shoulder, "Maybe later tonight."

"He wants to know your name."

"Jennifer."

Travis garbled his words. "Her name is not Jennifer it is kitten. Kitty, kitty, kitty…"

"We have to go. Time to get you in bed." They stumbled off down the block and could see Beaver Street and Delmonico's on the corner. There was another assembly of cars and limo's, all celebrating and partying. "I am not going there," she demanded. The surveillance cameras followed them as they turned in the other direction, and he still continued on acting like a drunk for another block. "What was that all about?" she asked under her breath.

"I'll show you." They went up about two more blocks to an old building that was barely lit. There were two military Humvees in front and a couple of guards engaged in conversation. It looked abandoned. "Take a look."

It was the Federal Reserve, the symbol of America financial strength. Travis lit a cigarette and passed it to Marla. He walked by it without saying a word. They walked for another block, and then they stopped and looked back. "What do you see?"

"Not much."

"Would you believe that our gold reserves are kept there?"

"That place, with two guards?"

They walked by another dozen or so buildings with mounted cameras that had been shot out or broken by rock or brick. Manhattan had had its share of dissenters too. "Come on." Travis took her hand and they walked away. He told her that it is believed that the gold reserves are all gone. America has been looted. He thought that is why they are celebrating. All the reserves are wiped out. He also revealed that they were clearing out the UN too. It wasn't a coincidence. They have been for weeks. "Do you know what is happening?"

"You've lost me, Travis. I haven't a clue?"

He stopped. "Something is going to happen, Marla. Take a look, look at it all. It could be days, or weeks, it might be months. I don't know, but they are clearing out. There is no money there; it is all gone so that should tell you something. They are all getting out; there's a reason."

A shiver went up her spine as he said the words. She

could sense it too. It was an odd feeling. The hairs tingled on the back of her neck like when you know someone is coming up from behind you. It was like a premonition, when you walk in a house and you know something is wrong. You get a strange feeling things are out of place, and you know it before you find the evidence. The old Federal Reserve building had the mystique of a deserted warehouse. She knew what he said was true. Things were wrong, terribly wrong. They hustled up the street, and the only workable camera followed them monitoring their every step. There lacked the notorious aurora downtown; the finance district was normally lit up all hours of the night but no more. The buildings were dark except for an occasional floor or office where they could see workers. They could see them hustling about in the night. It was strange, like they were packing. Then, a nearly empty transit bus came up Pearl Street. It was lit up so bright it was almost blinding, and a few older women were riding in back, probably maids that had just got off work. It stopped next to them on the street; the door opened. A middle age woman sat behind the wheel with her hand on the door handle, "Coming?"

They just stood there.

The woman raised her eyebrow, "It's either yes or no. This ain't a game show. You get no life lines." She laughed amused at her own sense of humor.

"Do we have to pay if we are just going a couple of blocks?"

"Get on. What the heck."

They sat in back as the rickety old bus made its way up the street. The old ladies smiled at the two of them sitting together with Travis's arm around her shoulder. The women in back were dallied in whispered conversation, and the driver bobbed her head listening to music on her earphones. They drove up a few more blocks, then, Travis stood up. "Here is good. Thank you."

"You sure? I'll take you as far as you want to go." She glanced down at Travis's hand and then looked him in the eye. "You don't have to worry. I have a son like you. I can always tell." She pointed to a picture of a young man stuck in a grove on her dash above the speedometer. "Haven't seen him in years."

Marla was touched. "Do you know where he is?"

She sighed, "No honey. I just know where he'll be. I'll see him again someday." She wiped a sniffle away and pointed to the door with a smile. "You remind me of him young man. You made my day."

Travis wasn't a young man, but he appreciated the complement. He didn't recognize the smiling face on the old photograph but had known many like him. Good sons that came from good moms. He and Marla stepped off the bus and the woman smiled at them. "Youse two be careful. My bus is 2296. You can ride anytime. I go all the way to midtown."

They thanked her, and the old bus drove off with the older ladies turning in seats grinning at one another. Marla and Travis crossed a few streets and doubled back down Trinity Street and passed by the old American Stock Exchange that had been closed for years. Across the street were Trinity Church and a cemetery. They scaled a wall and iron fence. "Come on."

They walked amidst the old gravestones in the shadows of swaying trees, and she could tell Travis was looking for something. Finally, he came to a monument different from the rest, "This is it." Travis knelt down beside the stone looking at it; his hand rubbed across the surface.

Marla looked around through the shadows and whispered.

"Whose grave is it?"

"Alexander Hamilton's."

She should have known. Travis use to talk about him all the time. Hamilton had been one of his idols, the architect of the American financial system and the man who started the treasury. Travis rubbed his hand across the monument and leaned his head against it like he was saying a prayer.

He asked her to go over to the wall by the street and keep an eye out. Marla complied reluctantly and she could see him digging in the shadows with something. Then, he whispered a hushed shout through the trees. "Come here."

Shadows from the tree branches covered his face, but she could see his eyes. They sparkled in the light, and he held something in his hand that she couldn't see. A cloud passed across the moon, and he leaned over, and his lips touched hers. "I want you to feel this." He put something in her hand. It was very tiny; it was in like a miniature box about the size of a lighter. It was a lighter.

"What is it?"

"Inside there is a flash drive, a code. It is our only hope."

At that moment, they heard a cage turn the corner. It drove down the street slowly along the cemetery with its spot light shining back and forth across the face of the buildings. The light then shined up and down the cemetery wall and then back to the stock exchange across the street. Suddenly, it stopped. They listened. They could hear the radio. Both their hearts were pounding. They heard the driver talking to the dispatcher. If they heard a door open and footsteps, they knew they had to run. They couldn't see what the MF was doing on the other side of the wall; they could only listen. Marla was scared they were being circled. Travis slipped the flash drive back in the lighter and covered up the hole. They crept to the edge of the wall, and then the cage drove on. They followed its lights down the end of the street where it turned the corner and went the other way.

Travis ran back to the grave and dug up the box. "Let's go." They scaled the wall and crisscrossed down through the streets towards Battery Park. Down on the waterfront, they saw a helicopter landing; it was a private craft and huge. Then, they saw another coming out of the sky. This one was blue, but it was too dark to see the emblem on the side. There was another limo with guards in the parking lot, and Travis figured they were flying dignitaries and bankers out. Finally, they passed through Peter Minuit Plaza, and she thought they were going back to the Trinity Plaza subway station; she was wrong. She just wanted to get back home; she had seen enough but knew better not to complain. Next, they went down to the old South Ferry terminal where they use to take ferries to Staten Island and the Statue of Liberty. It was closed; all the ferries were docked to the pier. Across the waters, a couple of SCABS on patrol were walking around the Ferry Terminal and were laughing it up. A fog was beginning to roll in. They watched them walking on a dock a hundred yards or so away. She didn't know exactly what Travis was looking for. He walked over to the edge of the dock and looked down to the water; it was about an eight foot drop.

"What is it?"

"Just checking." They could see the Statue of Liberty across the water through a gray rolling cloud. Then, they walked back up State Street, passed Battery Park toward Trinity Plaza when Travis stopped. She could tell he was listening. Suddenly, they both saw something moving in the fog. She couldn't tell what it was. It was too short to be a man. They quickened their pace, and the figure quickened his. Then, they could hear it. Its mechanical paws clinked along the pavement. They saw its red light emerge from the fog. He squeezed her hand, "Get ready."

It was a Big Dog.

"Run!"

It was about 150 feet behind them charging through the gray vapors sweeping across the street. They took off for the park running through a concourse of paths going in every which direction through a labyrinth of trees and shrubs. They could hear the mechanical hum behind them in full pursuit. Its titanium paws stroked the ground galloping in rhythmic advance like a metal horse charging across a battlefield. It was amazingly agile and gained ground quickly as they darted down the paths. Marla knew there wasn't any way they could escape its rapid advance. It was too fast, but Travis grabbed hold of her hand and rocketed like a hurdler through an obstacle course leaping over benches and brush. She ran with her hair flying and knew it was going to get caught in the limbs and with every turn the big dog seemed to be behind them gaining strategic ground. Then as Marla looked back, as the beast tried to cut off their path, it ran directly into a thicket of holly bushes. They heard it grinding and slashing its way through the shrubbery.

It was stuck.

Marla and Travis ran for their lives. Finally, they came up to a clearing where a round circular castle wall stood and ran around to the front where there was an old wooden gate. Travis cupped his hands forming a step, "GO!" He boosted Marla over the gate, and she dropped to the other side. He stepped back and ran leaping for the top grabbing it and pulled himself over. They hunkered down next to the gate and listened.

A few seconds later the beast came charging by. It was so odd. It sounded as if someone was galloping down the path behind them with a weed eater. Strange and peculiar, it kept going. The beast didn't stop; it kept running apparently following the path. They sat silently just on the other side of the gate as the sound faded away. Next, they heard footsteps running to the front gate. Her heart was beating against her chest. Marla was totally out of breath. Travis sat perfectly still. He didn't move; he just listened. She watched his eyes, listening. They heard a man panting, short of breath just outside the wall. Travis put his hand over Marla's mouth and she could tell by his look that he was instructing her to breathe through her nose. She did. Travis held up his finger to his lips signaling her to be quiet. They could hear him on a phone or a walkie-talkie. "I lost them. I don't know where they went." Panting, "Okay, alright, I'll go back to the ferry. You go to Trinity Station."

He stopped and rattled the gate. Suddenly, it was quiet. The man didn't move. They could see his feet underneath the big gate, and the sound of the Big Dog returning.

"It's right here. Yeah, well they lost the dog too. I bet they're on the waterfront, maybe under a pier."

His voice trailed off, and they heard the sound of the Big Dog following. Every time its head turned it made that hideous robotic sound. It was weird like someone turning off and on an electric shaver, a loud electric shaver at that. They listened to it searching for them in the bushes. If it had heat or motion detectors, they would have been caught. The Big Dog would have known they were just feet away on the other side of the gate. Travis thanked God; it must have been an older model or they would have been caught. Still, it was dangerous.

Neither one moved a muscle; they sat motionless for

minutes until they were for sure he was gone. They looked around inside the castle which was really more of a fortress built with reddish colored stone. It had a round open circular interior, a rotunda, with a roof that protruded over the middle. The moon cast a long shadow through the courtyard. "Let's get on the roof, so we can look out." Travis helped Marla up first, and then he hoisted himself to the roof. When they crawled up to the highest point, they turned around and were blown away. Across the glittering waters and lights was the Statue of Liberty. The moon's reflection bounced off the waters and pierced the opaque fog. The fog was lit up from beneath its vapors. It was a sight that neither of them had seen before. The strange illuminating effect created by the thin layer, like a sheet, that glowed almost as if it were alive, like a mysterious pale ghost with arms that stretched out across the waters surrounding the city. They sat there together hand in hand in utter amazement.

Marla took a deep breath and sighed. She could finally relax. She looked at the tranquil fog that engulfed them as if a gray vapor curtain was being drawn around them shielding the castle. "Do you always live like this, Travis?"

He didn't say anything. She studied his silhouette, his tufted hair. Travis stared out across the bay. She knew he did live like this, on the run. He was always pursued and chased. She didn't know how he coped. Day after day, night after night. He was so resilient and calm. He was strong.

She whispered, "How are we going to get out of here?"

"I haven't got a clue."

He took her by her arm and pulled her to him. They lay back on the roof. Marla curled next to his chest as if his whole body was a comforter. It was a beautiful night, cool with a slight breeze. They could hear the sound of waves lapping against the shore and a fog horn in the distance as a ship made its way out to sea. Both breathed in the refreshing smell of the ocean just beyond the bay. Marla stared up at the sky amazed that beyond the passing clouds were a quadrillion stars. Travis peered over the wall with his head low and listened. A moment later, he returned. No one was there; they were alone. It was a strange feeling for both of them; danger lurked right outside the fortress; they were in fact surrounded by danger, but neither seemed to care. They were alone together, a city of millions and no eye was watching them. Neither had to say it, they knew their freedom may end at any moment, and it may be their last night together. Sometimes, you take just what you can get. All they had at that moment was each other, and they had stumbled onto their fortress of peace.

Travis studied her face in the passing shadows. Blonde trails of hair blew slightly in the wind. Her body was still except for an occasional deep breath. The features of her face glowed in the soft light of the moon, and Marla's green eyes illuminated, appearing almost neon. She looked almost angelic.

Her voice was quiet as the breeze. "What are you thinking?"

His eyes smiled. She knew.

He leaned her back on the rooftop and unbuttoned her blouse. She felt his warm hand embrace her breast. Marla didn't say a word, nor did he. She moaned with delight from the touch of his palms roaming across her breast. His firm hands eased all her fears, as if he was squeezing the poison out of her body. She didn't want him to stop. He didn't.

They both keenly were aware they'd probably get caught. Neither seemed too worried at that moment. They realized it may be their last chance together, and they both were starving. They felt as if they were the only two lions left alive in the world, stranded on a metallic island. Time stood still. It was without motion or depth or space. They eased into a somewhat different dimension apart from the world they had lived in, apart from this world. Momentarily, it did not exist beyond their shores, beyond their fortress.

Travis lips caressed her breasts. His mouth filled with her flesh. He paused and looked up at her in the glow of moon light. He whispered softly mumbling, "Let… the… world… burn…."

She played with his hair unsure exactly what he said, "What?"

His eyes danced with hers as he unbuttoned her blouse all the way down. "…as I burn for you." The warmth of his lips began to radiate her whole body. Her hands stroked the top of his head with her fingers playing with his tussled hair. He went lower.

The fog then rolled in off the bay and covered their naked bodies as a sheet is drawn across a bed. And…he devoured her.

CHAPTER ELEVEN

At both our worst and best moments
in life, time stands still. Doesn't it? Some events are
capsulized in a film department somewhere in our mind to play
over and over again as often as our thoughts will allow.
Sometimes they are good thoughts, and sometimes they are
bad; sometimes our worst, but ultimately we are the director;
we get to choose what memories we play.

Neither of them knew how long they were there. They
lay huddled together after making love for the longest time
without saying a word. The view was beautiful from the roof.
It was their private island of serenity in the city. She leaned
forward and buttoned back up her bra. The fog began to lift.
"Travis?"

"Yes."

"What are we going to do now? How did we ever get
here?"

He buttoned up his shirt. "You mean this castle?"

"No, I mean this world. How did it ever get so screwed
up? How did we ever get so far off course?" She lay back
with her arms behind her head looking at the Statue of Liberty
across the water. "It wasn't that long ago; remember, in our
parent's time? They had cars and things. They had
refrigerators, television and planes? But it wasn't like this."

"I don't have an answer for you doll. We went from
freedom to slavery in a few short years. Technology first gave

us one, and then it gave us the other."

Marla put her arms through her jacket and zipped it up. "This world sucks, Travis. We once had businesses and factories. Our folks listened to music; they played radios and albums. There had money and good jobs. People could go and come, do as they pleased. We had liberty. We could eat what we want, there. And, there weren't rations. I hate rations. It wasn't insane like it is now. Why can't we go back?"

He lay beside her and stroked her hair. He didn't say anything. He laid his head on her chest and listened to her breath. She lowered her voice another octave. "Can we go back?"

Travis listened to the sound of her heart beat. He still didn't say a word; he just looked in her eyes. It was a peculiar puzzling stare. "You're awfully quiet hon."

"Just thinking."

"About what?"

He sat up and checked the device on his leg. Travis looked relieved and lay back down. "There is a place I'd like to take you." His voice filtered through her ear like she was being induced with an audio drug. The rich texture of his deep voice always aroused her. "There is a sea with this long white shoreline and rock cliffs that go on for miles. It has a bay. It is very private; you can be all alone. I've been there. I'd like to take you there, that is, if I can get you out of here. It is where we'll live."

Marla put her hand on his thigh and squeezed. "You don't have to ask twice, Travis." She looked out across the waters, "Do you remember a song I used to sing?" She snuggled against him and started singing in his ear a tune from long ago. *"That I still want you, and I want you to want me. My love is wider, wider than Victoria Lake. My love is taller, taller than the*

Empire State..."

"Sade?"

She was surprised, "You remembered?"

"I had lots of time to remember, remember?"

They watched a barge pushing its way out of the harbor. They could hear the tugboat with its engines throttling the water. They listened to the seagulls flying in the night. His voice was so low she could hardly hear him "You don't know how much I missed you."

"Yes I do."

She could tell something was bothering him, "What's the matter, Travis? Something else on your mind?"

He pulled out the lighter with the flash drive and just held it in his hand. "What if all this could be reversed, would it be worth it? What if we could stop it? The whole world, bring it to a halt?"

"What do you mean *reversed*?" The scar on her chin began to curl.

"If we could set the clock back...say...just forty years. Like what you were saying. Turn the clock back to your parent's time. It is not so much reverse as it is resetting the course. Do you think the world could handle it?"

"Is that possible?"

He nodded. "Yeah, it can be done."

Travis played with the chip in his hand. He told her it was more than possible, but there were issues. Travis began to reveal what he had; it was, in essence, one component of a worm designed to terminate hard drives and software. There were two other components that went with it. They were already out of the country. In fact, the one he held was more than a worm. It was designed by the military, for the military to take out all computer systems. It was a *neutron chip* and said it could destroy Trisix. He showed it to her and then laid it in her hand.

Marla's eyebrow arched in interest, "So *this* is what they are after?"

"Yes." Travis gave her a slow and methodical explanation. The problem was that though the chip was designed originally to attack computers, specifically enemy satellites; the neutron worm doesn't stop. It is indestructible. It would eventually eat through every firewall into every computer system in the world. It would down every satellite, terminate them, including even our own. It operates differently than other worms or viruses. At first, they developed a worm that duplicated memory, a data base. It multiplied information rapidly. It could not be stopped. A computer would implode from its own data overload and crash. He said it was a brilliant system, but there were too many backup systems, so they decided to deploy another type of neutron. This neutron would terminate everything, permanently.

"How?"

"Language." As Travis explained it, computers communicate in digital language. Computers receive information and then interpret the meaning and then respond to the directions. The neutron chip they devised changes the language from English to gibberish, from Chinese to gibberish, Arabic to gibberish. They can't communicate any more. It is all babel. The systems are still operating but cannot function. They are unable to communicate with each other and unable to understand the commands they read. Data that is sent to correct and destroy the worm cannot be read. Dates and times would be destroyed. All numbers become letters, all letters become symbols. Nothing would make sense anymore.

It would be worldwide, mass technological failure. Banking, utilities, cell phones would all become inoperable. Computer operated mass transit systems would come to a halt; computer engineered cars would be at a standstill. But it would also knock out all nuclear weapons and military missiles deployment systems. Everything operated by computers would be terminated. It would be a matter of days if not hours.

She was breathless. "This could do all that. Are you serious?"

"When this chip is integrated with the other components, destruction occurs, but alone it is just meaningless information. We looked at every aspect, and it all seemed so improbable. This is really the only way, complete termination of all systems. Otherwise one country holds too great an advantage over another; the political and economic systems are too complex, too interconnected. It is all or nothing. No chip would function any more. Yours wouldn't." He took her hand, "Your chip would malfunction. Your GPS would be gone. Your rations gone. Your banking terminated. Your job deleted. Think about it. Your office would just be a building with useless computers. But you would be free. The world could start over."

It was frightening and yet beautiful. The words "the world could start over" seemed refreshing, inspiring. Marla suddenly had hope, but at the same time, it seemed extreme. She thought about it. It was scary. "Travis, it seems so desperate though."

Travis took her by her hand and rubbed it where the chip was located. "Desperate times require desperate measures. Consider the alternative. That chip in your hand has stolen all your liberty. It has taken your freedom and future. It has stolen your dreams, and the new chip, the Trisix chip, will make you a slave. It is your choice; do you want freedom or do you want slavery?"

"That is all I want. To start over, to have this *thing* out of me."

"Then you will go with me?"

"Are you nuts? You know I will, Travis."

He was skeptical, "Are you sure, because there is always a price? Freedom is costly. It is never free. Everyone must weigh the cost for themselves. The price of slavery is the high cost of your soul."

Marla looked around behind her at the city, "I wouldn't care if we had money. It wouldn't matter to me if we didn't have electricity as long as we had food and I was free, with you. Give me that beach, or even a farm, a ranch, anyplace but this. I just don't want to be chased by robot dogs and watched by cameras and all the police and…"

He looked into her eyes. He had to be sure. "Shhhh, whisper." She was excited. He took the box from her. "Do you understand fully what this will mean? How it will change the world?"

Marla smiled, "Our parents got along without all this. Why not us? It is not an unfathomable thought."

Travis didn't know if he even understood the meaning of it. He had grown up in the computer age. He could not ever remember living without them. His doubts were overshadowed by his knowledge of government plans. He knew there was no alternative. Marla leaned over and kissed him. "Society functioned very well not that long ago. It could happen again, possibly. She wanted to hold the drive again. He let her. "I would miss my microwave."

"You might not have too; you'd be surprised at what can

run on circuit boards and transistors."

"Really?"

Travis looked at his watch. "First, I've got to get us out of here." He texted TD and told him to meet them at Pearl and State Street in thirty minutes. TD texted back and told him he would be there. Travis texted him again and warned him about the Big Dog. *"You can't be late."*

Marla was excited, she wanted to know more. She was enthralled by the possibilities. Suddenly, there was hope for a better life, a simpler world. Travis checked his monitor again, and it was running low; the batteries were almost out. He turned it off and crept up to the edge and peered over the wall. He could see through the trees far off down by the docks flashlights searching. He inched his back down where she laid and rechecked his watch. They had about twenty five minutes to meet TD; they couldn't get there early that was for sure.

"Travis," she whispered. "How did you, your group, get this chip?"

He seemed at first reluctant to tell her, but then she prodded. His answer was somewhat obscured. He said that *the people* that developed Trisix turned against it. They didn't realize fully how it was going to be used until it was too late. Then, several scientists began designing another system that would destroy it."

"So you were part of it?"

"You might say that."

"So when you joined the Body, the Frees, you helped them obtain this neutron chip? What, like after you escaped?"

He shrugged and nodded, then looked at his watch again. He didn't answer.

Marla twitched her lips in curiosity. "Will I be free?"

"If we can get your butt outta here."

"If you get me outta here, Trav, you can have all of it you want." She winked.

He chuckled and smiled; then, he reached his hand behind her and squeezed.

Her lips curled into a smile, "Humm, Travis. You don't know what you do to me."

"Ditto." He looked at his watch. He looked nervous.

"I've got a question?"

"Go."

"Did the people; was Trisix, also involved in building the neutron chip?"

"Of course. I can't tell you more because I don't know. Many people in government realized after the development that they had created a modern day Frankenstein. They were scared of it when they realized exactly what its purpose was. I guess it was when they discovered the design was for mass inoculation; that's what got people's attention. It wasn't for criminals; it was intended for everyone. Every mother, every father, every child. So the people involved realized they had to destroy the monster. Do you understand?"

"Were the makers of Trisix ever given the chip?"

"You ask a lot of questions. How would I know? If that happened, I guess the monster would have destroyed its maker."

"How frightening."

"It is sort of like the atomic bomb. Some of the greatest opponents were the ones that helped build it. They didn't know how powerful it was until it was completed. Then, it is too late. They gave a monster life, the bomb and then it ruled them, ruled us."

She noticed he was chewing on his nails, "So you were never forced to take the chip?"

"No." He looked at his watch. "Let's go."

Travis helped her down from the roof and then turned on his monitor to get a read. The Big Dog was in the vicinity but fortunately for them was about 300 feet away. They slipped back over the gate quietly and walked hand in hand through the shadows of the trees along a Promenade and then ducked into some woods. Travis checked his monitor again. The Big Dog was still far away. As quietly as they could, they walked as timid as deer along the path back to near the street where they stopped and knelt in the shadows of some bushes. They could see no one. He looked at his watch; it had been thirty-five minutes.

Travis was pissed. "Where is he?"

"It will be alright, Travis," Marla reassured him.

"I told him…" They saw car lights turning on to their street; they listened to it cruise slowly down to the corner. They couldn't tell who it was because of the glare until it got closer, and then he saw the Taxi sign on top. It was about the prettiest sight either had ever seen. TD pulled his cab over at Pearl and State. They could hear his music playing. Travis watched to see if other cars had followed. He grabbed her hand. "Walk swiftly, don't run. Let's go."

Just as they were reaching the cab, they heard footsteps running down the path way and a voice yelled out. "Halt!"

They jumped in, and TD sped around the corner as Travis clung to the handle trying to shut the door nearly falling out. The tires were smoking like they were on fire, and the stench of burning rubber trailed down the street. TD looked in his rear view mirror to see if anyone was chasing the cab. "Why don't you get a ride like normal people?"

"Why don't you show up on time?"

"Time, you want to know about time! I've been waiting

four hours for you people! I should be home in bed."

"Bed! What would you know about bed! You just woke up the whole neighborhood with that radio blasting! Why didn't you just have sirens blaring?"

Marla yelled out to both of them. "STOP IT!" She was panting and clearly shaken; she lay back in the seat and blew the hair out of her face. "Just drive."

Travis looked behind them to see if there were any cars coming. All he saw was an old bus crossing an intersection. The streets were barren. TD turned again down another street, and when they did, they saw a Raven flying by. TD slowed down his speed, but it was too late. The Raven circled in the air, and it began to follow behind the cab about thirty feet high. "Great!" He pounded his dash. "I knew it! We're busted."

Marla and Travis looked behind them from the back seat at the drone as it followed the cab humming suspended above the street. Travis knew it was sending a feed to a nearby cage; they would soon be swarmed. In a matter of minutes they'd be surrounded. "Just keep driving." He tapped TD on the shoulder. "Give me your gun."

"Shug?"

"Your 44."

He reached under the seat and handed it to Travis. Travis rolled down his window and leaned out. He aimed and steadied his hand. "Cover your ears."

Travis steadied his aim and pulled the trigger. The blast knocked him back. The gun's ferocious sound boomed like a cannon. The thing literally exploded in the air, and then they heard the metal debris tinkling as its pieces hit the pavement. "Go man!"

TD punched the accelerator and the cab shot like a yellow

rocket down the street. They roared around another corner with tires squealing onto the next block. It was a momentarily sigh of relief. As they were flying down the avenue doing at least eighty past abandoned cars and buildings, they all looked up ahead. All three saw it. About two blocks down, a Cage pulled into the intersection. "Ooooh no!"

TD slammed on the breaks and skidded to a halt. He made a U turn in the middle of the street. "This ain't my night." Travis and Marla were both looking back and forth as TD turned again on the next block. They quickly realized that was a mistake; it was a dead end. There was a barrier across the road, and the street was blocked off for repairs. There wasn't any way around the barrier. He turned the wheel sharply and came to another stop, then slammed the car in reverse when suddenly a red light flashed into the car.

"Look!"

They turned around and saw a Big Dog charging over the barrier towards the cab with a laser firing multiple shots. "Roll your window up!" His tires were squealing as he backed out. The Big Dog was charging at them full blast with its laser bouncing off the hood and window ricocheting like bullets. TD didn't think its laser was strong enough to penetrate the car's metal but if the laser hit his tires they would explode.

Just then Marla turned around and screamed. "Oh, my God!"

It was another one...charging from another direction. Red beams were ricocheting all around them off the buildings and glass. It looked like they were caught in night fire with lasers bouncing everywhere.

Marla screamed again when she saw a third. "My God! Just go!" TD then shifted into drive and punched the gas. His cab took off for the charging robot. He rolled down his window and stuck out his 44. Like John Wayne, he gripped the wheel with one hand and squint his eye steadying his bead as he raced back up the narrow street. Marla ducked her head behind his seat.

"Move over Rover!" TD pulled the trigger, and the explosion rocked the cab.

BOOM!

Its metal head shattered into a thousand pieces, and TD jerked the wheel sharply and swerved around it. Travis and Marla caught just a flashing glimpse of it as they sped by. Travis was utterly amazed. The Big Dog was still running on all fours like a blind headless dog down the street.

"Did you see that?"

"Ain't that something!"

Marla looked back and could see it still running. Sparking wires protruded out its neck as its headless torso and legs galloped along. The other dogs ran right past it and were still chasing the cab.   TD rounded the corner, and they disappeared. That's when they saw the Cage coming east from the next block, but TD turned back south again, then west, then north. They shot down a deserted street, and suddenly, he came up to a garage and turned in quickly just as the door was being raised. His cab came to a screeching halt. As the door was closing behind them, he turned around and shook his head. Nobody said anything. They all sat there stunned. He picked up a bottle of water and took a sip. Sweat was flowing down his face. They were all breathing heavily. TD then turned around to his customers in back. "Now this ride is gonna cost you. You wanna tell me what is going on?"

They looked around; it was an old dusty looking garage. Travis and Marla looked at each other; both were trying to figure out what to say when they heard the sound of the Cage coming down the street like a noisy tank. They all listened. Their hearts raced. Finally, it passed. They had escaped. For the first time, Marla felt like she could breathe.

TD got out and slammed the door. They could hear him cussing. He peeled off a decal and then walked around to the other side and peeled off another one, changing the numbers on his cab still cussing under his breath. Then, he walked to the front of the cab and knelt down; his plate was magnetic. He simply popped it off and flipped it around. It had another plate with a different number on the other side.

He walked up to their door and looked inside. "Sorry about that."

"Oh, don't worry. I am not offended. You oughta hear Travis on a bad day." She paused, "Well, every day."

"I figured youse two might be trouble, but I had no idea you'd be *that* much trouble." Then TD opened up the back door on Marla's side. "We gonna be here for a while. You want some coffee?"

Marla stepped out and took a deep breath. It was a sigh of relief, "You got something stronger?"

"Oh yeah, and I've got the good stuff." He looked at Travis, "You want something?"

"Just need a wall socket. I've got to charge some things." Travis looked around inspecting the garage. It was workshop actually, a mechanic's shop. Had tables all around with vices and bolts and rags lying about. A typical grease pit. He figured that TD must have been a tinkler, must have done his own work on his cab.

Travis knew he had to get the drive to a safe location. He couldn't be walking around New York with it in his pocket. He had plans but that all changed when the Big Dog spotted him at the park.

"I'll be with you in a second."

"We'll be upstairs." TD and Marla walked up some rickety wooden steps in the back of the garage to what looked like a little office. He watched them in the window and could see TD smiling; he had a bottle of something in his hand. Travis leaned against the cab lit a smoke. His hands were shaking; they never shook. He leaned against the trunk of the cab thinking. He had so much to do and so little time. First of all, he had to secure the drive, and Marla had to get back to work the next morning. He didn't have a clue on how to do that. But that wasn't his only dilemma; there was another assignment, someone he had to eliminate. He wasn't sure how he was going to do it. He wasn't even sure where his assignment was. Or how they were going to get out of the garage? He looked at his watch; he was running out of time. At that very moment, it looked pretty impossible.

He pulled out his cell phone and dialed.

"Yeah."

"How's it lookin'?"

"Quiet. How about you?"

"You wouldn't believe it man. Nearly got caught."

"Does she know yet?"

"Yeah, but not about you."

"You going to tell her?"

"Not yet."

"Did you get it?"

"Yeah, I'm still hot, and I don't know when we are going to get back."

"Should I still stay here?"

"It may be best if you don't leave until early morning."

"Whatever you say."

"Any word, Mac, on the location?"

"Yeah, they spotted your man. You have to do this. It has to be done before Exodus. But there is something else you need to know. Marla's been scheduled. Could be tomorrow, we don't know."

"Ahhhh, man. NO!" Travis smashed the hood of the car, "I gotta go."

CHAPTER TWELVE

Marla possessed a unique hypnotizing quality, one that amazed him to the point of envy. She could get people to do things that he never could imagine, and it wasn't just because she was so knock down good looking; people genuinely liked her. By the time he walked up the steps, TD would have done anything for her. Most men would. She smiled and lifted her glass, "So you got any other bright ideas?"

She started giggling almost like a snort. TD laughed too. With a big wide smile he reached for a glass and set it down on a desk and started to pour a drink, "Come on man, have one. We showed them…"

"No thanks."

"He doesn't drink."

Surprised, "Really? Well, I do. Got to. The only way I can make it in *this* city." He chugged the drink down and gulped, then grimaced as the scotch took a bite out of his throat. TD sniffed and wiggled his nose. "Man that's good!"

Travis noticed a magnetic key box on his desk. He picked it up and opened it. Taking out a key, he tossed it on top of some papers lying on the desk. "I need this." He put it in his pocket, and his eyes inspected the room. There was an old instamatic plastic Kodak camera lying on a shelf. He walked by TD, "Excuse me". Travis picked it up. "And I need this."

TD tilted his head sideways at the offense, "Well you know, normally people would ask…"

Marla giggled and handed him her glass, "Put in on my

tab." She snickered, "I'll have another, *thank you*."

"You got some shells?" Travis opened up a drawer and looked. He slammed the drawer and opened another.

TD laid down his glass, "Hey, man. You ain't going through all my stuff here."

Travis stood up. This was the side of Travis she didn't like. He could have the coldest penetrating stare. "Okay, then show me your shells."

TD knew there wasn't any use trying to extract a *please* out of the man. He went to a file cabinet and opened it. "Just don't take all of em'...I may have to shoot somebody."

Travis ignored the insinuation behind his remark and pulled out several boxes and dumped them on the desk. Marla sat quiet while he rummaged through the different calibers. Without saying another word, he took about a handful and then went down the stairs. Neither had a clue what he was up to, and at that moment, Marla knew not to ask.

She shrugged. "You know, he really is a nice guy, TD. You just have to get to know him."

"Let me guess; he ain't never won a Nobel Peace Prize has he?"

She rolled her eyes looking at the ceiling, "Nope, don't think so. Not Travis's style." She snorted.

"You guys are in a heap of trouble aren't you?"

She took a deep breath, "Let's just say this is not...our..." She took a drink, "typical date." Marla paused and put her index finger to her lip, "Come to think, yes, this *is* our typical date." She handed him her glass. "How about one more, TD."

They could see Travis downstairs on the phone talking to someone. He was pacing back and forth with a smoke in his hand. TD turned on a monitor. He had a camera mounted outside his garage. They sat there in his office looking at the black and white screen with grainy pictures flashing from different angles. Then, they heard Travis sawing. "What the….?" They looked downstairs, and he had clamped a pipe in a vise and was sawing it into. "Do you have any idea what that man is doing?"

"Not a clue. I've learned not to ask. Though he is pretty handy around the house."

They saw him measuring the pipe; he had several of them that he connected together, and then they heard him drilling holes. "What is that guy's problem?"

Marla smiled and took a drink. "I learned a long time ago, not to ask. Promise you though, he can put anything together. He's a genius." She tipped her glass to his, "and a geek." She burped, "Don't tell him I said that though."

After about thirty minutes, he came back up the steps sweating. "Duct tape?"

TD didn't bother to extract a please. He fumbled around and found some in a drawer, then tossed it to him. Travis rolled up his pant leg and took three pipes about a foot long a piece and a half inch in diameter and then taped them to the his leg. He had some other assembled instruments that had holes, and he wrapped duct tape around it and then taped it to his other leg. Travis then motioned to his watch, "We have to go."

"Well, I've got news for you *Mr. Bond*," emphasizing a degree of sarcasm. "You ain't going nowhere in my cab because the Force is going to be crawling the streets looking for you cats."

"Can we paint it?"

"You serious, man, you want to paint my cab?"

Marla nodded, "Oh, he's serious alright."

"You ain't touching my cab."

"Can you call another one, a friend?"

"Well, yeah I can do that."

"You call another cab, somebody that doesn't have a cab like yours. Then, you go with her back to her place and make sure she gets there safe."

"And what are you going to do?"

"I've got business to take care of."

TD didn't have to ask twice. He called a *brother*. Marla and Travis went downstairs. He told her what to do. He was worried about her; she could tell he looked troubled. He was worried about how she would hold up at the office. It was very important that she stayed alert all day. He told her to take something if she had to keep up. Marla looked at him; she knew something was wrong, "What is it, tell me?"

He hesitated, and then he knew he better tell her; she needed to know. "I got word that you may be scheduled."

"Scheduled?"

"For Trisix."

She was stunned. For a second, she lost her balance. "Me?"

He nodded. "It could be today, might be tomorrow or even the next. They are on to you."

Suddenly, she felt nauseous. Her ankles twisted in like she was giving way, going to faint. Travis held her by her arms. "Please listen to me; we are down to just days. In 72 hours, we are out of here. If you suspect they are going to schedule you, then text me, U2. I will know…and we'll try to do something."

"We?"

"Yes, we."

"Like what?"

"There will be a team in the vicinity."

"Where are you going to be?"

"I can't tell you, but this is what you need to watch out for." He said that if she was scheduled, they would more than likely ask her to attend some kind of meeting. It only took several minutes. It could happen behind closed doors. They will inform her that her chip has to be updated. It will only take a few moments. They strap a person down to a chair, secure them somehow; then she is given a shot to deaden the skin, usually Novocain. He pointed to his widow's peak at the top of his forehead and told her that many people are having it put there; however, if a person's eyebrow is thick like hers were, they were inserting them there. In a matter of seconds, they inject Trisix, and then they inject the transmitter near the temple which fuses to the auriculotemporal nerve. It is inserted right at the hair line, and never noticeable. Within minutes, it is activated. The person knows they have it but can't do anything about it. They can't even register a thought to take it out without suffering severe shock.

She looked sick, "I'm not going to work. That's it!" She pushed him away. "I'm not going in."

"You have to. You have to carry on like you suspect nothing. If you call in sick or don't show up for any reason babe, they are coming after you. Just where in the heck do you think you are going, Marla Jean, with that chip in your hand? You have to go in, see? You have to. Just avoid any meetings where they can get you alone. Do you understand?"

She leaned against him. Travis put his arms around her. He wished right then that he hadn't of got her involved. It was irresponsible; he knew that. His superiors had warned him to stay away. But on the other hand, if he hadn't, she was destined to get Trisix anyway. Everyone would. That was the truth he reminded himself. It wasn't that he was putting her in danger; he was getting her out. He thought she was about to cry, but she didn't. Maybe it was the scotch that had dulled her senses or just tired. Travis told her that he would do his best to see her that night, but if she didn't hear from him, not to worry. He would contact her somehow.

She didn't want him to leave her, "Will you go with me back to my apartment?"

"I can't. I have a job to do."

She knew it was useless to ask. They went back up to TD's office. He was looking at his monitor. Travis told him he needed a set of work clothes.

"Anything else?"

"A suit, if you have a suit, I'll need that too."

He wasn't happy. "I'm putting that on the tab too. Come with me, Mr. Bond. But you ain't getting my best suit. I've got an *old* one you can use. It is perfect for you; it is *out* of style."

TD led him through a door into his apartment that was attached to the garage. It was tiny but well kept. Marla and Travis couldn't help but notice several aged photographs of TD and a woman. They both figured it had to be his ex-wife but neither asked. He pulled out a teal suit with wide labels and handed it to Travis. "Suits you just fine. Got that Gumby look."

"Screw Gumby." Travis hung it back up and pulled out a dark pen stripe. "This, I like, thanks."

"That's my good suit. You ain't..." He looked at Marla and started to say something, then just shook his head. "It is going on the tab."

"I appreciate it." Travis dropped his pants right there and changed into the suit. He pulled a shirt off the hanger and grabbed a silk tie. TD started to say something but didn't. He just walked away mumbling something about white folks. Travis checked himself out in the mirror and then gave Marla a kiss. She held him tightly not wanting to let go.

"You remember what you texted me this morning?"

He knew what she was referring to. "Yes."

"You can't say it, can you? In person?"

"I live it. Isn't that better than just saying it?"

She knew he wasn't going to say the words, but he did always show it in his actions. Marla wasn't going to push him. It wasn't his style, or hers. "I love you, Travis."

"It is why I came back." He took her in his arms, and they kissed. "Just remember what you owe me, because I am going to want a lot of it". Then, he left.

A few minutes later, a black cab pulled up out front. His buddy looked very surprised when TD and Marla came out and got in the back of the cab. TD told him where they were going and gave him some story about his cab breaking down and yada, yada. About two blocks away, they passed Travis in a sharp suit walking down a dark street. He was carrying a brief case.

TD turned around, "Briefcase? That ain't my…"

Marla patted him on the leg, "We'll just put it on the…"

"Tab! I know!"

She looked back out the window as the cab slowed down for a light. He had already disappeared.

CHAPTER THIRTEEN

She was worn through like a cheap rug when she finally arrived home. It was somewhere around 2:45. Mac was dead asleep on the couch. She didn't bother to wake him; she was exhausted. The next morning she woke him up and thanked him for being there, though she didn't even attempt to explain what all she did. How could she possibly explain it anyway?

After the awkward departure, she felt nauseous. A combination of nerves and Scotch on an empty stomach did the trick. She threw up and afterwards felt better. Marla showered and dried her hair, and picked out a dress. She did everything she could to give the appearance; it was just a normal day. Then, she stood at her bathroom vanity trying to put the toothpaste on her brush, but she shook so much she could hardly get it on. She was dreading work, especially after what Travis said about her being scheduled. After she managed to finish brushing and gargling, she stood in front of the mirror and practiced smiling. No matter what she did, she couldn't get the nervous twitch in her lips to go away. She looked around her apartment and wondered if this was the last time she would see it. She didn't know if she would return like she was or would she return someone else. She fed her fish and picked up the empty wine bottle. Mac had left a note.

"Call me, if you need me. Thanks for dinner, Mac."

Marla smiled and tossed the bottle in the receptacle. When she left, Mrs. Goldstein was standing by the elevator, "Why don't you ride down with us?"

She didn't want to; she didn't want to indulge in idle

conversation that morning, but didn't necessarily want to take the steps either. As she was about to conjure an excuse to walk, the elevator dinged and the door opened. "Come on, ride with us."

"Hello Marla, where have you been?"

She tried to act normal. "Oh, I've been busy Mrs. Langley."

"Morning, Marla."

"Good morning Mrs. Portis."

They crowded into the elevator until Marla was pinned against the wall, "You look nice this morning. We've heard you're seeing a nice fellow. Baltimore is it?"

Mrs. Goldstein coughed, "What was his name again? Joe? Mac? I've forgotten?"

Marla was feeling the condescending vibes. "Joe. Mac is just a friend."

"Oh, I am sure he is, and a good friend he is to bring wine for dinner."

They came to the bottom floor, and they all got out. As Marla was heading out the door, Mrs. Goldstein called out, "Oh Marla, I am having trouble with my chip again. I went to get some milk yesterday and couldn't. I've got to get this darn thing fixed. If you would, could you get me some powdered milk on the way home this evening? I will repay you as soon as my chip is repaired."

Marla spun around. "Repaired?"

"I am scheduled to have it replaced."

Mrs. Portis fiddled in her purse, "Oh dear, I think I've locked myself out of my apartment again. Mine has been messing up too. I'm getting mine fixed next week. *I* have an *appointment*," she added rather smugly.

Marla looked at her watch. She had to get to her office.

"I'll get the powdered milk; just don't go in to have your chip fixed yet. Please, just don't. We'll work out something."

"But, but it is not working."

"I have to go."

Marla hustled down the block to the station and barely caught the train in time. She had already received a text from Travis. She knew the code well enough to decipher it in her head. It said he had a *pick up* the next morning at 9, in the park. A few minutes later, she received another code. The message said, '*Meet you tomorrow at noon. Be packed.*'

Tomorrow, at noon? She didn't like the sound of that. She worried all the way into work that she wouldn't be able to see him again until the next day. She felt lonely and scared, and the old feeling of abandonment began to creep back. Her doubt began to choke her like hands wrapped around her throat, and it took all her might to shake it off. She couldn't doubt him now; she had no choice but to believe him. She knew deep down inside that everything he told her was true. If he said he was coming back, he would; she had to believe it.

Marla was one of the first in her office that morning. She did as she had done the day before and went straight to her cubicle and began work, but it was difficult. She couldn't get her mind off the old ladies in her building. Maybe, she thought, she was just overreacting. There was nothing to be concerned about. Maybe it was just an ordinary malfunction? It happened a lot, and the elderly seemed to be the most susceptible. Hackers often stole their rations. Maybe that is what happened? Their thin skin caused problems too. The oils, lotions, and rubbing alcohol they used were known to have caused *disruptions in service*. These were miniscule problems compared to the rash of skin cancers that were attributed to the chip. She was one of the fortunate ones; she had never had a breakout of sores which were common.

Marla knew she had to quit thinking about the ladies and get her work done. People came by that morning to chat. It helped to settle her nerves, and as the day progressed, she felt better. She felt more comfortable, somewhat protected when others were around. What she feared was being alone. She never in her life craved a mundane boring uneventful day, but that is exactly what she wanted. She had this dreadful fear; she would look up, and there would be the secret police. They would grab her by the arms and zap her in front of her co-workers. The thought terrified her, that they would shock her senseless in front of everyone, and she'd jerk and convulse and in the process defecate on herself. Her co-workers, friends would then turn and walk away. Go back to their cubby holes as if nothing happened. It tortured her, thinking about it. So when people came by that morning to talk, Marla kindly obliged them. To her surprise, she saw very little of Charlotte who went downstairs for a meeting and hadn't seen her since.

Marla watched the clock all morning, and when it hit twelve, she was stepping on the elevator. She was thankful she made it half way through the day and contemplated not even going back. The elevator took her to the first floor, and she wanted desperately to run when she got off, to get away, to put as many miles as she could between her and her office. She decided to have lunch and think about it. Though she hated it, she decided to carry on through the rest of day as if everything were normal. She stopped at a Deli shop and ordered a sandwich. The lettuce was wilted. They did have tomatoes slices that surprised her because it was about the only place in town that did, but it cost more than the sandwich. Marla passed on the tomatoes and then tossed the lettuce away. She felt a twinge about throwing it in the trash. The birds looked so hungry, but only certain items were allowed to be given them, and lettuce wasn't one of them. She managed to eat her rather tasteless sandwich as the birds hopped around her bench looking at her.

When she finished, she started to toss them the remains of her bread, but she couldn't remember if Animal Management had ruled if white bread was permissible for the birds to eat. She thought that wheat and rye were, but she couldn't remember if white bread was. She looked around, and no one seemed to be noticing her so she coyly dropped the bread in some bushes behind her and walked to another bench. Marla then listened to the people talking as they strolled by. Their conversations were all so typical of the day: Macy's was having a big sale, the baseball players were going on strike, no fans; and she heard them say it was supposed to rain that weekend. But, the talk of the town was Chocolate. There had been a two year government moratorium on it while the Department of Health conducted studies on its effects contributing to obesity. It appeared that after years of controversy, chocolate was about to be taken off the restricted list, and they would begin rationing it that summer.

Just then, two ladies that Marla knew from the ninth floor came by. They were ecstatic about the news. "Did you hear? We're getting chocolate!" They licked their lips, "We are planning a big party when it comes out."

"Yes, I heard." Marla rolled her eyes. "I heard already." She wanted to get up and leave, but it would have been too obvious that was being rude. She asked them out of curiosity, "How are you going to have a big party with four bars a month?" She scooted over as the ladies sat down.

They giggled and whispered. "We have connections, shhhhh."

"Your secret is safe with me, but I don't know how you are going to afford it. I know I won't be able to, not on my salary."

The looked like two big round tires deflating. "What do you mean?"

"They are going to tax it under the 'fat' tax, just like they do sodas, chips, and ice cream. It will be better if it stays in the black market. It is cheaper, and at least, you can get all you want. I've traded coffee for it and soda."

The women hadn't thought about the tax. All they had thought about was the chocolate, and so with dampened spirits they changed the subject and inquired about her love life which seemed to always be an interest to the women in the building. For some odd reason, they were always curious. She told them it had been dormant until recently, but she had started dating a guy. He had potential she said.

"And?"

"I'll let you know. We went out last night. So far so good."

"Did youse guys watch the show?"

"Nope. Not exactly. What show?"

"Last night, the finale. The contest. You *didn't* watch?" They were shocked.

The other one interrupted. "It was so suspenseful!"

They talked to each other with Marla in the middle. "I think last night was the best season so far, don't you?"

"Of course. I told you at the beginning of the year who would win."

"No, you picked the other one."

"No, I picked him."

"No, you didn't. I picked him."

"I think I know who I picked!"

Marla looked at the time. "Excuse me. I have to get back to work." They were still arguing as she walked away. She walked by a fountain and sat down. The sun felt great on her legs, and a slight breeze fluttered her dress. She didn't want to go back early. She wanted to stay away as long as she could and hoped that maybe, just maybe, she might turn around and Travis would be there. She wanted so badly to see him. Marla wondered, was it her, or was the world wallowing in insignificance? Then she realized; it was her. She had not been much different than those women in the park. Something changed the world was the same; it was digressing into irrelevance. She had changed; she was enlightened.

A very handsome younger man walked by and stopped. He was about twenty- five, if that, and had thick wavy chestnut hair. He asked her if she had the time. He was tall, about 6' 5" and had strong almost Grecian looking features. She couldn't help but notice his eyes; they were beautiful for a man, a dazzling turquoise with dark eyebrows and an olive complexion. She could also see his watch tucked back under his sleeve and his wedding band. She knew the spiel before he even began. He started some conversation wanting to know where such and such building was, and then he asked where she worked. It took her all of about ten seconds to size him up. She knew his lines even before he said them. She stood up and walked away resisting the urge to reach up and pinch him on the forehead and go Buzzzzzzzzzz. She grinned, thinking about it. Trisix may have a use after all, keeping husbands faithful!

She went back to her office dreading, like the plague, the rest of the day. After her lunch, she felt a little better but very tired. She drank a triple mocha to juice herself with caffeine, and she needed every bit. Charlotte kept coming by intermittently, going from the meeting to her office and then back to her meeting. It was to everyone's relief when she was gone. In the last month, she had become a real pain. She wasn't the only one to go into the meeting though. Al was in it too, and then as the day wore on, others were asked to attend. She had no idea how she made it, but she plowed through her work; and the next thing she knew, she was looking at the clock above the elevator. It was 4:58. She couldn't believe it. Marla shut her computer down, and a minute later, she was gone.

She couldn't remember a better feeling than when the elevator doors closed. It wasn't just that she was tired. It was that work, the whole environment, everything was insane. Marla hurried down to the subway and was thankful it wasn't that crowded. It was the usual assortment of professionals heading back to their tiny apartments. They jostled around on the old trains stopping at graffiti-decorated stations along the way. She was tired and sat alone, paying no attention to those around her. Marla didn't know how she had taken it all those years like the women from the ninth floor. *Geez*, she thought, *get a life*.

She wondered how people, a somewhat sophisticated society, became obsessed over the most ridiculous things. And the man, the young guy, looking for his next prospective affair. The city was full of them, every age, every kind, and every profession. She knew the drill; she practically wrote it. The boob would have fallen in love or been too egotistical to comprehend what it is. They usually had a pretty little wife and one or two cleverly named kids. Then came the holidays and Christmas, she'd sit alone with her one present and card expressing how deeply *the relationship* meant to him. Sometime between opening presents with his kids and the traditional dinner at the relatives, she would always get the text again, saying how much she meant to him *if only* they could be together. Same thing on Thanksgiving, Valentine's Day, her birthday. Same old thing. The sex was good; the company at times charming, but the lines just grew old.

Marla leaned against the glass of the train reflecting on her life. All of her years were spent in relationships like that; only Travis had been different. She had spent years of her life changing men like other women change dresses, but instead of styles, she changed occupations. The football player, lawyer, politician, stock jock. They really were all the same; only Travis was truly different. Marla glanced around the train at the faces. They all looked the same. Everyone. They were just bees going back to their hives.

She wanted to close her eyes and think about last night, but she was afraid she'd fall asleep and miss her station. She thought about her and Travis on the roof of that castle with the moonlight over the water and the fog. Travis was so bold, so determined. It wouldn't have mattered to him if the whole Russian Army had them surrounded. He was not going to be stopped from loving her. Nothing was going to stop him from her or her from him. That's the man she would want to have her baby, a man that loved her that much.

What she realized in the last couple of days was that he proved he really did love her; they weren't just words on a card bought in a gift shop. Travis came back for her, and he risked his life to do it. That meant more to her than flowers or dinners, presents or jewelry. Other men had given her things. Travis risked his life. He wasn't empty like most of the others; he would do anything for the things he loved, his country, God, and now her. Other men, in comparison, seemed to only love themselves.

Her train finally pulled into the station. Marla was relieved to almost be home. She almost had forgotten and then turned back to get the powdered milk from Tannebaum's. Mr. Tannebaum knew she was tired when he saw her. She tried to be bubbly, but by that time, she had gone two full days and a night on about two hours sleep. The little store was busy, and she had to stand in line and wait to be waited on. She couldn't help but notice Mrs. Tannebaum staring. She was never personable, but her expression was completely flat, her eyes dormant. Marla knew that she concealed her jealousy, but even for her, her demeanor was cold. Finally, Mr. Tannebaum checked her out with her milk and then whispered, "Tomorrow, we have steak". He held up his finger inquiring, "One or two?"

"Two."

He smiled with a soft glint in his eye, "Get some rest. Tomorrow, then."

She hurried down the block and dreaded walking up the flight of stairs. She was fortunate the elevator opened just as she entered her building. Marla then knocked on Mrs. Goldstein's door. Usually that time of the day, she could hear her favorite game show on, "WHO WANTS A DIVORCE?" It was a clever show where contestants get to recant how bad their marriage is, and the audience decides how much they'll get, or if *they* have to pay their spouse.

"Knock, knock". Marla didn't hear anything. She listened thinking maybe she was gone, and then the door opened just as she was turning around. "Yes."

Mrs. Goldstein looked at her almost like she didn't know her. She looked drossy like she had just waked up, except her hair was fixed. "What do you want?"

Marla looked at her flat expression, "I got you the

powdered milk, remember?"

She looked at her for signs that maybe she had a stroke. Her words weren't slurred, and the muscle movement in her face appeared normal. Marla handed her the milk, "Here."

Mrs. Goldstein took it and looked at it and then shut the door without saying another word. Marla was stunned; she had never like that, if anything she was grilled about her work and relationships. Marla had always been a bevy of gossip even if most of it was contrived.

She fumbled for her keys, startled at the bizarre behavior of her neighbor and then collapsed on her couch. She couldn't believe how tired she was. The sun was beginning to set across the city, and she closed her eyes, they were aching and tired. All she wanted to do was sleep and for Travis to be with her. She wanted to lay with him, to be in his arms, the only place in the world left she felt safe.

CHAPTER FOURTEEN

She felt floating as through an opiate induced fog when she heard him call her name. She never heard him come in. His voice blew softly across her face like a breeze. "Marla."

She woke, and Travis was by her side on the couch. The room was dark except for the light glowing from the fish tank. The features of his face formed slowly in the soft light as she rubbed the crusts of sleep from her eyes. She felt such relief seeing him. "How long have you been here?"

"About an hour."

She wiped her eyes again, regaining her consciousness, and felt immensely better though she didn't know how long she had slept. "I thought you said you weren't coming?"

"I wasn't, but I had to see you."

"Are you not going to stay?"

"No. I haven't completed my assignment."

She told him how her day had gone, and though he already knew, he didn't say anything. He just listened quietly and sympathetically to her recall the events about Charlotte and the ladies in the park. She didn't mention the young man in the park but told him of her strange experience with Mrs. Goldstein.

Travis was concerned about that; he said that if she had been chipped with Trisix, *marked*, then she couldn't be trusted. She would report any and everything especially if she was questioned. "Avoid Mrs. Goldstein at all cost and tell her nothing." He said that there were reports that massive numbers of elderly were getting *super chipped*. He didn't know about this himself until recently, but the elderly were being targeted, and retirement homes nationwide were being marked in an *accelerated program*.

Marla sat up. She curled her legs in a lotus position on the couch and grabbed a smoke from her purse. She shook her head as if to get the cobwebs out and rubbed her face. "But why, they're old?"

"Expediency. They are no longer useful."

She lit her cigarette and tossed the lighter on the table. "But they are to their families."

"But they are not to the government." Tens of thousands were being chipped daily, and they had just started doing entire living units. Their usefulness to society was over; the elderly had become a drain. Within days or weeks after taking the chip, *Re-assignment Units* would show up and pack their things. They were taken away without resistance.

She refused to believe, "It can't be! Our government can't be that cruel."

Travis took the smoke out of her hand and took a drag. She didn't realize until Travis stood up, he was dressed like a cop. He had on a uniform, a MF uniform. "Travis?"

"Yes."

"How did you get that uniform?"

"Let's just say, it wasn't voluntary."

"Are you going to tell me more?"

"No. Hope you like it. I nearly came home a SCAB."

"Boo."

"Let him pass. He stunk worse than the East River." Travis shrugged. "Decided I'd poach me a cop instead."

Marla swiped the smoke back out of his hand and gave him a mischievous grin. Her eye arched in approval, and

Travis knew what she was thinking. She motioned with her finger to come over to her. Travis didn't. He walked over to the window and looked out. He looked serious. "Listen, we don't have time, babe. Not now. I've got to tell you something, so you understand. The door is slamming shut. Trisix is being implemented faster than we anticipated. Tens of thousands are being chipped every day. It is Mrs. Goldstein today; probably you tomorrow. Do you understand?"

"I...I...I don't even want to think about it."

"You have to. It is very close. Within a week, everyone in your office could have it; everyone you *know* could have it, nearly everyone in this city. The beast is taking over everything, now."

She sighed, wishing now she hadn't woken up. She felt like she needed a break from the mental strain. Suddenly, she felt a headache coming on. It was too much to fathom, but if it was already next door, across the hall, if Mrs. Goldstein was getting it, then it had to be true. "How are they getting away with this so soon? I don't know how they could do it?"

"Everyone has been prepared, Marla. Massive brainwashing and propaganda. No one challenges what the government does or says anymore. And, everyone is in fear of resisting. What do you think all the talk about sustainability was? They have taught this for over thirty years. This is the price we pay when the environment is placed at greater value than human life. Seven billion people in the world and two billion over the age of sixty-five. The solution has always been to eliminate the unproductive, all unproductive: the old, the feeble, the sick, the mentally and physically handicapped, and dissidents. This is what it has all meant. Trisix is their perfect solution. It is the tool they needed to form their perfect world."

Marla fidgeted on the couch. She suddenly turned cold. She trembled to the point that her teeth shattered. Travis pulled a blanket off the chair and wrapped it around her. She sat there just shaking. Staring. Mentally, she seemed in shock.

Travis went to the blinds and scanned the street, and then he texted. She babbled something, and Travis turned around and looked at her. Her lips were shaking; her voice nearly inaudible. "Ho... ho.... ho... horrible."

Travis knelt beside her and took her hand. He rubbed warmth back into her cold chill and put his arm around her. He had not wanted to tell her what was going down because he knew how deeply she felt about her neighbors. He didn't know what to say to her either. It wasn't appropriate to say some trite comment like *it will be alright*. It wasn't. It wasn't alright at all. He sat there with her silently until she finally seemed to come out of her shock.

"I have to tell her. I am going next door and tell her to get out."

He assured her, "You can't do anything, Marla. Once they are marked, it is over. It is like they are not even human from that point because they don't have the ability to discern right from wrong, good from bad. They are just robots obeying commands."

"But what if we take it out?"

"She wouldn't let you. Do you understand? Once it is in, you are the enemy." He squeezed her arm to emphasize his point. "Listen to me." He spoke sternly. "You do *anything*, and you jeopardize the entire operation. You'll get yourself killed, and me. Think about that."

"But...she needs to know what they are going to do to her."

"Her only hope is that we succeed. Hope we shut the

system down. That is the only chance she has. The neutron chip is the only option left. That is her only hope, and if you do anything, I mean *anything*, you will sabotage the only chance she has. Have you got that?"

She sat there solemnly smoking her cigarette and then went to her window and opened it looking out across the buildings and listened to the traffic below. She couldn't believe how easily society relinquished its rights to the government. It happened so easily and across the hall, a little lady, a friend, her neighbor waited like a sheep for slaughter. Marla wanted to scream. She hated it. Finally, she flipped her cigarette out the window and watched it flip end over end, a faint trail of smoke disappeared to the street. She turned to Travis, "Hold me."

She didn't know if she could stand another moment, another hour in the city, but he encouraged her; it wouldn't be long. They talked for another hour or so. Neither mentioned Trisix, they talked about their life, what it would be. She wanted kids, at least three. She wanted to live on that beach that Travis talked about or some island where every day she could take them down to the shore where they would look for shells, and she could read them books. He could do anything he wanted. That's what she said. It wouldn't matter to her if he was a fisherman or painted houses, built schooners. It wouldn't matter to her if they lived in a hut with a thatched roof made from reeds and slept on mats on the floor.

"You know what I always wanted? Children. Travis, how many do you want?"

"As many as you'd like."

"They might even be a scientist like you."

"Let's hope not. I'd like them to be thinkers. Writers. Maybe someone like Thomas Paine, Shakespeare or Orwell."

"Emily Dickinson, perhaps?"

"Don't care, as long as they are happy."

Travis then showed her something. He pulled out a key, a small one. He looked around her apartment and then went to her refrigerator and pulled out her ice trays and emptied the ice into her sink. He placed the key in the tray and filled it up with water and placed it back in the ice box under another tray. "If anything happens to me and someone comes for a key. You know where it is."

"How will I know I can trust them"?

"You'll know who it is."

"Where does it go?"

"They'll know." He looked at his watch, and she could tell he was about to leave. Marla couldn't understand why he had to go. She wanted to make love to him again but figured it wasn't any use. She could tell things were heavy on his mind.

"Can you tell me what you have to do?"

He took her by the hand and stood with her by the door. "There is a terrorist cell in the city. They have been plotting for some time to detonate a bomb."

"A bomb?"

He was matter of fact about it, "Not just any bomb, they have enough plutonium to build a sizeable weapon of mass destruction. They are very close."

"You're joking right?" She realized as soon as she had said it that it was a dumb thing to say. Travis's eyes were cold. He said nothing. "Do you know where they are?"

He nodded.

She squeezed his arm, "Travis, then you must tell the police."

"Marla." He whispered to her. "They know."

"Then, why don't they do something?"

Travis took a deep breath, "Think. If all the money and

gold is stolen, and we are all wiped out, where is the trail? Who is left to trace it? Why are they clearing out? Why? The UN is nothing but a shell, has been for weeks. They are loading up trucks in the dead of night? What were they celebrating on Wall Street? Why is the Federal Reserve empty? People in power, the elite, know what is going to happen. It is why I had to see it for myself."

"You can't be serious; our government would stop it."

"It has been done before many times in history. It is how governments advance their agenda. The burning of the Reichstag, the sinking of the Maine. After it happens, there will be an outcry for the nations to implement Trisix worldwide. It will be mandatory in every nation to stop terror. That is how their system works. They rob, steal, destroy, kill; and with every atrocity, they turn around and implement more control over you. Our government is the terror. Can't you see?"

The cold chill of fear ran through her. Her body jolted at the thought. She had never been more stunned. She couldn't believe that the federal government could be that callous. Marla felt weak, "I have to sit down." She walked over to the couch nearly stumbling, and Travis poured her a glass of water. Her hands trembled as she took a few minute sips. He really hadn't wanted to tell her about the assignment, but she needed to know the gravity and urgency of getting out. He hoped that she would now fully understand why he had come back for her.

"I didn't want to tell ya, Jean."

"I wish you hadn't."

"You asked, so I guess you needed to know."

"So you have two assignments?"

"No, I've had dozens."

She took another sip and set the glass down on the table. Marla covered her face and was about to cry. As she did, Travis dropped something in her drink to calm her down. She didn't realize what he had done. Her only thought was of an atomic bomb being built within the city, somewhere in the streets, in some building. It unnerved her. She wanted to pack at that very moment and leave. She wanted to call everyone she knew to get out.

Travis took her hand, "Look at me, Marla Jean. Listen to me very, very carefully. Do you understand what I must do?"

She was breathless, "I think." Then, she shook her head, "No, I don't know."

"I must terminate the cell. The night we met, just an hour before I met you at the Hog's Breath I hid a rifle with a scope on top of a building. I would have taken care of them then, but the man I'm after changed locations. They never stay one place long. We found him again, but I missed my opportunity this afternoon. The engineer, the one that was assembling the bomb, came out of the building just once. I wasn't in position. I blew it. I won't make that mistake again."

Marla sipped on her water and looked out her window at the city as if she was stoned, "And what if you don't get him?"

"You don't want to consider the thought."

"And what about the neutron chip? That will stop them right?"

"We sure hope, but we don't even know for sure it will work. It has never been tested. We'll find out soon enough if we get it out of the country." Travis looked at his watch, "I've got to go."

Then it dawned on her, the danger he was in, "Travis, what will happen if you don't return?"

His answer shocked her, "It might be a good thing. One

way or another, you'll know."

She grabbed him, "You can't leave me. I'll go with you. Just don't leave me alone. I won't be able to make it through tomorrow thinking about this."

He took her hands off him gently, "What you have to do, babe, is concentrate on the next 36 hours. That's all. Just take care of yourself. Nothing else. I am more worried about you than me."

He kissed her and then was out the door. She stood by the window and looked down her block. Several buildings down she saw him exit from the stone Henderson building down the block. The same car was sitting outside her window that had been there the previous nights. They didn't appear to have seen the officer in blue step from the enclave. The crowd dispersed down on the corner as he walked by. Little did the public know the danger they were in. Even less did they know that the only man who could save them had just crossed their path.

Travis stood at the corner for a moment, and then a Metro Force cruiser pulled up along the curb. She thought for a second he would run, but instead, he opened the door and got in. It sped away.

Like that, he was gone.

She sipped her water and began thinking. She wanted desperately to go next door to Mrs. Goldstein, but she knew she couldn't. She had to trust Travis; she had no other choice, really. He had after all never lied to her; perhaps, the only man that hadn't. Marla suddenly felt sleepy. She went to bed thinking, *just thirty-six hours. Just thirty-six hours... just... thirty-six... six... six.*

CHAPTER FIFTEEN

She slept as gently as water, flowing from one dream to the next; that is, until her alarm rudely shook her from her sleep. She looked at the time, surprised just how exhausted she had been. Marla quickly showered and put on her mascara and eyeliner, chose a pant dress and wore some comfortable shoes in case she had to leave rapidly. This day, she wanted to be dressed appropriately; skirt and heels wouldn't do.

From the beginning, it was an utterly awful day. Her office, encased by glass windows, felt like a terrarium slithering with vipers. She was the mouse hiding in her little cubicle as their tongues flittered the air for her scent. She threw up twice because of nerves. Everyone became suspect, and though she wasn't an expert in physiognomy, she recognized the distinct signs of the mark on various co-workers. It wasn't just Charlotte and Al; she suspected Trina in payroll, Mark in administrative affairs. They acted robotically. Their faces were nearly completely void of expression, and what expression they did have seemed mimicked. Smiles weren't smiles, but lips trained to bend in rehearsed fashioned features. It was as if their entire countenance was molded to simulate human emotion. Eerie.

Periodically, she checked the news to see if there were any reports of a battle that ensued in the city or a shootout which would indicate perhaps that Travis had accomplished his mission, or....been stopped. She saw nothing, but that didn't always mean anything either. So much of the news wasn't reported, censored for whatever reason. Now, she knew. It all made sense. Every program, every commercial, every news story, it was all part of the lie. Somehow, though she managed to clear her head and make it to lunch before returning back. Her morning had remained relatively uneventful. Marla realized that in less than twenty-four hours she would be gone. Maybe? That is the thought that she kept trying to keep ever present all throughout the day. She found herself daydreaming as a way to get her mind off the seriousness of the mission. She fantasized about ocean waves and a sailboat anchored in a cove somewhere along a Caribbean island. Those are the thoughts that preoccupied her mind for most of the day.

It was rather strange, the paradox of feelings. On one hand, she was deathly afraid; on the other, she felt liberated. With each hour intensified the seductive feeling of freedom. It was strangely erotic. Marla caught herself several times rubbing her legs together thinking about escape. Somehow the feel aroused her. She wished she had a picture of Travis on her desk to intensify her stimulation. She wanted to look at his face and think about him chasing her down a beach into the emerald waters. She imagined being in the waves, holding onto the side of a weather worn boat swaying in the tide as he held her from behind. She could see him, lean and tan with broad shoulders gripping her with his masculine hands. She could taste his salty skin and the smell of oils, and the sea. Down below her, in the waters, she envisioned brilliantly colored fish brushing against her legs, nibbling down to her toes.

"Marla?"

Startled, she spun around. It was the pugnacious Charlotte, "Are you alright?"

She realized she was breathing heavily and felt flushed; totally unaware that Charlotte had been standing there. She looked up at the clock on her screen; it would not be long, and she'd be off. Composing herself, she blew the hair out of her face, "Um, yes, yes, I'm ah…fine. Just finishing my reports." She hit the send button. "See, I'm done." As soon as she said that, she realized she had made a mistake.

"Good", her boss smiled fiendishly, "You have time then for an upgrade."

"What upgrade?"

"Oh, it only takes a minute. There are some people here who will take care of it in minutes. All chips are being upgraded." She stood back and waved with her hand to her office, "No more viruses or bugs."

Marla peered around Charlotte to her office. There was a man and a woman standing there. He was tall with droopy skin hanging from his neck, but she was athletic and firm. They were waiting. They looked very odd standing there looking at each other and neither was saying a word. The woman stared at Marla over the maze of cubicles. She was expressionless. The man's eyes reminded her of a monitor lizard peering behind wire rim glasses.

A chill surged up her spine. She remembered what Travis warned her. Her purse was laying on her desk with her cell phone in it. She needed to call but was caught by surprise. Marla knew if she ran she'd be apprehended. She couldn't make it to the elevator or to the stairs. Security would have the doors downstairs locked down if she made it that far. It was hopeless. She was caught. Her instincts told her to leave during lunch, but she didn't. It was 4:19; another forty minutes and she could have left.

Marla tried to think, and then saw the bathroom at the far

end of the office. She slung the strap of her purse over her shoulder and smiled incredulously. "Why sure, but let me go to the bathroom first."

Charlotte grabbed her by the elbow and tugged, "It will only take a second."

Marla mimicked a straining wince and put her hand on her bladder. Her lip twitched nervously, "I won't make it. I'll be back in a few minutes, promise."

Charlotte reluctantly looked at the clock, "Well, hurry. They have a schedule."

As Marla walked through the 22nd floor of cubicles, she glanced over her shoulder. She was going to bolt for the stairs if they weren't looking, but they were watching her every step. It was pointless to try to run. She went to the bathroom and ducked into a stall and texted U2. She sat on the toilet trying to think of what to do. She thought about crawling out of the bathroom with her head down and making it around the cubicles to the stairs and then run for it, but even if Charlotte didn't see her, all the other workers in the room would. Marla began to cry. She texted U2 and sent it again. She fought back her tears and tried to gain her composure trying to think of anything she might do. Above the stall were removable acoustic tiles in the ceiling. Maybe if she was able to hoist herself into the ceiling, she could disappear and hide until evening and then leave after the office closed. She could find a way out. She knew she had to hurry. She stood on the toilet stool, but the ceiling was too high. She thought that if she stood on the commode tank she might be able to climb onto the stall wall and get out. That was the only option she had. She knew she couldn't go back. She'd end up like Trina in accounting, an emotionless, brainless robot debasing in front of a monitor.

As she was about to get on the commode tank, the bathroom door swiftly opened, "Marla, they need you." She recognized the whiskey voice. It was Gail from IP. She took the stall next to Marla. "Well, aren't you going to go?"

Marla reluctantly flushed the toilet and came out. She went to the sink, still trying to think of any possible way she could escape. Her mind was blank. She touched up her make-up so it wouldn't be noticeable that she had cried. It was 4:32. She had no choice but to go. It was the longest walk of her life across the floor to Charlotte's office. It was like walking to the gallows. All her co-workers watched as she moped down the aisle towards Charlotte's office in back. She could see her on the phone, and then she hung up. The two people stood up and turned toward Marla as she approached.

Charlotte looked agitated; her lips were drawn tight like fist, "There is someone to see you."

Surprised, she looked around. "There is?"

Behind her a man stood up in the waiting area. She recognized him immediately; it was the man she had seen at Tannebaum's a few days before, the handsome man in the suit and gray top coat. He smiled and stuck out his hand, "Hi, Marla. I'm Clark Davidson with the Mayor's office. They have requested an interview with you."

She was stunned, confused. She turned to the people standing inside Charlotte's office looking at her in a cold blank stare. Charlotte pointed to the office clock. "Mr. Davidson, she doesn't get off for twenty more minutes. We would hate for you to wait, perhaps you could come back tomorrow? Make an *appointment*."

Mr. Davidson was not deterred. He said he would wait if necessary but didn't know why she couldn't leave then. He suggested maybe she could come in twenty minutes early tomorrow or work through a break. Charlotte objected, saying they had rules and procedures, and if they were broken for one person, then everyone would want to break them. They had to keep the order.

"Then, I will wait. I can watch Marla work right from here and give a report on how she does, if you don't mind."

"I'm actually finished with my work. I've been finishing early each day."

"Great, we've heard you're very proficient." He turned to Charlotte. "Is she?"

Charlotte was clearly upset. "Sometimes." She walked into her office and shut the door.

He put his hand over his mouth. "U2."

Marla looked at him inquisitively. "U2? You're U2?"

He nodded his head and didn't say anything more. They could see her talking to the others; it was so obvious they were trying to figure out what to do. They were all whispering none too discretely with their eyes on Marla the entire time.

Marla thought the man looked familiar somehow. She thought she recognized him, like she had known him, she whispered, "Who are you?"

"Stay calm. Let me handle this."

Charlotte came back out and relented, saying that Marla could get the *upgrade in the morning*. It was a real inconvenience for them to come back, but they would. She then buzzed Trina Kamenski, and Trina came to her office and then left with the two to a room down the hall.

Marla's knees were shaking; her fingers trembled. She didn't know who the man was, if he was really from the Mayor's Office or someone else. She didn't at all care; he was a Godsend. Clark told her to grab her coat and umbrella if she had one, and they left. As the elevator doors closed, Marla stood back and looked at the stranger, "Who *are you*, really?"

"Don't you know?"

"Haven't a clue."

"I am Travis's brother." He put his arm around her and patted her on the back, "We've been watching you all day. We knew your name was on the list, but that was close."

She was flabbergasted. She had never met him, but she could see the resemblance in his face, though Clark was ten years older. She thought about it, another minute, and it would have all been over. The bell dinged, and they were on the bottom floor. He escorted her out to a waiting car in the garage. "Well Clark, you are just like Travis in one regard."

He smiled, "How's that?"

"You could have at least given me a warning what was going to happen."

"We tried, but you blew us off." He opened the back door to the car, "Get in."

She got in the back. There was a petite Spanish looking lady in the front seat, and then the driver turned around. She recognized him too even with his sunglasses, by his chestnut hair. "So, we meet again. Remember me?"

"Oh, my God!" Marla reached across the seat and slapped him on the shoulder.

The black sedan squealed through the parking garage and out onto the street into the foray of afternoon traffic. Clark, Travis's brother, turned to her and shook his head, "Now, that was close."

Before she could say anything, he was on the phone.

CHAPTER SIXTEEN

She felt exhilarated as if she'd just escaped over the Bedford Hills walls. They sped away, and if anybody was following, they would have lost them. Clark stayed on the phone most the time. The driver, Chestnut, darted through traffic with adroit precision. Marla never got a good look at the woman in front. She wore dark sunglasses and was constantly talking on the phone, half the time in Spanish.

Chestnut made so many quick turns that Marla had no idea where they were until they finally turned onto the FDR Expressway going up the East River. Clark told her to sit back and relax; she was safe, for a while.

"What about Travis? Is he alright?"

"Yes."

He didn't elaborate. That seemed a bit odd, but she concluded that maybe they don't say very much in their business. She folded her arms and leaned back against the door. Marla's heart was still racing; she wondered if this was like routine to these people? They seemed so calm, all of them. She wondered, did they go home at the end of the day, have a drink and push the games of espionage, narrow escapes and clandestine operations behind them? Marla didn't know what to expect. Chestnut was on the phone practically ignoring her, looking back over his shoulder making sure they weren't being followed. As he was talking, Clark, (if that was his real name) pushed a button to a black leather console between them. It opened up, and there was a small bar with an ice dispenser. The selection was limited, but she didn't care. Marla didn't bother to ask or to wait for him to show he was a gentlemen; she poured herself a gin and tonic and slug a few quick shots down her throat. Within moments, she felt the effects of the alcohol spread down her body like a warm massage down to her feet. She felt better. She downed the whole drink in a couple of more large gulps, then immediately refilled her glass. She couldn't believe it, but her hand was still slightly shaking. The bottle rattled against her glass as she poured. She put the gin bottle back in the console and held her glass as if gesturing a cheers, "So, ah, you driver, is this just a normal day for you or what?"

"There are no normal days." He zipped between two eighteen wheelers and crossed over a few lanes. "How about you?"

"It sucked. It really, really sucked! Burp!"

Clark smiled. Marla was understandably shaken, and he knew it.

He kept talking on the phone to someone, "Yes, she's safe." As he was talking, she thought to herself, *Whadda ya mean safe?* She didn't say anything, but it didn't necessarily make her feel any better that she was driving through traffic like a maniac with three strange people that she didn't know for sure who they were. She leaned back against the door and stared at *Clark* and wondered if he was who he said he was. He did indeed resemble Thomas. His hair was the color of a pecan nut, sort of silver with dark gray streaks, very distinguished looking. He was taller than Travis too and would catch the attention of any woman. "Want a triple?" He took her drink and poured her another one.

He had an easy way about him. Clark told whoever he was talking to that they rescued twenty-seven more that afternoon. He smiled at her, almost seductively, "Yes, she looks *alright* to me." He then hung up the phone and indulged her in a bit of small talk as they sped along the freeway. If Marla didn't know better, she almost got the feeling he was trying to seduce her. He was polite, cordial, and very charming. She could tell he was trying to make her relaxed, and it helped. "So, you want to tell me how your day went?"

Chestnut in the front laughed, "I tried to let her know I was in the next building."

"You people!"

They all laughed. She then apologized; she explained that she thought he was trying to pick her up. They knew that; it was okay. The plan was going to be that if she U2'd they'd send him over and pretend like he was there to score a date, or pick her up, but when she rebuffed him like she did, they decided they had better switch to Clark.

"We thought you might tell him to blow off when he was there to help."

She couldn't believe she didn't connect the dots. But it was good it worked out the way it did. Clark told her that they had people in the vicinity for days, and to her great relief, he told that she wouldn't be going back tomorrow.

"But she said I have to come back in the morning."

"Relax, it's Good Friday. You are off."

Marla had never heard more beautiful words in her whole life. They didn't celebrate Easter anymore or Good Friday as a holiday. The government replaced Easter with the Mid-Solace break, the spring festival of the rising *sun*. Many government offices were going to be closed. She had forgotten, obviously. Lucky for her, otherwise, she'd been marked.

A light rain came down across the city. It was a gray overcast day, but even still, the penthouses overlooking the East River were elegant. As they talked, she realized that Clark was a bit more personable and intenerating than Travis. She could see how he could be in government affairs. Both men, though, displayed an unmistakable confidence about them, yet it was different. Clark was a charmer; Travis could be too, but Travis had an unmitigated, unwavering, undeniable courage about him. You could see it in his eyes. When Travis looked at you, you immediately knew he meant business. He was just strong.

Just then, the petite Hispanic woman in front handed her phone to Clark. She didn't know who he was talking to, but Clark was very matter of fact. He didn't say much. He pulled his sleeve back and looked at his watch; it was expensive. Then, he handed the phone back to the woman in the front seat, "It is done. Go to 125th Street."

"You sure?"

"125th Street." Chestnut floored it along the Expressway, and it wasn't until then that Marla realized whose car she was in; it was the Mayor's car, or one of them. A jet black sedan with crushed leather seats. There was a dossier next to Clark with the city's logo on it.

Amused and impressed, and also feeling the effects of the gin soothing her anxieties, Marla smiled, "So, is this typically how you pick up women?" She took another sip, "Or, do you...."

Clark could tell she had had enough. He took the drink from her and dumped it in a bucket. "Bars closed."

"Ahhh." She pouted her lips. "Come on. I don't get to ride in the Mayor's car every day."

"Sorry, Travis said no more than two. He was right."

She sat back with her arms folding in a protesting gesture and looked out the window. A light rain was beginning to fall. They passed by the UN, and she could see the tanks and army personnel stationed all around. There were moving trucks and lots of activity, but they drove by so fast she didn't get a good look. They passed the Queensboro Bridge, and she had no idea where they were going. It certainly was not her route home. She figured they knew what they were doing. Clark was texting on his phone to someone. She felt so odd because none of them said that much. He put the phone back in his coat pocket. "Your apartment building is crawling with agents. We've spotted at least five secret police on your street. You are going to have to be careful."

"What do you mean; *I* am going to have to be careful? I am staying with you guys right?"

"No. You are going to go back alone, but we are going to be watching."

"Why?" She didn't understand why she was such a target? "What's the big deal about me? I don't know anything. For Christ sakes, don't they know that?"

"You're the bait, and you are all they've got."

"Bait?" Her eyebrows squinched together, "Bait! Whadda ya mean, bait?"

"Calm down." Clark explained she had been under surveillance for weeks, long before Travis arrived there. They've been expecting Travis to show up. They knew there was going to be a pickup and delivery in New York. They knew, or believed they knew, who was going to be doing it, but they didn't know when or where. The secret police had been fed a lot of disinformation. If they moved in too quick, before he picked it up, it would blow their opportunity to confiscate *it*.

"It?"

"You know what we mean. *It.*"

"Oh, yeah."

"They've been planning on marking you but didn't make the decision till today, but it was close."

"Why didn't they just do it earlier?"

"Are you kidding? Travis would have noticed. He knows what to look for better than anyone. If you were dirty, he would bolt...or be forced to terminate you. They wouldn't get the information."

The significance of his words stunned her, "Terminate?" She swallowed with noticeable discomfort. "Me?"

"If it was the other way around, Marla, you'd have to do it to him. You know what is at stake."

"But terminate?"

"Do you realize how many tens of thousands of people were rounded up just today? Do you realize how many more tomorrow, or the next day?" As he was speaking, he was also texting on the phone. "Look at the millions of lives in this city, the danger, the threat that awaits them. No one person or life is more important than the rest. Do you understand?"

"Yes, but..."

"Don't worry. It didn't happen. Remember? We got you out. You're safe."

"But I am going back to my apartment, and you said it is crawling. That's what you said, right?"

"We've got you covered. We'll be there too. We are watching them watch you. You are vital to us."

"But, how?"

"Haven't you figured it out?"

"What?"

"While they have been watching you, we have saved

thousands this week. You are our decoy."

"I am a decoy? I have been put through all this to be a decoy?" She was furious.

"You are looking at it all wrong. Look at how many lives were saved because they have been focusing on *you* all week. '

The driver, Chestnut, turned around, "There are a couple of hundred people that owe their life to you if it makes you feel any better."

Marla took in a deep breath and exhaled. She was both upset and then relieved. In a way, she was flattered.

"Don't be mad at Travis. We used the circumstances to our advantage. Understand?"

Bewildered, Marla looked at the traffic passing by. It was a dreary rainy afternoon. It slowly began to sink in. He really did love her. He didn't say it much, but he showed it. She couldn't be mad at him. It was almost too much to comprehend.

"Marla". She turned to Clark, "You aren't mad at Travis, are you?"

She bit her lip. And, shook her head, no. He thought she was about to cry. "Because he is not to blame for any of this, you understand that, right?"

She looked out the window holding back her tears. The sound of car wheels splashing in the rain hissed by her window. She listened to the rhythmic sound of the wiper swishing across the glass. She thought back to that first night when she saw him on the street in front of the Tavern. It seemed like so long ago. So much had happened in one week, and to think, he came back for her after all those years. It was almost beyond her ability to comprehend the significance of it. No one had ever cared like that for her. Ever.

She sat there quietly alone watching the traffic bottleneck

at the exits, and then they finally turned onto 125th Street and meandered through traffic. She had no idea why they had gone such a long ways out, so far from her apartment, but she knew not to ask. These types of people always have reasons. The sedan was stalled in traffic. Chestnut gave her passing glances in the rearview mirror, or she thought it was at her; she couldn't tell. Clark was texting on one phone, and then his other phone rang. He pulled it out of his coat and answered it, "Yeah, she's right here." He handed her the phone. "It's Travis."

His deep voice immediately comforted her. "Jean, you alright?'

"Me, what about you? You're the one that…"

"Shhhh. I'm okay. I could hardly get my mind off you. I was worried sick about you all day."

They talked for a few moments more. He assured her everything would be alright. He told her that he couldn't wait to see her and that was all she needed to hear, his voice just saying the words. She felt better immediately; it would all be okay. She didn't know what would happen next, but for her to just follow directions, it would be okay. They were down to hours; and it would all be over. They would be able to escape. They would be gone. "Think of our beach."

"When do I see you?"

He wouldn't say, or couldn't. "Soon." Then, he hung up.

She handed Clark back the phone breathing heavily. She could see the place he was talking about in her mind even though it was dark and drizzly outside. The windshield wipers flipped back and forth across the glass. The cars stood in line; their taillights shining, horns were honking, people scurried by sloshing in the rain with their umbrellas bumping into each other. She was leaving it all behind, and she couldn't wait.

Clark's voice was calm and reassuring, "You'll be alright."

She nodded and didn't say anything. He could see a tear roll down her face. She turned and looked out the window staring off to the crowd. She reached her hand across the console, and he took it. She squeezed his hand firmly.

"Just a few more hours. We'll make it." He reassured her. "We have to."

Marla couldn't say anything. She just nodded. She wanted Travis with her.

They pulled over to the curb. "You need to get out here."

Marla turned around somewhat dazed. She looked at Clark, "What?"

He pointed to a bus and told her to get on it. They would follow it the rest of the way. She should be safe. "Will I see you again?"

"Tomorrow."

"What about Mister, ah, exactly what is your name?"

"Jazz."

Clark reached over her lap and opened up her door, "Don't miss the bus. We're around." Marla slipped back on her shoes and stepped out. She ran up the street and jumped on. It was another half a mile ride down Central Park West before they came to her block. She was woozy from the gin, and when she stood up to get off, the bus she felt wobbly. She looked behind in the traffic but could not see the sedan. Yet, she had to believe what he told her; she was being watched, and they were close by.

The rain had stopped; it was just gray and dark. The first thing she did was light a cigarette. Her pack was almost empty, and then she remembered they had some steak at Tannenbaums's. She thought, why not? It would be her last night in the city. The cigarette helped to relax her nerves as she crossed the street. Suddenly, she felt great. The traffic was light; many people were already home. A few people were walking their dogs, but other than that, she didn't see anybody else out. As she walked along, she checked her messages on her phone; she couldn't believe it had been an hour and a half since she left her office. In one way, it seemed like only minutes, and in another, it seemed like days. She realized that she was definitely buzzed. The colors of lights and the way the water shimmered on the dark streets played tricks with her eyes. Her head was spinning. She took another puff and tossed her cigarette into the trash and then ducked into Tannenbaum's. She almost tripped on the step walking in; it was strange. Just three drinks and she was buzzing.

It seemed like every face in the store turned toward her when she went in. They all looked at her and then panned away. It was odd, like they were all on cue. Mr. Tannenbaum smiled and waved as he checked people out. It was busy and crowded. She noticed a pretty young woman standing in line, or at least she used to be pretty. She turned and smiled at Marla. Marla gave a customary grin, but she couldn't bring herself to say anything. The young woman had disgusting sores about her lips and forehead. It wasn't acne; the sores had festered and gotten worse. They were all the way down her arms and hands. Behind her was an elderly man, with these soft hazel eyes. He stood in line holding a can of soup and a small package of crackers. It was pathetic, really. That was probably all that was allowed on his rations. He worked his whole life for this?

She went over to the vegetable aisle and took a look. She remembered when it was full of fresh vegetables. Now, the bins were nearly empty. She picked up a couple of potatoes, though they were very small. Marla hesitated; they did have cauliflower and turnip greens. It was the only thing they had in abundance, but she had never acquired the taste. She looked at the price of carrots; they were sold individually and were way too expensive, but she picked up a dozen anyway and put them in her basket.

They were down to two lines at the register, and the faces were rather glum. The people were mysteriously quiet; perhaps, it was the weather she thought that had put a damper on their sprits. Marla stood waiting to be checked out. It was orderly, mechanical. She looked with amusement at the tabloids at the checkout line. Rubbish. Distractions from the things of importance. Dalliances in trivial nonsense. But, it still sold. It always had. They all put their items on the counter and scanned their hands and put them in the little green bags and walked out.

She wanted to scream. She had the urge to jump up on the counter and yell, *"What is the matter with you! What are you doing?"* Instead, she smiled politely, hiding her ridicule in a mocked grin. It wasn't any use. It was like they were all programmed. She realized this is the way it was going to be. This is the world that was created by us, for us. This is the best we could come up with. They would all go home and watch their stupid shows with canned laughter and eat their pathetic tasteless meals. They would all work until they completed the end of their cycle. Then, it would be simply a matter of disposal. This is what they all bought into, sold out to, and relented to.

This is what they chose. Collective obedience. Bees.

"Hello, Marla."

She was startled; she hadn't been paying attention. She was daydreaming in line.

Mr. Tannenbaum pulled out a small package wrapped in white paper from the refrigerator. He laid it on the scales. There was a glint of enthusiasm in his eyes, "I've saved this all day for you."

"Oh, thank you." When she saw the price, she realized perhaps she had spoken prematurely. The cost almost half a week's salary, and for eight ounces she thought that was a little excessive. "Ahum...." She hesitated. There was no way she would have spent that much, ever, but then she realized it was their last night in the city. It wouldn't hurt to splurge. "Oh, go ahead. I'll take it."

He could tell she was not too excited about the purchase. She scanned her hand, and as he put her things in the bag, he walked back to the refrigerator and pulled out another package and slipped it in. He gave her a wink.

She wanted to say something. He was such a good man. His wife stood nearby or otherwise she would have given him a big hug and a kiss. There wasn't anything she could do. The city still had many people just like him, good people, wonderful people caught in a hopeless situation.

She would miss him.

Marla hurried home and up to her apartment. There was a note on her door from Mrs. Goldstein. Said she needed some help with some boxes. Marla's heart sank. She quietly closed the door to her apartment. It wasn't that she didn't want to help, she did, but she had things to do. She didn't know when Travis would be there, but she wanted to have a meal cooked and for them to have a quiet dinner together. She wanted for their last night to be special and so she sliced the potatoes and put them and the carrots on the stove to boil, and then she laid out her favorite dress and took a shower. She wanted to fix herself up for the occasion.

After she finished showering and drying her hair, she checked on the stove and turned the heat down. She wasn't going to cook the steaks till he got there. Marla unwrapped the packages. They were dreadfully thin, disappointing, but with some spices she had, she could make them taste delicious. Just then, she heard a tapping at her door, and she looked through the peephole. It was Mrs. Goldstein. Marla really didn't want to talk to her right then. She listened quietly. Mrs. Goldstein knocked again, this time louder.

Finally, the elderly woman went back over to her apartment and closed the door. Marla felt badly, but she didn't want to be bothered, not then. She sat down on her couch and lit a cigarette. The rain had stopped so she opened her window. The sun was beginning to set through some clouds in the west. Its red glow across the wet streets produced a rather spectacular effect. The streets looked like rivers of fire almost like molten lava, but it was cool. It was marvelous; it looked like an impressionist painting obscuring the lines of buildings blending them in with the puddles reflection in the street. She rolled the ashes along the rim of the ashtray and then held the cigarette just above the skin where her chip was embedded.

She marveled at the absurdity, how something so small could have so much control. That little instrument, the tiny gadget no bigger than a grain of rice, took complete control of her life. It was her chain, everyone's chain. It was more powerful than all the other chains that bound and enslaved society throughout our brief human history. It was greater than iron or steel. It was a marvel of ingenuity, if you want to call it that, and the most perplexing thing is that it is probably the first chain that the slaves willingly took.

As inhuman as what it was, there was still another chain that would turn them all into obedient zombies like the loquacious pithy Al. They would all become just mindless sub servants subdued by their skullduggery. The thought horrified her. Marla held her fire from her smoke just above her implant. She wanted to press the fire into it, burn its circuitry up, fry its little components and wires. Instead, she took a long drag and looked out across the city she had loved. Then, she heard her phone buzz, the phone Travis gave her.

Enthusiastically, "Yes."

"I'll be there in five minutes. Be ready."

CHAPTER SEVENTEEN

She strolled silently as a thief past the other tenants' doors and crept quietly downstairs. At first, she almost didn't recognize him when she opened the back door. Travis was dressed as a mechanic wearing overalls and a rather filthy cap. She pulled him into the stair well and shoved him against the wall. Marla ripped off his hat and gave him a long wet kiss. Her breasts pressed up against him and she breathed. "You don't know how I've missed you."

She took him by the hand, and they went upstairs. Together, they tip toed down to her apartment where they snuck in. He noticed the note still on her door.

"What's that?"

She explained it was nothing. Mrs. Goldstein needed some help with some things; she would see her later. Marla insisted he take a shower, *a good one.* She put the steaks into the broiler and prepared the setting. She laid out cleaned pressed clothes for him, and when he came out, she had everything ready, table cloth, candles and all. He had never in fact seen her look more radiant. She wore a red dress with a V neck that revealed her rather spectacular cleavage. Her hair was pulled up in a French braid, and a black onyx gem with diamonds draped around her neck. But, it was her eyes which stood out in appearance, green emerald dazzling eyes, sparkling over the flickering flame of the single candle burning on the table. Her face and everything about her glowed. He had never seen anyone look so spectacular.

"I wish I had more to give you."

They shared, (she shared), about their day. Travis enjoyed just listening to her talk. She told him all about the horrifying experience at the office, which he already knew but didn't interrupt her. She, of course, talked about his brother and the ride, and all the while, he just listened. Marla knew the meal wasn't much, but Travis complemented her on it several times, and she could tell he was truly hungry. Even though he was famished, he was careful not to insult her by devouring it so quickly, so he ate slowly with manners. It was after all their last supper.

When they were done, he helped her wash the dishes, and though the night had turned a little chilly, they both decided on a whim to go up to the roof to look out over the city one last night. Marla grabbed a blanket and poured herself a tall glass of wine, and then they sneaked down the hall and up to the rooftop. The city looked spectacular, though not as brilliant as it used to be, New York was still an ocean of lights shining off the fresh wet pavement in the night like as the stars do off the surface of a placid sea.

Together they sat down on a bench, and she pulled the blanket over her lap. Marla had been curious so she took a sip and finally asked. "Can you tell me what happened?"

Travis had been unusually quiet, almost melancholy. He wasn't reveling in his mission. She wondered if he failed. He confessed to her that he never had gotten use to *a hit*. There was no jubilation of victory, not for him. He described the job as one of the toughest he had ever done which told her immediately that for sure this wasn't his first job. His target was a Middle Eastern scientist, a brilliant man by all accounts who had become involved in the jihad against the United States, either willingly or by coercion. He didn't know, and it didn't matter. He had to be eliminated. The hardest problem was finding a suitable position from a building opposite the cell. The buildings were too tall to *perch* from a roof top and so he had to find an office window across the street. That was the difficult task because there wasn't a set hour. He didn't know when he might exit the building or when he might return.

Marla curiously asked. "So what did you do?"

He finally found a suitable vacant office, but it was the next building down, further than what he wanted. He entered the building as a policeman; then picked the lock to an empty office where he set up. Travis told how he assembled his barrel together with the pipes he made at TD's. They had tried to secure a rifle, but they couldn't get their hands on one in time, so he made one, equipped with a shoulder butt and even a tripod. He commented on how it was very efficient for relatively *short range targets*. The principal problem was detonation because it obviously had no trigger or hammer, but Travis revealed how he solved that problem by devising a muzzle loader style igniter.

"A what?"

He took out the flash from the camera he took from TD, and taped the wires into a hole at the end of the barrel which he had sealed and packed with powder that he procured from the shells. It worked just like a regular muzzle loader. When his target was in view and his aim steady on the tripod, he put the button that connected to the flash between his teeth. He waited and at the right moment squeezed down.

She marveled. "And it worked?"

"Perfectly. I even made a silencer. Poof. He never heard

it. He never took another breath." Travis explained that the shot was easy. "Getting him in the open was the problem."

Marla pulled the blanket around her shoulders and looked at him with her raised eyebrow. "And, how did you do that?"

Time was running out. Their leader had only been outside once in three days and that was for just a brief moment. He had to do something. So, as he described it, he "baited the scene". He got the idea sitting there in the window looking at the graffiti on the neighboring buildings. He still had the workmen's clothes he snatched at TD's. So he changed clothes and went and found a can of spray paint and walked along one of their cars out front and when no one was looking painted some inflammatory slogans along the side of one of their cars. It took a while. It was about an hour before it was noticed, but then when it came to their attention, they all came out. Travis was ready and waiting. His man stood in the street looking at the graffiti making a perfect target. "He stood exactly where I wanted him."

The expression of Travis's face was noticeably solemn. She could tell he didn't want to talk about it, but he wouldn't have said anything if he didn't feel compelled to get it off his chest. Obviously, he did.

Marla tried to comfort him. She wrapped the blanket around both of them, "You did your job, Travis."

"Yeah, I suppose. It's called war…and I hate it."

"You saved the city."

"It is not how I look at it. He was doing the job they assigned him, and I did the job I was assigned. That's all. Today, I just did mine better. Tomorrow, it starts all over. It's insane." He didn't say another word about it. They sat together on a bench leaned against an old crusty incinerator wall and looked out across the city. The lights began to turn dim in all the buildings as curfew went into effect. The traffic's noise quieted as people turned into their homes. They could hear a few buses trolling. On the next block, they heard the distinctive rattling sound of a Cage roving down the block. She felt his body tense up listening to it.

Marla wondered how Travis viewed his cause, whether he considered himself as a freedom fighter or revolutionary. She could tell by his demeanor that it might not be the time to ask. The *hit* definitely bothered him. She could tell. The muscles in his jaw rippled up and down. He was edgy and silent. His head hung down. She didn't know what all he did for the Body, but she knew that this was a job he did because it had to be done. There was no glory in it, not for him. It wasn't like those Hollywood movies. No big hooray. No special effects or applause. Marla reached her hand over and wrapped her fingers around his palm. He finally looked at her and a trace of a smile showed on his face.

Suddenly, it dawned on her. She hadn't thought about her family. They didn't live in the city but still. "Travis, what about my parents? They're still in Omaha and my sister is in Abilene? I can't stand the thought of leaving them behind."

He pulled a smoke from a pack, there weren't but several left. Travis flicked a lighter and held it to the cigarette. He took several puffs and leaned back. "We are doing all we can. We all have families. Everyone on the mission does. Clark and me, we have our mom. Jazz has four sisters. None of us are comfortable with just saving our own skin. But if we don't save ourselves, their days are numbered anyway. They haven't got a chance."

He spoke to her in a very matter of fact way and not condescending; nevertheless, there were lots of questions he never answered; she wanted to know. "And what will happen when you activate the neutron chip? You said it will shut everything down, right?"

"Correct." He took a puff and blew the smoke in the air. It drifted like a gray cape hovering about the roof.

"So what happens to a plane if it is flying? Or a train? What happens to the cars driving on the interstate? You haven't told me about that. I need to know."

Travis flicked his smoke and popped his neck, "What happens when the power goes out now? There are power outages every year. What happens when there is an earthquake? Subways stop on their tracks; electric trains come to a halt. Planes will crash, that is for certain. Some are equipped to fly manually, some not. There will be deaths, no doubt. But, it is far fewer than the alternative."

"Deaths? How many?"

"Too many, but we have no choice. None. We can't afford the other option, to do nothing." He turned facing her. Marla always marveled at how he could be so handsome when he was serious, and at times unbelievably kind. Travis bit his lip tentatively thinking about what he was going to say, "Babe, every question you've considered is one we've already asked. Believe me. What we do know is that there are plans by the elite rulers to eliminate roughly one third of mankind. Think about it, one out of three people you know will be eliminated. So the question becomes *not* how many lives will be lost if we take action, but how many lives will be lost if we don't. You see?"

"A third of all mankind? The human race?" She was in disbelief. "No way."

"At least a third. It may be two thirds. Ask yourself how many people are truly productive today? Is the old man in the wheelchair? How about the retarded boy at school or the child with spinal bifida? How about all those other drains on society? What about people with low IQ's, the disabled, the overweight? Think about it Marla, because the rulers have, and the world they envision will function better without these people. Look around you. Take a real hard honest look at humanity because they have. Only about one in three is really worthy. Functional."

"You can't be serious."

"I am dead serious. They can't manage a wet dream, and yet they want to rule the world. It is all about function and purpose. And you know there was a book that was written a long time ago that said it would be this way, but what the heck? Let's just ignore it."

"The Bible?"

He shrugged. "It was our past, and our future. Call it what you will."

"But still, what you are doing seems so drastic. So many people will die when you activate the neutron chip."

"We tried to best determine the date in which the fewest number of people will be traveling. The problem is that we are running out of time, so as soon as the neutron is operational it will be activated. We anticipate that it will take three days to fully shut everything down. The good news is this; as soon as planes start to malfunction, the rest will be grounded. It's the satellites that we are really after, because all communication, all information, all internet is via satellite. And most important Trisix can't operate without it."

"And the highways?"

Travis flicked the smoke, "It will be mayhem. Stranded cars everywhere, except of course the older ones. If the GPS is removed before the worm, the systems should still be operational." He shrugged, "That is what we hope."

Her shoulders slumped; she hadn't thought about that. It hadn't dawned on her exactly what would happen. Travis knew what she was thinking, and he tried to console her. "Marla, don't you know that we have thought this thing through. We've looked at it from every angle. We thought about a coup, but this is worldwide. It is not just here in America. It is the whole world. All the nuclear weapons from all the countries, all the stockpiles, it is the only way to disarm it completely."

"I hadn't thought of that." Travis felt her hand slip across his thigh.

"Remember, this was first designed by the military as an end all solution to shut down everything, but everything means everything. And then, there is the little matter of the world wide banking system, the corrupt morass that it has become. How do we free ourselves from the financial imprisonment we've been relegated too? Do you see? There is only one way to end it all. We can't be naive and believe that to alter the system here or tweak it there will make any difference. We are way past negotiations or even reform."

"Are you absolutely positive, this is the only way?"

"Positive. There was a chance a number of years back, before the chip was ever installed, before people were forced to take it. Our country was bankrupt, and it was corrupt, but the seditionist could have been routed out. We had that option. Our finances could have been restored. Our infrastructure and the judicial, executive and legislative branches purged. It might have taken a generation, but it could have been done. Our generation blew it. We didn't take our future serious enough."

"Why didn't we?" Her hand slipped lower between his legs.

"Don't you remember? No one would listen. The country had set its course. There was a time that the political process and the corrupt leaders could have been thrown out, but that movement was hindered by individual greed, and complacency. People made the fatal choice that had doomed many nations."

She pulled the blanket around his shoulders and squeezed him tight, "What was that?"

Travis's voice was a bit hoarse, perhaps, from the night air. He coughed trying to clear his throat. She could barely hear him for the traffic below. He leaned his head against hers and took a drag off his smoke and blew it across the roof. "Babe, we chose security over freedom. Freedom has always been our security. And we chose government over God."

Marla was perplexed, confused. She took a smoke from the pack and lit it. She wrapped her arm completely around his leg, and squeezed. She didn't say anything; she just thought about what he was saying and took another sip of wine. It didn't set well, probably nerves. She was feeling uneasy, maybe anxious. It was the most unusual feeling of her life. She was elated that she was leaving, escaping, but on the other hand, she was sickened to her stomach that it had gotten to the point it did. How could people be so barbaric? How could humans connive to do the insidious things they did? She laid her head down on his knee and gazed at the lights dimming in the city, her city. She whispered, "How did all this hate happen?"

Travis ran his fingers through her hair and stared out across the city. He listened to the sounds of traffic down below. He looked up into the sky and leaned back with his arm stretched out on the bench. "The world can google for solutions all it wants, but there was only one answer. It comes back to that every time. The only chance mankind ever had was God. When you don't respect and love the God that made you, you aren't going to respect or love anything else. We brought this crap on ourselves. You might say we are really getting what we deserve."

She rubbed her cheek against his leg. Her voice was quiet, almost a whisper. "So, what is the answer?"

"So, it is really that simple?"

"Let me clarify. There is no such thing as rejecting God. That's the great fallacy. You become obedient to one god or another. See, we choose. Whenever you give something dominion over you, it becomes your god; you become its slave."

Marla sat back up and held up her glass and stared through it thinking. Personally, she hadn't thought much about God, nor did anyone else she knew. She liked the way Travis talked about it though, because he simplified it. It wasn't complicated. It wasn't religion. It was just plain talk. It was digestible, understandable. She stared at the city lights through her glass and rolled the last of the wine around fascinated by the colors that swirled. The thought about the demise of humanity made her sick.

Marla set her glass down next to the bench and looked out across the rooftop to the lights. She was amazed she had never thought about these things, but now that she considered it, it was all true. Man had brought destruction on himself. Humans didn't treat humans like humans anymore. Life had become disposable. Marla closed her eyes at the revelation. She sat silently thinking. Travis pulled up his pant leg and checked his monitor. He stood up and crept to the edge of the roof. She could see him texting against the backdrop of the city. She heard the sound of a sax somewhere down on the street, and then she heard a guitar; someone was playing it from their apartment. The sax was on one side of the street and the guitar the other. The musicians seemed to be playing into the others song. It was beautiful. Travis stood there listening and then finally sat back down.

"Is everything okay?"

"Yeah, just checking. Everything looks cool. Hear that?"

"They are awesome." Marla took the pins out of her hair and shook it out. "I am going to miss New York."

"One day, we might come back."

"You think?"

"I hope. I love this city."

"Little do they know, I am with the hero that saved the city?"

He shook his head. "It's insane! What did I save them from? What if we can't stop Trisix? Would it be better to be annihilated in an instant by a bomb or turned into a human robot? A soulless Charlotte? Or Al? A mindless bee. Which is the worst fate?"

Consoling, "Travis, you can't think of it like that."

"I do. What are we saving ourselves from? When a person saves a child from a speeding car, rushes into its path and grabs him, what are they really saving him from? You don't know the future. What if that child grows up to become a drug addict and dies with a needle hanging from his arm? Did you save him or did you just postpone hell? And what about the doctor that saves a patient on a table? What did the operation accomplish? Really? Is anyone saved? Extended maybe, but saved?"

"Travis, baby, you can't look at life like that." She blew the hair out of her face and pulled him tight.

Travis contemplated undressing her right there but didn't. He kissed her on her forehead. "I have to. We must

231

study the real purpose of it all. I wonder sometimes what good it would do if we destroy Trisix. Because even if we could go back forty years and start this all over, what lessons have we learned? We would just do the same old thing. Repeat it all over again because we haven't learned. I take no gratification in killing that man today because I am not sure what I am saving us from. Do you understand?"

She shook her head, no. "You think too much. You can't torture yourself with all these thoughts."

"It is all for nothing, Marla, if man doesn't change the way he views the world."

"So how do we do that?"

"We were given a very good example. *Love your God with all your heart, all your mind, and all your soul. And love others as you love yourself.*"

"You are quoting Jesus Christ, right?"

"Absolutely." He reached over to her hand and took her smoke and drew a long drag down into his throat and then exhaled it into the air. He looked at the embers radiating in the ash and held it against the backdrop of the city. "What is so hard about accepting that truth? Would we have *any* problem in the world today if we lived like that? It's that simple."

She paused, thinking. He watched her green eyes in the lights of the city. Travis leaned over and kissed her. She smiled. She was so beautiful and sometimes so innocent, like a child. "You might be right."

"I know I am. If we disable Trisix, there will be chaos for sure. But out of that chaos must come a new revived direction. There must be a commitment and purpose to do things right. We have to see the error of our ways. For the next generation, we must do it...right. Man must live by a higher set of principles and not his own or we will just repeat the failures of the past, and doom is inevitable again."

"Let me see if I have this right. Government sucks." She nudged him and snickered. He started to say something, and she put her fingers on his lips. "Shhhh. I got it. Okay?" Marla rolled her fingers across his lips. "I understand, and I do want to help. You're right. I want to help those around me. I want to help out." Then, it dawned on her, "What about Mrs. Goldstein, Travis is there any way we could take her?"

"We can't, babe; there is no room left, and if she has been chipped...it...it...we just can't risk it. I'm sorry. I would like to."

"But I want to tell her good-bye."

"I know you do, but it is not a good idea. Maybe in the morning right before we leave."

"So when are we leaving? I'm ready."

"First thing in the morning. I've got to go to Grand Central with the key to get the drive. It is in a locker. I am meeting the woman you met earlier today. She is going in. Then, I am meeting you down at the dock, same pier we went to. You have to be there at 10:00; that is when it is leaving."

"What's leaving?"

"Just get on the Ellis Island Ferry. I'll meet you there; there will be others."

"We are going to Ellis Island?"

"No, we are taking a ferry to Ellis Island. There is another boat waiting for us but don't worry about that now. You have to be on that ferry. Now, can you see there is no way you are going to get her on that boat with you? It's just impossible."

"Okay, I believe you." She tugged on his arm, "Let's go inside."

They went back down to her apartment and tip toed

down her hall. Mrs. Goldstein had left another note. She didn't want to, but she knew she had better go over. She surely didn't want her coming over later and interrupting their last night together. Marla put her glass in the sink and began to unbutton his shirt. She kissed him all the way down his chest.

She was breathing heavily across his neck, and her tongue rolled across his shoulder. Marla undid his belt with a tug. "Now, I won't be long, and when I get back, I want you in bed waiting." Her lips kissed him across his nipples, "Have I got a surprise for you."

"That's not a good idea."

"Trust me, I won't be long." She turned the kitchen light off; the candle was still burning. Reluctantly, Marla went across the hall and tapped on Bernice's door, hoping she had gone to sleep. No luck.

She unbolted the door. It was quiet. She saw some boxes packed and taped on her floor.

"Are you moving, Bernice?"

Her face was expressionless. She looked tired; her eyes were droopy like someone that had just been awakened. "Yes," she said flatly, "I am moving with my children."

Marla hadn't ever heard her mention much about her children, and when she started to question her, Mrs. Goldstein cut her off. "I need you to get some things down in my closet. They are too high. I am afraid I might fall."

Marla was glad she had come over. She would have felt terrible if she had fallen on account of her not helping. "Why sure. Where are they?"

Mrs. Goldstein escorted her down the hall and opened the door. Marla walked into the bedroom unsuspecting. The door slammed shut behind her. She turned around. There was a man standing there in a dark trench coat. The closet door opened, and another man came out. She saw the rag in his hand. Instantly, she smelled the odor of chloroform.

Then suddenly, everything in the room went dark.

CHAPTER EIGHTEEN

The face of betrayal has always worn a mask. It can be our brother, our lover, sometimes a child, or even our friend. Marla returned to her apartment after about forty minutes. Travis was nearly asleep when he heard her come through the door. He saw her open the refrigerator and could see her still in her red dress standing in the soft light. She retrieved a bottle of water and then went to the bathroom. Travis waited anxiously. He heard her fumbling through the medicine chest, and then she came back out. All the lights were off except for a tiny plugged-in night light by the bathroom door.

He asked how things were, and she said *fine*. She helped Mrs. Goldstein get some items down from the shelves in her closet and then packed them. Travis then took off her dress and undid her bra. His hands roamed across her breast. She slipped off her own panties and slid under the sheets. Her body was very warm, but the sex was not as good as he hoped. It was brief, and he suspected that the long day and all the anxieties had gotten to her finally. They had for him, but obviously, to a much lesser extent. It was not long thereafter, and she had fallen asleep. Travis was actually relieved. He knew that both of them needed their rest before tomorrow, their last day.

He put his arm around her as she lay on her side facing the wall, and before he knew it, he was out too.

To his surprise, Marla was up before he was the next

morning. In fact, she was already dressed and texting when he walked into the living room.

"Saying good-bye to some friends?" he asked.

"Yes, breakfast is in on the stove."

Travis looked at his watch. There wasn't much time, and they had to leave. He took another shower, a quick one and then came back out drying his hair. She was on her computer and then shut it down when he came in. He ate his bagel with jelly. It was a beautiful day out; the sun was rising over the city. He talked about the island with the local village nearby and the beautiful indigenous people. She seemed busy, that was understandable, but she listened and fed her fish. Then, she put a load of clothes in the washer.

"Hon, you don't need to worry about that. We have to go in fifteen minutes."

"Okay, I'll turn it off. I'll stop."

Travis went to the blinds and peered out the window. He dialed his phone, "You guys still down there?" He flipped the blinds once. "Everybody ready?" She listened to him talking for a few more minutes. It was obvious he was excited. She heard him ask, "Is the ship ready?" He then went over to his belt and pulled out a detector and a stun gun. "I'm traveling light. Okay, see you at the point."

He turned around to Marla, "Are you ready?"

"Yes."

She didn't look that excited, but then Travis knew that her nerves had been shot by the whole ordeal. He knew that her emotions shouldn't hinge on his expectations, or vice versa. As she stood there in the center of the room, he went over last minute details of what they would do. He pulled out the ice tray and dumped it on the counter and then ran warm water over the cube with the key melting it. They were going in different directions. She acted somewhat removed, a bit distant. He dried off the key and slid it into his belt, "Are you listening?"

"Yes."

"Good, because this is it." He went on and explained he was leaving over the rooftops. He would exit from the Henderson building. Travis said he had to get to Grand Central before eight o'clock where he was meeting that woman. After she retrieved the drive from a locker, he would walk from there to the port. He would meet them all at the ferry.

"Who do you mean by all?"

"We are the last dozen. Clark is already out; he got out last night. All the other components are off shore. They are just waiting on us." He pulled the gloves out and tossed them on the counter.

"What about my work?"

"You will need to wear the gloves. When you don't arrive at work on time, they will issue an APB and track your GPS. So it is essential that they can't track you. Your office will be one of the only ones open today, we already know that. It's Good Friday, remember." He shoved them across the counter toward her. "Alright?"

Marla rubbed her forehead and smiled. "Yes."

Travis observed her as he put on his overcoat, the same coat he wore the first night they met. He fixed his belt underneath his shirt, and inquired again. He knew that the strain had been tremendous, "Babe, are you okay?"

"Yes, I'm fine." She nodded politely.

He took her by her arms, "We have to all be on the 10:00 ferry for Ellis Island. Get there early if you can, because they leave right on time."

"And where will it go?"

"I don't know. They don't tell me everything. I just do what I am told." Travis took a deep breath. He pulled her close, "Now, you are going to be okay? We are only…" He stuck out his arm and looked at his watch. "About an hour and a half away. It won't be long."

He pulled out his phone and called someone. Travis walked by the blinds again and looked down the street. "How many are left? Okay, why don't you guys clear out? I've got it. Yeah, yeah, ummm." He looked at Marla. "She'll be wearing a blue dress. Yes, yes, she knows where to go."

Travis went over a few more last minutes details. He instructed her to leave her cell phone there, only take the one he gave her. As a precaution, wear a coat and don't forget to put on the gloves. She needed to go out the back door. The team was leaving; everyone had last minute assignments before they met at the dock. If she got into any trouble, U2. Someone would be there.

Travis looked at how beautiful she was. Her long blonde curls draped across her shoulders. Her eyes that normally sparkled like green effervescent gems were dull. He took hold of her long elegant arm in his hand and pulled her to him. They kissed. He squeezed her body next to his.

"This is what we've always dreamed, right?"

"Right."

He turned his head sideways and looked into her eyes. Travis took a deep breath and brushed the hair back from her face. "I am so glad I came back for you. Life without you would be meaningless. You know that, don't you?"

"Be careful. Don't be late."

He went to the door and started to open it. Travis turned to her still standing where she was. "Marla."

"Yes."

"I love you. I always have."

"Yes. Travis I know."

He stared at her expressionless face. Her eyes were glazed and cold. He started to say something else, but there was nothing else to say. His heart sunk like sand down to his feet. She turned away from him, and he quietly shut the door and left. She went to her window where she texted on the phone. Her head was pounding like a hammer chiseling away into her scalp. Her heart was racing too. She waited and watched, and then she saw him come out the building down the block. He was walking briskly down the sidewalk with his overcoat and hat passing through a crowd of pedestrians. He was nearly half way down the street when she saw the car doors fling open, and the men running to him shouting with their guns drawn. Instantly, the street swarmed with agents. They piled out of cars and rushed from various buildings like a swarm of black ants.

A bead of sweat broke from her brow, and Marla pressed her hand against her temple applying pressure to the pain. She gasped for breath and inhaled several long deep breathes. She felt like she was going to faint. She braced herself on the window ledge and could see Travis spread against a car; the handcuffs were already on him. A dozen uniform officers and even more plain clothes men surrounded him talking on walkie-talkies. A Cage then roared onto the street. She was surprised there was no siren. It was so astonishing quiet, and quick. A group of bystanders were quickly shooed away.

She could see him clearly with his face penned against the hood. An officer's gun was pressed against the back of his head. Marla could see him straining to look up towards her standing in the window of her building. She could see his face, and his eyes met hers. She stood there watching; her temple pounded with pain, and a tear began to roll down the side of her face. She began to cry from the agony. He could see her even as they frisked him. His face and chin were smashed against the hood.

They jerked him up off the car and patted him down. An officer pulled off his belt and held up the key. "Here it is!" Another agent was on a walkie-talkie and gave a description of the woman Travis was to meet at the station. As they shoved him into the back of the cage, Travis was still trying to get a glimpse of her, but her shades were nearly drawn now.

The shackles were clamped on his legs, and they secured his arms and hands to the wall of the Cage. Travis knew what would happen from there. He knew all too well what they would do to him. He knew what was ahead. They slammed the steel cage door shut, and the siren was finally turned on. The loud rattling Cage then turned around and took off down the street.

Marla's phone vibrated; she read the text. It read simply, job *well done.*

The pain began to subside. She took several deep breaths and wiped her tears away. She could still hear the sound of the siren fading off in the distance. She looked down on her table at something he left behind. It was her portrait. She looked for a mere split second. She had a strange urge to cry again, but as the thought and emotion began to well up inside, an incredible intense jabbing surged back through her lobe. It was like an ice pick, shoved into her nerves. Very sharp bursts of instantaneous pain shocked her entire cranium. Her knees suddenly buckled, and she closed her eyes. Marla Jean felt around on the table till she had hold of the portrait in her hand. Then, she crumbled it. As the paper portrait was crushed into the palm of her hand, the pain began to subside. It gradually went away. Finally, it was gone. She felt relief. Marla opened her eyes and went to the kitchen where she tossed it away.

The pain had dulled to no more than a slight headache.

Just then, her phone vibrated again. She didn't want to look; she wanted to crawl in bed and pull the drapes. She felt sick to her stomach. The phone rang again and then again. It was from Charlotte. The message was brief, *Come to work.*

She sighed and took some more deep breaths. She went to her bathroom where she put on eyeliner and touched up her eyebrows. She couldn't even see it herself; it was just beneath the skin at the top of her forehead. It wasn't even noticeable. She looked around her apartment and then at the time. She looked out across the city and the street where traffic was resuming as normal. It looked like a spectacular Mid Solace Day.

She told herself repeatedly as she stood by the window; *it was such a beautiful day, such a beautiful day. She liked to work, she liked to work, she liked to work. It was Mid Solace Day, and…such a beautiful day.*

Shortly thereafter, Marla left her building and passed her neighbors along the street.

"Good morning, Marla."

"Morning, Marla."

"Yes, good morning."

"Yes, good morning."

She gave them not a second glance. She just stared straight ahead walking down through the tall glass menagerie of buildings. A group of men standing at the corner turned her way. She appeared oblivious, weaned of thought. Marla walked trance-like to the station. Saying to herself over and over, *I like to work. I like to work. I like to work.*

The pain in her head had almost completely receded. It dissipated literally with each step she took. Gradually, every other thought disappeared. Gone.

By the time Marla caught the subway to work, she wasn't even sweating anymore. She sat alone as the old train passed through a series of graffiti painted tunnels. She sat solitary, focused on the seat in front of her saying to herself over and over, *Yes, yes, yes, yes it is, it really is…a beautiful day.*

CHAPTER NINETEEN

It was maybe thirty minutes after she had left to take the train. A man stood in the stairwell of the Henderson building texting on a phone. He looked outside at the streets after all the agents and police had cleared. He was a tall man with long hair pulled back in a ponytail. He emerged from the building as a cab pulled up out front. He jumped in back, and the cab quickly pulled away from the curb and shot down the block.

"Can you believe it, Mac?"

He shook his head and looked out the window in back making sure they weren't followed. "We all told him it would happen."

"So you think he knew?"

"Yes, he knew."

"What did he say?"

"You know how he is; he would never say anything against her. He said, *We were right; they finally got to her,*' and then he handed me the drive." Mac held it up in his hand.

"So, when did it happen?"

"Last night. He could see it in her eyes this morning before he left."

TD looked alarmed. "He didn't tell her about the plane did he?"

"Nah. She thinks the plan is to leave from the ferry." Mac looked at the chip in his hand and put it back in the lighter. "They think the chip is at the station. So it all worked as planned."

"Damn that Travis. She was a great lady, but why would he take the risk?"

"Freedom didn't mean anything without her. You know how he was."

TD shook his head as their cab turned on to the entrance ramp to the freeway. He checked his watch and looked at Mac in back. "Man that sucks. He has gotta hurt."

"Don't you know it? You know what is killing him though? He wasn't even thinking what they would do to him. He was thinking of what they will do to her. He said it was like the life was sucked out of her. She was a living corpse. It was like she wasn't even Marla."

"He tried."

"Yeah, he tried alright."

They accelerated down the freeway through relatively light traffic. The two men looked solemnly at the river as they cruised along, knowing it would be the last time they'd see their city. TD kept shaking his head; he couldn't understand it. "Why would a man do something like that? Why make himself a sacrifice?"

"That's what love is. It's a sacrifice, bro. What would you do for your wife?"

TD looked out his side mirror making sure he wasn't followed. "But did she know?"

"You mean, who he really was?"

"You mean, who he had been?"

"No. He never told her that he created Trisix. He made up something, I guess. It is hard for some people to understand just how much a person is capable of changing. If we did get her out of the city, alive, without the chip, we had strict orders to never to tell her."

Mac looked at the drive and placed it back in the magnetic container. He handed it across the seat to TD who put it under the dash. They drove for a few more miles, and then Mac looked at his watch, "Punch it, TD; our plane is waiting."

In less than an hour, a rather obscure older aircraft with props eclipsed the edge of the city. Henry and Mac and the dozen or so passengers looked out the port holes taking one final last glimpse of Manhattan as they made their way to sea. Their mission was accomplished. It had all gone as planned, except of course for Marla and Travis. They didn't make it; though, they came close.

It was a spectacular sight; the sun was shining down on the glittering city. They could see the ships pulling into ports and the planes circling preparing for landing. Beyond the harbor were hundreds if not thousands of merchant ships waiting to dock. It looked like an armada of cruise ships, cargo ships all carrying their goods to port. And as they looked back one last time, from a distance, the city appeared a radiant golden color, golden as honey, shimmering in the crystalline light.

They all knew then, they may never see the place again. If the neutron chip failed, the city they loved would virtually become what Travis always said it would be; a colony...a Trisix Colony. The future of the world was in their hands. They knew not whether they would be successful or if their efforts would fail. All they knew for sure was that it was Good Friday, and they were free.

OMEGA

The Afterword

Originally I had thought about writing a book based strictly on fact that would be informative but not too entertaining. Now that you have been entertained, I would be remised if I did not present you with the facts which were the motivation for writing the Trisix Colony. All the technologies mentioned in the Trisix Colony are already in use or are being developed for deployment. Laws have been written on both a national and international scale to strip of us our freedoms and impose implementation of human micro chipping. Most of these laws I might add have never withstood public scrutiny. They have been adopted through a long series of Executive Orders or written into treaties, but nevertheless are on the books, yet to be enforced.

I might add, we have made incredible advances in technology, and we have all no doubt benefited tremendously. Technology is not the problem, nor is it necessarily the companies that manufacture and design them. The problem is how they are being used, and who is using it. In America, we are fortunate to have the very best and most inventive companies who have led nearly all major technological advances. The problem that is occurring with more frequency is the use of technology at the detriment of personal freedoms and liberties. Our constitution has for all these years been the great protector of our freedoms and liberties. We've had laws protecting us against unreasonable searches, laws that protected our privacy, a court system that guaranteed us fair trials. We had the right to ownership of property. All these are being attacked, stripped from us like clothing one tear at a time.

This book was written for you, your freedoms, your children's freedom. It was written with the sole intent to free you. Many in our country have lived blind, "comfortably numb." Television has tranquilized their perception of reality and confused them with half-truths. For them, for you, I have outlined here for your convenience a brief synopsis of what is happening in the United States and around the world. I urge you not to take my word. Let me repeat, I urge you not to take my word. Research these things on your own using the means you have and your God-given brain and thirst for knowledge. You have the ability to become informed and intelligent. Let nothing and no one stop you from truth. Challenge me and my assertions; that is good. I would challenge you. I am suspicious by nature and have always questioned authority. Discover for yourself what is truth and then take action. Confront tyranny or be enslaved by it. That has been the historical challenge of all mankind.

May God help us, help you, and help our children. He is good. He is our only hope.

GENERAL TECHNOLOGY

1. Big Dog. Big Dog is a four-legged robotic creature which can carry a payload in excess of 200 pounds and leap with the agility of a deer over a fence. Big Dog was funded by DARPA, the Defense Advanced Research Projects Agency and Boston Dynamics. www.Bostondynamics.com

2. Drones. Every size drone is being produced by our government today for use on both the federal and local levels. Here is a list of

the most popular deployed UAV's (Unmanned Aviation Vehicle) in use today.

Raven: RQ-11 Made by AeroVironment, this craft can fly up to 6.2 miles and weighs no more than 4.2 pounds. It is the ideal spy drone and contains an array of spy equipment including cameras with infrared lenses. The Raven was used extensively in Afghanistan by the military in reconnoitering operations. www.aeroviroment.com

Hummingbird: This drone was also built by AeroVironment and funded by DARPA as well. It is an amazingly adroit spy craft with a wing span of 6.5 inches. The Hummingbird weighs only 19 grams and looks and flies just like a hummingbird moving backwards and sideways. It is the perfect spy craft though it is limited in air flight time. It can move outside a window just like a hummingbird, view the occupants and then fly off to a secure location. www.areoviroment.com

Predator: Built by General Atomics Aeronautical Systems, Inc. (AF-ASI). This drone was built originally to just be for surveillance, but in late 2000, Hellfire missiles were attached. It has been used extensively in Afghanistan and in time will also be being replaced with the Reaper which is also built by General Atomics. The Reaper flies much faster with speeds up to 260 knots and will have an attitude max of nearly 50,000 feet. It will be able to carry ten times the payload (two tons) of its predecessor.

www.ga-asi.com

The X-37B spy plane: This new spy plane recently made its test debut. It is a large drone plane that can orbit for over 250 days and land itself in similar method as the space shuttle. This is the ultimate spy plane or big eye in the sky. This plane can fly easily at attitudes of 180 miles up making it vastly superior to all previous spy planes. www.boeing.com

3. Future Attribute Screening Technology (FAST):

Created by the Department of Homeland Security, this technology is in essence a lab module that will be used in airports, borders and other locations to detect "mal-intent" by screening people using a variety of techniques including pupil dilation, pulse rate, breathing speeds, skin temperatures and various other physiological factors as well as psychological indicator. [www.theatlantic.com/technology/archieve/2012/04/homeland-security-pre-crimescreening]

4. Advanced human monitoring capabilities. Closed –circuit television (CCTV). There are believed to be now over 30 million surveillance cameras in use in the United States, but other technologies are emerging. Here are a few.

Video Content Analysis (VCA):

VCA can detect unusual patterns such as people walking faster than others in a crowd or in the opposite direction. More importantly it has the ability to virtually track people on a map by calculating their position from images and link it to other camera feeds and track them through an

entire   building.
[www.2020imaging.com/brochures_whitepaers/vi
deo_content_analysis_(bsia)pdf]   bsia (British
Security Industry Association).

Facial recognition systems: This system
automatically identifies a person (suspect) via
digital facial features. It will eventually be
integrated to pick up and identify a person in a
worldwide   data   base.
[www.epic.org/privacy/facerecognition/]

IP (Internet Protocol) cameras: Integrated
technologies allow an individual to monitor others
through one or multiple cameras from remote
locations anywhere in the world using Local Area
Networks   (LANs).
[www.wilkipedia.org/wiki/Internet_Protocol]

Remote audio spy monitors:

Sigard, a Dutch company has developed an
audio spy system that is connected to CCTV units.
Amazingly, it can monitor a conversation from a
hundred yards away and filter out background
noise in environments such as airports and
subways.
[www.telegraph.couk/technology/news/7870928
/Surveillance-system-monitros-conversations]

THE CHIP

The microchip was approved by the FDA to
be implanted in the sub dermal   (under the skin)
in humans on October 13th, 2004. The technology
has gained growing acceptance mainly in the medical
field but also has met resistance. Several states have

already banned companies from forcing workers to take the chip. These states are California, Wisconsin and North Dakota.

Applied Digital Solutions which is one of the world's largest makers of GPS and RFID products owned a percentage of VeriChip Corp. and then merged VeriChip with another company called Steel Vault, a national credit agency. This new company is now called Positive ID and is a leading developer in microchip technology. In 2010, the company discontinued making the human implantable chip due to reports about cancer that resulted in lab rats. The concerns about this technology are growing not only for medical concerns but because of privacy issues, and as a result, many privacy groups have formed to challenge the use of this technology. Linking personal information, medical data, credit (banking) information in a chip with possible GPS applications is considered by many to be a threat to civil liberties. [Wikipedia.org/wiki/microchip_implant_(human); www.wilkipedia.org/wiki/PositiveID; www.wired.com/threat/2009/12/positive_id/; www.cbsnews.com/8301-505123_162-42843185/microchip-implant-controversy-a-mark-of-the Beast-or-the-coming-singular, by Jim Edwards; Spy Chips by Katherine Albrecht and Liz McIntyr.

House Bill 3200 in the original Affordable Health Care Act (ObamaCare) did have language which would have made mandatory medical data sub dermal implants of the ObamaCare recipients. This version of the bill was restricted; however, it came dangerously close to becoming law.

Nevertheless, governments have not been deterred from implementing microchips. Recently, our military has authorized the use of chips to be imbedded in U.S. soldiers. The array of features in this chip is somewhat startling in that they can monitor a soldier's physiology during combat. Furthermore, it is capable of dispensing medicines to the carrier. [www.mobiledata.com/news/134354html] Kate Knibbs.

In India, measures are being taken at this time to use biometrics to keep a data base on all 1.2 billion of their citizens. The biometrics will include iris scanning, DNA and fingerprinting. It is the first of what many consider to be the first national data base system using primary biometrics for citizen identification.

GOVERNMENT USE OF SPY TECHNOLOGY:

Federal and local governments are combining efforts to now use drones to spy on citizens. Here are just a few of the latest reports.

1. Drones are now being used by government agencies to spy on farmers. A North Dakota family was arrested for not returning six cows that had come onto their 3,000 acre ranch. Local law enforcement agencies used the Predator to spy on them from the air. [www.dailymail.co.uk/news/article-2073248/Local-cops-useddrones]

2. The EPA is now using drones to spy on cattle ranchers in Nebraska. Fox News reported

that EPA officials said that flights are being used on farmers. Spying "over a swath of Midwest the agency calls Section 7 which is composed of Nebraska, Iowa, Kansas and Missouri." [http:wisupnorth.com/2012//06/epa-using-drones-to-spy-on-farmland/]

3. The city of San Francisco is said to be installing 288 new cameras in buses, subways and other transportation systems according to The Daily Mail. The new systems built by BRS Labs "have the ability to track up to 150 suspects at a time; the cameras build up a "memory" of suspicious behavior to determine what constitutes potential criminal activity."

[www.infowars.com/san-francisco-to-tet-pre-crime-surveillance]

CLONING

Cloning has been going on for some time. Here is a historical list of the developmental advances.

1952 Briggs and King cloned tadpoles.

1996 The first mammal was cloned. Dolly the sheep became the first   clone from adult stem cells.

1998 mice were cloned.

2000 dogs were cloned.

2001 the first cat was cloned.

2002 rabbits were cloned

2003 a mule was cloned, the ass wasn't. They figured we already

had enough of them in the world.

2004 a bull was cloned from a cloned bull, called serial cloning.

2001 the first human embryos were cloned but only to a six cell stage.

Today, we are eating cloned products. "The Advisory Committee on Novel Foods and Processes (UK) authorized the sale of foodstuffs from cloned animals. The panel's conclusions mirror those in 2008 of the US food and drug administration's five year study which found that cloned meat and milk were indistinguishable from traditional meat and milk."

[www.guardian.co.uk/uk/2012/nov/26/scientist -all-clear-cloning]

A growing consensus among scientist is that cloning (advanced cell technology) is not normal in the human or mammal environment except when twinning. As of today, cloning still results in a high number of birth defects and clinical failures; nevertheless, it is even being advanced and advocated by many international groups. [www.actionbioscience.org/biotech/megee.html]

INTERNATIONAL AND NATIONAL LAWS:

Agenda 21: In 1992, 177 assembled in Rio to adopt Agenda 21. Under the guise of a green movement this agenda uses the terminology "Sustainable Development" as the catalyst for controlling all aspects of human life including reproduction, private property ownership, energy use, single family homes, private cars and transportation and even family farms. It supersedes national law and is an affront to national sovereignty. Unfortunately for us the tenants of Agenda 21 were signed into law via Executive Order #12858 in 1995 without consent or preview of Congress.

[www.theblaze.com/stories/is-the-soros-sponsered-agenda-21-a-hidden-plan-for-worldgovernment-yes-only-it-is-not-hidden/]

House bill 347 made it a federal offense to cause a disturbance at certain political events. Signed into law 2012. The National Defense Resources Preparedness Executive Order gives the President power to grant the Secretary of Agriculture authority to allocate food resources, livestock and farm equipment. Five other agencies under his command have the authority to control various utilities such as energy sources, water and transportation in any state emergency. [www.rt.com/usa/news/obama-executive-order-national-9291]

MANY MORE ORDERS GIVE THE PRESIDENT VERY GREAT POWERS TO CONTROL COMMERCE IN CASE OF "EMERGENCY."

Revelations on a Stranger Passing Truth

Condensed volumes of enormous truths
Outside my window one evening fell
I awoke and...much later a stranger...
Their revelations to all I can now tell

What we think is, is not
What we think has been, will be
We learn to know God
Or godlessness is all we learn,
The Universe is a state
*   of perfect balance*
Man is unsettled in unparalleled contradictions,
In revolution the earth constantly turns
In rebellion man will never change

Why me I pondered on this night
Where else on earth might these volumes fall
Watching meteors rocket cross the sky
I read their signs, I studied them all

We can never be self-governed
Until we relinquish our control
We are slaves to liberation
When freedoms are our master
Substance is immaterial
When we are filled with emptiness
We have succeeded in achieving failure
When we cannot find our mistakes

So long I've wanted to be touched by truth
Outside my window...the stranger moved...
Throughout my mind these thoughts were felt
As a woman's fingers through my scalp

...their gentle touch was smooth

We can be united by the boundaries that divide us
Or separated by the things we share
Our greatest battle has been with peace
We take great pleasure in seeking misery
We hate to love each other...
We love to hate ourselves
We are rapidly going nowhere
But we are arriving there right on time.

Inspiration is kindled from the splintered spark
of truth
The stars are the light of another world's day
Comfort awaits me in the wee hours away
Heaven is never more than one heartbeat away.

Technology is not the answer
But the mass production of a lie
We consume tons of information
Spoonfuls of knowledge
And wisdom in droplets over time,
The greatest discovery in science to come
Will be how it is used by man
If history repeats itself
Our future has long been past.

Condensed volumes of enormous truths
Outside my window one evening fell
I awoke and...much later the stranger...
In me moved to tell *(you)*.

1992

Victims of the Night

A shadow chases her in her sleep
Down long and deserted mean city streets
Bricks burn hot boils to her bare feet
No place to run...No place to hide
She is just another Victim of this Night...

SCREAMS of passion...cryyyys of pain
the drunken neighbors said
    they sound the same
but one was dead, and one was slain.
A crowd came together to watch
chalked silhouettes pose for the camera flash
and as a stranger leaves
    clues are tossed into the trash.
Walkie-talkies later play
a top ten serenade
a door is kicked down in a midnight raid
the long arm of flashing blue light
pulsates on top of a black and white,
a megaphone yells, the orders given
the answers follow in rapid gun fire
black bleeds red in every hour
And miles of neon haze away...
two cops dunk chocolate doughnuts
and soak their cuffs in coffee stains
the hooker likes hers creamed filled
the junkie likes his glazed

in walks the pimp who's been short changed
Bang! Bang! Bang! Bang!
Add to the nights tally
    another four more
Blood across the counter
    Blood's across the floor

The city is quiet by the morning sun
    rising from the trash bins climb the bums
    newspapers plop on the suburban steps
    and a father leaves the bedroom
    where his oldest daughter slept.
    The city is rampant with crime in the streets
    but hidden from the public's view
    are the (quiet) crimes
    on flowered covered linen sheets.
And, a shadow chases her in her sleep
    down the long and deserted city streets.

MAXWELL

Words of wisdom from father to son
   please don't do all the things I have done
   in those loving eyes of yours I see
   me, in my youth, looking back at me
Oh, my precious loving son
   if you only knew all the things I've done
   perhaps you could not bear to see
   all those things that I would be
But I want you to learn the lessons of life
   that in my youth I wish I was taught
   to be courageous, honest, unselfish and kind
   for these are things that I was not
I want you to be a better man than me
   to resist temptation, to fight for good
   I want you to know that I have failed
   to do many things that I knew I should
When I look into your loving eyes
   I pray you'll be spared my heartaches
   so I've opened my life to you as a book
   for you to see where I made my mistakes
And I hope someday that you might say
   when looking at your loving son
   that if he's to find great joys in life
   that he should do just as you have done.

WILL YOU WALK THE STREETS ALONE?

Where will you be when He comes
Will you walk the streets alone
      Will you be one that He will greet
      Or will you be like the people
      Vanished from the city streets
         Hiding in their homes?
Will you be there to see the light
Will you hear the trumpets blare
      Or will you hide in your shame
      For you did not really care?
      And if *you* were God, how would it feel
         The creator of the Universe
         The greatest giver and forgiver
         The mother and father of all birth
         If this is the reception you received
            When *you* returned to earth?
Will you my brother, my lover, my friend
Will you, yes *YOU*
      Come take that long walk with me
      Past the churches, past the steeples
      Past all the hidden little people
Will you take that long walk with me
      Hand in hand down the empty streets?
Will you meet me on the corner
      On that day the world will end
And will *YOU* walk the streets alone
      If no one else is there, for Him?

Polar

She hadn't taken her medicine. Debra Ann had just run out when she opened the medicine cabinet and found the clear finger nail polish hiding behind the band aids. Trevor wouldn't be back till Sunday evening. He was on a hunting trip with Carlton, if he really was hunting. She gripped the tiny clear bottle in her hand, *'I'll find out.'*

They were supposed to be married in two weeks. There would be a slim chance of that now. She had evidence, and it was a good thing she had already began moving her things into his apartment or she might have never known. Debra Ann was filled with rage. Trevor had told her he wasn't seeing anyone else, but Debra Ann knew he was. Liar. All the signs were there. He was always late; nobody worked as many long hours as he claimed. Supper would be cold when he got home, and sometimes he said he was too tired to eat. Sure. But, there were plenty of other things too like the way he always seemed to quickly end his conversations on the phone when she entered the room. "I've got to go. She's here." Besides nobody talks to their mother that much, or their boss. Trevor always seemed to have good excuses, but Debra Ann knew better. He was charming and handsome. He knew he could get away with anything.

Debra Ann went all throughout the house that morning looking for evidence, letters, cards, anything. Trevor wasn't stupid; he wasn't about to leave messages on his phone machine to give himself away. She went to his laptop and checked his emails. He would have been way too careful to leave love messages from some skank on his phone. Not Trevor. She knew that, the gall of him. As she scrolled through the deleted messages, she kept looking for a suspicious name to pop up. He knew lots of women, men too for that matter; but as a sports writer, he covered many women's sports on campus as well as men's. There were indeed lots of emails from women, tons! "Thanks for the article, Trevor." "Our tournament starts next week, hope you're there." "The nationals are next month, can you come?"

"Yeah, right, come you slut!" Debra Ann could barely stand to read them. She knew he was probably banging all of them. She couldn't remember how many times she had called him on the road, and he said the game ran late. That was always a convenient excuse, and then of course, he had to write the article and get it in before the deadline. He couldn't talk. *Yeah, right.* He probably had a soccer player spread out like a cheap blanket in the back of his car or a cheerleader doing the splits in his bed. Trevor was good looking and smart. She knew he picked a profession where he could get away almost every weekend for a romp. There would be an endless supply of women and excuses. He had done nothing but lead her on from the first year in college. No one is such a total fake to help a girl with a broken leg get to her classes. He liked playing the Good Samaritan, the all American boy. Made it easier to get his way, to use people. That's all.

Debra Ann lit a cigarette and tried to think. She knew he didn't like her smoking in his apartment. He was so bossy, but she didn't care. He was a jerk about it; he kinda rubbed it in. He was the epitome of health, never smoked and rarely drank, ran three times a week, lifted weights. What was he trying to prove? That he was better than she was? She wasn't good enough? She slipped the ashes on the carpet and rubbed them in with her foot. She hoped the smell wouldn't go away. She didn't care. Screw him and the patches anyway. Some gift! The conceited bastard. Who gives smoking patches to his fiancé as a present? Only jerks do that.

That morning, Debra Ann scrolled through hundreds of deleted emails, maybe thousands, reading each and every one of them. She realized Trevor was probably way too smart. He surely used different email addresses. He had several; so she began to check them all. She knew all his pass codes; that was easy. They were all boring work related junk. Staff meeting, deadlines, travel schedules, crap. There had to be more; she knew there was. Debra Ann ended up going through emails until midafternoon when suddenly she remembered Trevor's Facebook page. She was a complete idiot. She should have started there first, of course.

Goldmine. He was probably screwing fifty women. OMG. They were everywhere. Mr. Popular. Sure, most of the friends were guys, jocks, fans or bloggers, but there were loads of chicks, loads. Old classmates, girls from church, women sports' announcers, players. They were everywhere. The marriage in comparison seemed a ruse. There were pics of them, of course, but he never put the best ones of her on there. She looked too fat in her ski outfit last spring in Aspen. And the one on the beach, she had burned in the sun that day, and her hair was a mess. In all of them, he was always smiling, sure he was. He was a cheat and getting away with it.

It made her sick to look at his page. There were his "friends" (ho's) who all said they were so happy for him getting married to his love. *Make me sick.* "Congrats, Julie!" "Will miss you, Brooke." "Ahhh, what a sweet couple, Kat." Ho's, all ho's. Shelly from church is enough to make one sick, the little saint slut. "May God richly bless you two always. Friend in Christ, Shelly."

Debra Ann was furious. It was like he was flouting it in front of the world. Rubbing it in her face, but she caught on. She knew what was happening. Sure, he told her he loved her, and he adored her sense of humor. Sure he did, he loved to laugh alright. He was probably laughing every day at her. She was the fool. How cruel can you get? Two weeks from getting married, and he's still carrying on with these sluts. How can a guy just diss his finance like that? What kind of psycho pimp is he anyway?

That night, she went on his Facebook account checking out all his friends. It was total bull, complete cover; especially how Shelly and Kat, the whores, said he was such a wonderful friend. She hated both of them. Kat was everything she hated, looked like a model in all her pics, blonde, blue eyes. Probably spent all her money whoring to get plastic surgery. Nobody is that perfect. And Shelly, that fake, it is all an act. Nobody is that humble. Mission trips, feeding the poor? Yeah, right. Who in their right mind would want to go down to the jungles of Costa Rica for a year and help children learn to read? *Give me a freakin' break.* Just a front for a tramp. Probably some nymph. Shelly does a village. Who is she trying to impress? Trevor, that's who.

Debra Ann couldn't stand it anymore. It was getting late; she had had enough. She turned off the laptop and went to bed, but even the sheets smelled funny. He had been using a detergent with Febreze lately. Why? He used to use the cheap stuff. Why the sudden change? Was he trying to cover up some chick's perfume? Surely it wasn't that humble mousey pathetic Shelly. No, it had to be that tramp Kat, the reporter for KXIM. That's who it probably was. They hooked up while she was at her parent's house making wedding plans. It's why he didn't answer her calls that night after the game was over. He wasn't finishing a story. He wasn't too tired. That's bull. It was the tenth inning, and he rounded all the bases and was heading home. That's what was happening. He was diving in head first. Score. That bastard!

Debra Ann couldn't sleep. She tossed and turned, wringing the sheets in her hands like they were somebody's throat. She couldn't take it. She would not be humiliated like that anymore. She rolled over on top of the pillow straddling it and started beating it with her fist wailing away, crushing her competitor's face with each blow. Debra Ann swung and swung, punching the pillow and squeezing its throat. Her knuckles turned red and started to bleed. Speckles of blood were all over the pillowcase and on the sheets. She stopped, finally, and sat exhausted in bed before getting up and going to the next room where she curled up in a blanket on the couch. She slept like a kitten for the rest of the night having gotten her revenge. It felt good, real good, satisfying.

She wasn't through though. She wanted more.

-SUNDAY EVENING-

She was all smiles when he came in. "Hi, honey." Debra Ann laughed and leaped off the couch as he set his gear by the door. "Tell me. How did you do? Come on, where's your buck?"

He put his rifle in the closet in the entry way. "Do you have to ask?"

"Of course."

"Carlton got a ten point. I got my usual cold. Swear all I saw all weekend were does."

"Ahhh." She kissed him. "I'm so glad your home, babe. I've missed you."

Trevor leaned against the wall bracing himself and slipped off his boots and left them by the door. He knew better than to track mud all throughout the house. "So what have you been doing, D. Ann?"

"Nothing. Just washing clothes, sheets."

He smiled, "Can you believe it? Less than two weeks now. Did you finish with all the arrangements? Everything done? Set?"

"Oh yeah, it's all I worked on. Why don't you relax? I've got something cooked for you, new recipe. I want to see if you like it."

"What is it?"

"My special homemade stew." She giggled, "It's to die for."

"Give me a few minutes. Lemme shower first."

Debra Ann said that was okay and set the table while he washed in the shower. When Trevor came out, he noticed there was only one setting at their table. Surprised, "Aren't you going to eat?"

"I did, honey." She patted her belly. "But I have to lose a few more pounds before the wedding."

"You look fine. Come on."

"No I don't. I look fat."

"You're not fat."

"Well plump."

"Whatever." He rolled his eyes and began eating the stew. It tasted different. A little strange, but a man doesn't want to hurt the feelings of his new wife so he finished the bowl and then had another. He was hungry, starved in fact. Carlton was a great friend but a terrible cook. The eggs had been bland and soggy that morning. He hadn't eaten much all day, and so the stew was great. It had lots of vegetables which he needed. He planned on running the next morning and would need the energy.

As he ate, they talked about the wedding. Debra Ann was bubbling with enthusiasm. She kept going on about St Croix, what they would do and see. She hadn't applied for jobs, but she would when she got back. It wasn't really a concern though to Trevor. He had a job that provided ample income for the two of them.

After dinner, she cleaned up. He stretched out on the couch and watched some NFL highlights. The pennant races were heating up, especially in the National League, but Trevor was always more of a football fan than anything else. He could hear her washing dishes in the kitchen and putting things up. When she was done, she went to the laundry room and pulled out some fresh sheets. She came back in to where he was lying, "Getting sleepy yet?"

Trevor reached over and picked up a corner of the sheets and took a whiff. "Um, smells good. Need some help?"

"Nope. I've got it." A few minutes later, she came back out after making the bed. "All done. Ready? You have a big day tomorrow."

Trevor groaned and sat up. He was exhausted and perhaps ate too much. He rubbed his stomach and then rubbed his eyes, "Yeah, I'm hittin' the sack. Big week coming up for sure. We're playing Bama."

"Come on. Your bed is ready."

Trevor turned off the T.V. and went to the bedroom where he climbed in under the fresh sheets and comforter. He had indeed caught a cold that weekend and felt a chill. Before he closed his eyes, he set the alarm and was out like a light. Debra Ann smiled, "Good night my dear. Sleep well...forever".

It was the last thing she said if he heard her at all.

The dispatcher at 3:00 am recorded the call. It was most unusual to say the least, especially for calls at that hour. Most people that call in are hysterical. She wasn't. The voice on the line was soft and meek. She didn't say a lot only that her boyfriend had been hurt. "They might want to get here quick. It looks bad."

Debra Ann warmly greeted the officers at the door almost as if it were an open house. She had dressed, and her hair was done just like she was planning on going out. She smiled strangely at the officers when they arrived and pointed to the bedroom. "He's in there." The rifle was lying on the bed, almost at his feet. His hands were tied to the bed post with neck ties, presumably slipped over his wrists while he slept. There were things scribbled on the wall in blood, names. They were hard to read because the letters dripped over each other in long slender red runs. There must have been seven or eight names written on the wall above the headboard. There was the splatter of blood everywhere, the wall, lamps, the clock, chest of drawers, everything. It was definitely a close range blast, probably no more than two or three feet away.

As the first two officers looked in, Debra Ann calmly went to the living room and sat down reading a People magazine, lightly humming. Instantly, the officers stepped back. They knew not to go any further. They looked in the room at the carnage and then over to her reading perfectly composed on the couch. She just smiled.

"Ma'am."

"Yes."

"Did you do this?"

She turned the page and winked at them. "That's right, Sherlock." Then she began humming again and turned the page.

Other officers arrived soon thereafter then the coroner, and it wasn't long and the street was filled with cop cars. They took Debra Ann down to the station where she was interrogated. Veteran Detectives Riley and Jones conducted the questioning of the mild mannered little woman with her hair in curls. She seemed so matter of fact, stunningly calm. Trevor had been cheating on her. She knew that. He was about to lure her into a marriage, a "death trap." He was running around on her, and she knew it; she had discovered the evidence that weekend.

"Like what?" The detective asked.

"Nail polish. Some skank left it there."

Curious, "What kind of nail polish?"

"Clear. Don't know the brand. Something cheap I think."

"And you said he is a hunter, right?" The two officers looked at each other confused. "Is that it?"

"Oh, and the pantyhose. I found them in his dirty clothes. The dirt bag didn't even try to hide them. That's why he didn't get any deer. He wasn't hunting, not deer anyway. He was screwing around."

The two men looked at each other. They had already checked out Carlton. He had gone hunting alright. Two other friends had gone along as well. They spent the weekend together, and it rained both Saturday and Sunday.

The two detectives couldn't believe what they were hearing. It was beyond strange. They couldn't figure this woman out, but both were hunters like Trevor. Some things made sense.

Detective Riley looked at his partner then at the petite young woman. She was cute, nothing breathtaking but attractive. Debra Ann seemed amazingly calm. She was polite, courteous and even cheerful. They had never seen anyone quite like her in all the years they were police officers. Riley leaned over and whispered to Jones. Jones listened and then nodded. Riley then asked, "Debra Ann, may I ask you another question?"

"Got all day." She smiled sweetly, "Well, I guess I have all night, right? Go ahead, shoot."

"Have you ever gone hunting? Ever go hunting with Trevor?"

"Nope. The woods are not for me."

"Ever camp much?"

"Never. I like my bed way too much."

"Do you know what chiggers are?"

"Oh, I've heard, and you can keep those things away from me."

"They are little bugs. Can't see them, but they itch like crazy. They get under the skin. You know how to kill them?"

"Not a clue. Medicine I'm guessing?"

"That would be a good guess, but that would be wrong. People use finger nail polish. Clear. It covers up the sore where they have festered, and they can't breathe."

The expression on her face suddenly turned chalky flat. The perky smile vanished. Washed away. It was gone. Suddenly she looked confused. "Nail polish?" The words barely made it out of her mouth.

"That's right. And do you know what hunters use sometimes to insulate their legs? Especially deer hunters because deer hunters sit up in deer stands for hours at a time. It gets cold, and the wind turns their legs to ice especially when the temperatures are near freezing and it's been raining. They can't move around, and it is easy to get frost bite so they have to insulate their legs you see. You know what some use to keep warm? I've done it."

"What?"

"They use panty hose. And sometimes they will put a layer of long johns over that if it is really, really cold".

Debra Ann sat there looking bewildered at the two cops. "Panty hose? Are you sure?"

"Yes ma'am. I'm afraid we are".

She looked dazed. There was no pain in her face just the look of confusion like someone who had just been told something she couldn't comprehend. She looked away and down to the floor like maybe there might actually be something resembling reality. There wasn't; it was all dreams and nightmares, nothing in between. She had drifted in and out of them her whole life. She seemed so dazed that for a second they thought she might have gone to sleep or something. She looked like she was in a trance.

"Debra Ann."

She looked up from the floor and smiled. "Yes."

"Is there anything you want to say? Anything you want to add?"

She shook her head, no, and stared back down at the floor again. The two men gathered their notes and the recorder and were about to leave the room when she spoke up. "Yes, there is one more thing."

Jones unlocked the door and asked, "What's that?"

"I think I'm out of medicine. There was none in the apartment and I really need to get some or I, ah, I sorta go off…the deep end. I'm ah, a…."

"We know Debra Ann. We know. The doctor is on the way."

-the end-

WHO, WHO ARE YOU?

She heard a board squeak down the hall
  the shadow of death crept along a wall
  alone and frighten she could only stare
"Who are you?" she whispered
  "Who is there?"
No one else was at her home
  the batteries were dead in her cell phone
  she slipped her feet down to the floor
  but it was already standing behind her door
  then...the cold figure entered her room
  frozen in fear she could hardly move
  the figure of death crept closer still
  she knew it was there that night to kill.
There was no sign of struggle
  when her roommate returned,
  nothing out of place; and nothing they would learn
      just cold and naked
          lying dead
    with her little bottle of pills
          beside her bed.

dedicated to Amy W.

Note: According to the National Institute of Drug Abuse, 20,000 deaths occurred last year in the US that are attributed to prescription drugs, equal to deaths attributed to illicit drugs. More people died from prescription drugs than were murdered. The National Survey on Drugs found in 2006, 2,000,000 youth met the criteria of drug abuse and/or dependency in America.

your mother and I...

Why do you hate me? Hate us?

Why do you hold me in such contempt?

Did we not defend you? Nourish you?

Make you? Your grandparents too?

You are so self-righteous, so smug

Disrespectful; intolerant of others views

So set in having your own way.

Did I not give you the best years of my life?

Is this the love we get, your mother and I?

You look upon us as the enemy. Why?

Just answer me, (if you have the courage)

Give us some explanation for your rationale.

But before you condemn me further

May I ask why you constantly lie?

Why must you cheat us and steal from us?

Why do you abuse us, the hands that feed you still?

Why are you such a pompous hypocrite?

Don't you know it is you who needs us

And not us who needs you?

I know the answer to that, but you don't

Your mother and I have one last question...

      why are you our government?

THE SWITCH ON THE WALL

Someplace inside of me
   there is a switch on a wall
   Sometimes it's at my fingertips
   sometimes it's down the hall
   Sometimes I turn it on
   to do what I need to do
   or do whatever I can
   Sometimes I must search to find it
   to do what I have to do
   in order to be a man.
Someplace deep inside of me
   there is a switch on a wall
   Sometimes I'm afraid to find it
   when it gets dark down the hall
   Sometimes I turn it on
   just to take a good look inside of me
   to find the courage I lost
   Sometimes I don't like what I see
   and I turn the switch off.
Someplace deep inside of me
   there is a switch on a wall
   but isn't there a switch
Someplace inside us all?

THE FACTORY

It was his first month on the job. Times had been tough, and Johann was thankful for work. The Editor told him to write a feature about the industrialization. The world was in a great depression, and Johann himself knew the pangs of hunger having himself struggled through three years of unemployment. Personally, his family had lost everything. Outside their meager abode, beggars trolled the streets, and shameful faces hid behind dark hoods and rattling tin cups at the passer-byers. The industrialization was thought good.

Johann looked at the clock; it was 5:00, time to leave. He put his papers in his satchel and grabbed his hat and coat, then whisked down the flight of stairs into the street. He had three days to write his assignment and could write it at home. Along the way, he decided to stop at a bodega for a beer which he hadn't done in a long time for he hadn't a mark to spare. It was rather dark, and the air was full of smoke, but the beer came from his favorite brewery. It poured from the keg with lathery foam and tasted wet and rich like a woman's lips after a long day of work.

Johann waded through the shoulder-high smoke and took a spot at the end of the long dark mahogany bar in the dim lit room of rowdy older men with felt hats and dripping mustaches. Their conversation was lively and boisterous. He took the first drink and licked the suds from his face like he was licking a woman's body, his wife's. The beer was delicious. He leaned back and listened. They hardly noticed him. When he was almost done, he decided to ask them what they thought about the "industrialization." He knew they all had opinions. "Was it good?" Every head in the room turned toward him in silence as if he were a ghost.

Afterward a long awkward moment, they all clamored together, "Das is goot!"

"Yah, we're building auto. Arbit (work) is goot," said another. That was true; many people were driving now instead of walking.

"Yah, and we're building planes too. Das is goot."

Johann took another sip and questioned them whether it was good the government had taken over the factories. Specifically, he asked if it was good they were building tanks instead of tractors, and some factories were building bombs, or so he had heard.

An old man with burly sideburns and a mustache slammed down his beer on the counter. "That is for our defense! To protect us from our enemies! Arbeit macht frei!"

Johann knew the sentiments of them before he asked. He knew the sentiments of his paper, of nearly everyone. The economy had been wrecked because of the dismal leadership. The whole nation was bankrupt, because of the corrupt politicians. A full day's wages (if one could find work) couldn't buy a loaf of rye. He heated his apartment during the last brutal winter with wood he pried off abandoned buildings in the neighborhood. The industrialization was changing that, but few questioned what it was about, and yet there were reports that things weren't right. Some were suspicious; there were questions without answers.

Johann finished the last of his brew and set the stein on the counter. All the faces in the room were staring at him, "So, you all agree it is good?"

Before they could say another word a voice came from a

dark corner across the room, "No." A short man stepped from the shadows of a booth. His cardigan hat was pulled down to the brim just above his eyes. He walked with a limp and cane. His cane sounded like a judge's gavel in a courtroom, a slow methodical pounding as he crossed the wooden floor. All the other men were silent. Johann recognized him; perhaps, the other men did too. He used to be a person of notoriety in the city, a distinguished man of great respect and influence. He hadn't shaven in a while and had been obscure for years. The men parted as he came up to Johann.

His voice was quiet, tired, almost a whisper, "Nix, das is nix goot."

The others started to shout at him because of his statement. Two men grabbed his arms like they were going to throw him out in the street. The old man raised his cane in the air defensively and looked toward Johann with pleading eyes. Johann shouted, "Let him speak! I want to know. Why is it not good?"

They let him go, and he looked about the other men in the bar; his eyes were haunting, fearful. His voice was coarse and weak. His expression sullen, almost shameful, "You don't know what they are building. You don't understand. I know. I've seen it with my own eyes. You can see it from the autobahn, the factory." He shook his head. Johann leaned forward; the man's voice was almost a mumble. "The buildings, the smokestack, the fences four meters high with razors."

"Ah, he's an idiot," one scoffed, "a fool."

His eyes glared back, "Fool? You'll see who's the fool. Why build fences around a factory?"

"It is going to be a meat packing plant," was the retort.

"Yah, they've even built a railroad to haul the cattle in. You think cattle are going to just sit out in the field and wait to be slaughtered?" They all laughed at the old man. "The factory is good! We want to eat."

"You'll see," the old man replied, "You'll all see."

Another man at the end of the bar with big broad shoulders came forward. He was younger than the rest, closer to Johann's age. His hair was curly and his jaw square. "Don't listen to him. I have been there." He pointed to the man with the cane hobbling back across the floor to his booth, "He's crazy. That's why he was fired."

Johann was curious, "So, do you know about the factory?"

"Ya, I'm a bricklayer. I built the smokestacks. It is for meat processing. Trust me, I know."

"Smokestacks?" asked Johann.

The voice from the dark corner shouted out, "Tell him Hans, tell him."

"Ya, for the ovens." He stretched his arms out wide, "Big ovens. Ya, I know. Don't listen to the old man; dat is why they fired him. He is crazy."

"I designed them you fool!"

The rest of the men scoffed at the old man and raised their mugs in the air for more drink. Johann looked at his watch; he had to go. "You designed the factory? It was you?"

He nodded, "I can't tell you what das is for, but it is not good. It is horror, young man." He would not give out his name. He told him to go see for himself, and so Johann grabbed his hat and pouch and headed back out into the night. "Ob vertisan."

"Chow, Chow."

He hurried along past the hostels and a new hauptschulen

under construction; there was a fence around it too with razor wire protruding outward toward the street. It was dark and street lights were few. There were still a few beggars along the way, but not as many as there used to be, the polize patrol kept them to a minimum. The demonstrations were down too; the government made sure of that. In fact, there had not been any in years.

Johann reached his building and ran up the three flights of stairs to his flat. When he walked through the door, his children screamed in delight. "Surprise!" His beautiful wife hugged and kissed him and then stood back and spun around. She was wearing a brand new dress with lace that tied in a bow just above her breasts. Johann was pleased; she looked so good, and the new soft fabric was pleasing to the touch.

"Look at Heidi," she said.

His young daughter tugged on his pant leg, smiling at his feet. The tooth that had been chipped was repaired. Her smile now as beautiful as her mothers. She skipped around singing a nursery song holding a mirror admiring her new tooth.

"Little Johann, did you see him?"

A soccer ball bounced off his leg, and his son raced proudly through the cramped kitchen in his new pair of shoes. They weren't used with scruff marks and patched holes in the soles; they shined and smelled of new leather. It had been a year since they bought him his last pair, and the soccer ball was to have been his Christmas present. Its arrival was late, and they explained, "Santa had run out. But it was coming as soon as the elves acquired more leather." They had!

That night, they ate a hearty stew with fresh vegetables, and all slept soundly with full stomachs. Early the next morning, Johann awoke and went to his typewriter while his family still slept. He looked out their tiny window at the city.

Across the town, plumes of smoke rose from the auto factories and drifted across the skyline like a long gray nightgown. A year before, they weren't even running, closed down, and hardly a light was in the city. He sat there in silence with his fingers on the keys wondering what he would write. He thought about the new plants, and the autos. That was good. He thought about the planes, and that was good too. It was progress; they needed advanced transportation. Johann then begin to think about the production of tanks (if it were true), and the sentiments of the people. They needed defense; there had been a war. That was good too. Johann paused, reflecting. He thought about the bodega and the men there, what they thought, and he wondered about the strange man with the cane, the man who hobbled from the shadows.

What was it he was saying about the factory? He had warned them they would all understand one day, but then it would be too late. What did he mean? Johann had seen the place himself once from afar when he had travelled from Munich. It was off in the distance but clearly visible from the autobahn. He tried to picture it in his mind; it was so strange. There was something about it that was eerie. It was secret and mysterious. He had heard rumors, awful rumors, from the anti-fascist, but there had always been arguments against progressivism.

The man with haunting eyes had to be wrong. It was good; it was all good. "Arbeit macht frei." The government wouldn't do anything to hurt the people. It wanted progress; that's all. Johann looked out across the city. He could see the factories running. The people had work now. People were fed. In an hour or so, the noise of the traffic would fill the streets. He looked down from his typewriter; next to his feet was his son's soccer ball. Christmas had finally arrived due to his job and the monthly check. Next to his papers was his daughter's mirror. Johann thought for the words to begin his story, but there was something that he couldn't get out of his mind.

He sipped on some coffee and pictured the factory in his mind. He pictured it as he last saw it from the distance on the autobahn. There was something strange about it. He tried to figure out what it was. The fences around it were high. Do cattle need fences four meters high? They don't climb. There was something else that was out of place; something else that was very unusual. He tried to think. He thought of the hamptschulen. It had a fence too and with razor wire; it was necessary to protect the new school from thieves. But the factory bothered him, and he didn't know why. It was different.

Johann closed his eyes and tried to focus on it in his mind, but it faded in and out like a dream, and then he saw it. He saw it clearly. The razor wire. He could see it clearly. It wasn't like the razor wire at the new school; the wire didn't bend out over the street. The wire at the factory tilted in. It was not for cattle, not at all. And, it was not to keep people out, but to keep people in. And the railroad, it stopped there. It was the end of the line. There would be many, many, and many on that train.

A shiver went through him, and then a cold sweat beaded on his forehead. He felt nauseous. The rumors had to be true. He looked out across his beloved city through his trembling fingers. He knew. The old man at the bodega wasn't crazy; he was the architect. The smokestacks were for incinerators. And from what he heard, it would be operational soon. He had never given it much thought; there were always rumors. There were rumors too of another war. He hadn't believed that either. The government he believed was for peace.

The truth went through him like a cold chill. He had to write his story; was it good? He felt ill. Johann looked down at his feet at his son's new ball, and at his daughter's mirror. Times had been so tough. He had a choice to make. Freedom is costly, and truth is not always popular.

Tears began to roll down his face. He put the paper in the typewriter. He hoped his family would someday forgive him. He hoped they would understand. He knew all too well the repercussions journalists faced because of dissent. He knew what his family may face. Johann scrolled the paper through the carriage and lined his margins. He took a deep breath and another sip of coffee trying to think of what to say. He lit his pipe packed full of fresh tobacco and set it on the tray. His fingers sat on the keys, and he began as journalists do pecking away the words that flowed from his heart and mind. He began.

"Work does not set man free, only the truth does…"

〰〰〰〰〰〰〰〰〰〰〰〰〰〰〰〰〰〰〰〰〰〰〰〰〰〰〰〰〰〰〰〰
Seventy Years Later

Allen sat at his desk in the early morning hours looking at the picture of his father and grandfather. Grandfather Ottoheimer died years before he was ever born, but he had heard the stories. Like Allen, he had been a journalist. The old weathered black and white photo of his father and grandfather was one of his most cherished possessions, if not his most. His family came from meager beginnings, and like most, there had been almost nothing left after the Great War.

He sat there in the glow of his desktop looking out the

window. Some skyscrapers were lit even in the predawn hours. Other buildings were completely dark, abandoned. They hadn't been turned on in years or since the great "recession" began. They were just dark symbols of the past. Work had been scarce. People held on to jobs like lifeboats from the Titanic as the economy just sank lower and lower.

He was fortunate. He had a job now, finally. On his desk were pictures of his wife and kids, all upstairs asleep. In the tray next to his computer were bills that would get paid that month: credit cards, the mortgage, utility bills, and insurance. He breathed a sigh of relief not to have to negotiate payment again, a task he always felt ill-equipped to do.

He had been asked to write about the "recovery." It was his first big assignment for the magazine. Optimism that things were going to get better had waned. The expansive power of government seemed to be the only thing that grew. Government was growing at record pace as the industrial sector declined. One industry after another had been taken over, health care, financial services, auto, agriculture. There was talk that they would nationalize other industries as well; meanwhile, the recovery didn't seem to be recovering. In comparison to the other "emerging economies," America limped along like a three-legged dog at a Greyhound track. It wasn't good, nor pretty.

His hands rested on the keys; the story was his to write. He had heard from his father many times stories about his grandfather, a brave man he never had the opportunity to meet. He looked at his picture and then looked at his screen. Outside the window was their car in the drive, with twenty-two months of payments left. Down the block were home after home with the all too familiar "For Sale" (foreclosed) signs in the yard. Writers filled the ranks of the unemployment lines just like auto workers, roofers, secretaries, real estate agents, and mechanics. Millions had been laid off; millions had lost their homes, but he had a job, at least for now.

There on his desk next to his mouse pad were tickets to the ball game, box seats courtesy of the company that hired him. Allen had promised his son for years he would take him to a game. Now, he could fulfill that pledge. He looked at his daughter's picture next to his wife. She was in her ballerina outfit. It was her dream and love. It had been two years since they could afford lessons, but they were about to begin again because of his new job.

Allen sat there in the dark that quiet morning and wondered just what he would say. Was it good? He knew the sentiments of many other journalists and of his superiors who never seemed to question the continuous reports, dismissing them as "conspiracy theories." They were all just rumors. Allen contemplated what he would say, the method he would approach the subject. How does one write about what was going on? What was the truth about the "recovery?"

On his desk were dozens of stories about mysterious prisons built throughout the country, twenty-two by some counts, many more by others. He had files full of pictures sent to him. They were in diverse places, most being in the vicinity of a railroad. This bothered him and reminded him of things he remembered hearing about back in the day when his father was a child.

Allen looked at the picture taken of him and his father in front of the Washington Monument. He had always loved his country and what it stood for, the sacred rights of freedom. He knew what it meant more than most. Then, he looked out across his beloved city. All these things ran through is mind. He knew what his grandfather would do. He knew the price he paid. But that was a different time; people didn't have as much to lose, or did they?

Allen felt his courage slowly dripping from him like a leaky faucet drips into the drain. He felt empty, alone. His hands began to tremble. Truth has a price; popularity doesn't. He was taught that courage is gained not in triumph, but in the face of fear.

He looked at the reports and articles accumulated on his desk. Allen hoped his family would understand. He held the picture of his wife and kids in his hand and kissed their faces, then drew a long breath. He lit his pipe, his grandfather's pipe, and began to write. He studied the photographs of the camps one last time. He began to type his story, "When we do not challenge our leaders, the price we pay is more than freedom; it is our life. In the history of man; apathy is the noose by which most liberties are hung…"

Allen could see from the photographs which way the razors turned. And, he knew very well what happened when the railroads end.

the end.

The famous slogan, "Arbeit macht frei!" (Work makes one free), was posted above the entrance to the death camps in Nazi Germany. Thousands entered the camps believing they were there for work.

AN AFTERTHOUGHT TO
THE FACTORY

Did you know that during the last century, there were four times more people killed by their own governments than were killed by foreign armies? RJ Rummel came up with the term 'Democide' in his book *Death by Government: Genocide and Mass Murder since 1900*. His evidence shows that 25 million soldiers died in World Wars I and II and another 12 million were killed in other wars and revolutions totaling 37 million worldwide. During the same period 1900-1999, millions more victims were killed by democide in the last century. He defines democide as "the murder of any person or people by a government, including genocide, politicide and mass murder".

Here is a short list of atrocities committed by governments.

*The Soviet government became one of the world's greatest killers. Under the Communist regime of Stalin and Lenin between 1917-1953 (the year of Stalin's death), the Soviet Union executed or starved some 40 million people.

*Mao Tse Tung declared millions of citizens 'class enemies'. Two million dissidents were shot; another one million Tibetans and Turkestani Muslims were 'liquidated'. It is estimated that 30 million people were starved to death during the Communist Cultural Revolution.

*In Germany, the Socialist Nazis regime and Hitler put to death some 12 million people, half of them Jews.

*In four years between 1975 and 1979, after the collapse

of Vietnam, the Pol Pot Communist regime in Cambodia killed an estimated 2 million people.

*Many other nations have slaughtered millions of their own citizens. Some of these nations include Iraq, Libya, Pakistan, Bosnia, Rwanda, Ethiopia, Indonesia, Somalia, and countless others.

Do you know the countries that are on the UN Human Rights Council? Here is a partial list: China, Cuba, Russia, Saudi Arabia, Kuwait, Angola, Bangladesh and some other countries that have had serious human rights issues including Libya, which wasn't removed until March of 2011. Feel comfortable?

Did you know that "detainment camps" have been built in the United States? The obvious question is why?

Suggestion, considering the history of governments on planet earth, you may want to check it out. Don't be silent.

SILENCE HAD BEEN LONG AND STILL

Silence had been long and still
  Before the soldiers could be heard
  Marching through the farmers' fields
  And choppers flew overhead
  And beat the winds above the earth

Silence had been long and still
  Not a word was heard in this town
  Before the schools had been closed
  And every business was closed down

Yes, Silence had been long and still
  Before the voices knelt beside the road
  And shadows scampered in moonlight
  And tanks rumbled above the ground.

Oh yes, silence was very long and still
  Before the churches were boarded shut
  And pews were stacked against the doors
  And stained glass windows were covered up

Shhhh, silence had been long and still
  Before they gathered around the candlelight
  And young faces in the darkness glowed
  Before they heard the shots of rifle fire
  And the hands trembled of the old

Yes, the silence got very still
  Before the flashlights filtered through the cracks
  And soldiers pounded at the door
  And they heard them cock their rifles back

Yes, silence is always long and still
   Before people wondered what goes wrong
   And those few that lived to tell the story
      -always say-
   THEY WERE SILENT FOR TOO LONG.

ABOUT THE AUTHOR

Wade Rivers was born in Oklahoma City but has resided in Arkansas most of his adult life. As a young man, he lived in Europe and travelled extensively before returning to the states where he attended the University of Arkansas and then the University of Oregon.

Out of college, he became the Director of a consumer affairs group where he was very involved in lobbying on legislation and travelled frequently between Washington D.C. and Little Rock. Afterwards, he became an investment banker (stockbroker) for ten years and specialized primarily in trading for banks across the country. In the 1990's, Rivers retired from a lifestyle that was very destructive and nearly killed him. He became sober and left the investment business preferring a less stressful and more serene life. He became a painter and eventually a realtor where he bought the farm on the Ouachita River where he now lives with his doting wife and daughter.

Though he is still somewhat involved indirectly in government affairs, Rivers' primary ambition is just to write. It is his love. He also covets his time with God and nature. A naturalist, (in the truest sense), he and his family live on a farm surrounded by a river in a virtual wilderness. When he is not tending to his orchards and "chores", he is on the river with his dogs, fishing and kayaking.

Currently, Rivers is working on his fourth book, another thriller, and is deeply immersed in his lifelong interest, the pursuit and discovery of mass alternative energy sources. For more information on Mr. Rivers, go to www.waderivers.com.

www.ingramcontent.com/pod-product-compliance
Lightning Source LLC
Chambersburg PA
CBHW070305260626
47160CB00003B/717